Signature of a Soul

Riona Kelly

An American Rose Abroad

Suspense Romance Novel

This edition is published by:

Pynhavyn Press

First Print Edition: July 2021
http://www.pynhavynpress.com

ISBN: 1-942622-12-0

ISBN-13: 978-1-942622-12-3

This novel is a work of fiction. Names, characters, businesses, places, events, and incidents either are the products of the author's imagination or used in a fictitious manner. Any resemblance to actual persons, living or dead, or actual events is purely coincidental.

Cover Art by: CoverInked.com

Dedication

For my friends and family.

Acknowledgments

Thank you to my beta readers, my editor, and to the wonderful people of Spain and Portugal, who made my trip there a fabulous memory. Thanks also to Barb Hoeter at Coverinked.com for designing the stunning cover.

Table of Contents

Chapter 1

"Well, damn."

Lindy Morton kicked the back drivers-side tire, not needing any more observation to know she had a flat. In the twenty-two years since she'd received her driver's license, she'd never had to change a tire herself. Hands on her hips, she turned to gaze down the coastal highway, looking for someone likely to help.

"It's flat," her niece, Michelle, noted as she came around the car to look at the deflated hunk of rubber.

"I know," she answered. "Do you know how to change one?"

"Uh-huh, Dad taught me." Michelle flashed a grin at her. "Don't you?"

"No, my dear, I don't. I've always had a white knight come along when I needed one."

"Really, Auntie?"

"Yes, really." Lindy popped open the trunk to check for the spare tire. She wasn't sure her rescuer would show up on this Spanish highway, but she had hope.

Smoothing down the lines of her white linen slacks, she stretched her torso to remove the two suitcases sitting on top of the spare tire well. Her pants pulled snugly against the rounded shape of her backside, presenting an inviting view to any man passing by, a technique she'd used more than once to obtain unplanned roadside assistance. It didn't fail her this time. Before she even straightened up, she heard the sound of a motorcycle pulling up behind her, and her mouth tightened into a sly smile.

Perhaps the Spanish *policía*, she reckoned, then turned to greet the gallant man who had stopped to help. Barely hiding her surprise, she faced a young man who was closer to Michelle's age than hers. He removed his helmet and strode over to her with confident steps.

Beside her, she felt a jostle as Michelle reached for the wheel well release, then paused. She glanced to see her niece's eyes had fallen on the newcomer.

And why not? A handsome hunk of virility smiled at her in a swarthy, Spanish way if you went for his type. Clad sexily in black jeans, with the collar of a dark gray shirt peeking out of the traditional biker leather jacket, he looked quite dashing and perhaps a little dangerous.

"*Buenas tardes.* Good afternoon," he greeted them in both Spanish and English.

"Good afternoon," Lindy answered before Michelle could speak. "Thank you for stopping. We blew a tire a little bit ago."

"I guessed as much. I spotted a broken wine bottle on the road and just missed it. I suppose it was what you hit."

Although he spoke with an accent, his English was quite good. "Is there something I can do to assist?"

"Well, I could use some help changing the tire," Lindy replied as she affected her helpless female expression.

He looked her up and down in a quick glance and took in Michelle's tee shirt and blue jeans in another second. "You don't want to change the tire in those clothes. I will do it for you."

"Oh, that's very kind of you. But I can help."

He waved her off. "No, no. You would get dirty. Perhaps

the *señorita* could assist with the tire?" His gaze shifted to the young woman.

"The *señorita* would be delighted to help." Michelle inserted herself between her aunt and the young man. "I'm Michelle … *yo soy* Michelle."

"Roberto Aponte. I live in Marbella. Are you going there?"

"Yes. Isn't it lucky?" Michelle flashed a sunny smile.

He grinned, and she blushed a bit. At seventeen, she was a little reserved, but not naïve.

"What a coincidence," Lindy said. "Do you work at the resorts in Marbella?" She didn't want her niece getting any ideas about seeing the young man there. At the moment, she was concerned it might not be the best plan to have a passing biker change the tire on a rental BMW. Did her insurance cover this?

He laughed. "No. I am an artist."

Dare she ask? Lindy wondered. "What kind of artist, Roberto?"

"A painter." He pulled leather gloves out of his pocket, took the bolt-tool bar, and knelt to loosen the nuts on the tire.

Michelle stood to one side, holding the spare tire upright, ready to roll to him.

"I paint all kinds of art. Landscapes, people, hotels, whatever my clients want."

"You're a contract artist then," Lindy concluded with a nod of understanding.

"Not so much." He rose, removed the jack from the trunk, and went to the driver's side to fit it under the car. "I do murals and paint designs for some of the hotels and restaurants, but mostly, I do paintings for sale at the street shops."

The tire rose off the ground, and any misgivings Lindy had harbored about whether she should call the rental company to change the tire sailed away as Roberto seemed to know what he was doing.

"Do you make a good living doing with it?" Looking at his motorcycle, she wasn't so sure. It looked like it was quite a few years old, although he seemed to keep it in good condition.

"I make enough to pay the rent, but not enough to say I make a good living." He punctuated this with a grunt as he removed the last nut and lifted the damaged tire off. Running his fingers over the rubber, he located the cut quickly. "There it is. A big tear in the tire. You take it to a garage, and they might be able to fix, but it may be too big."

"You're probably right. By the way, I'm Lindy Morton, and I'd be very interested to see your artwork."

Michelle pushed the spare to Roberto and said, "My aunt is an illustrator. She does book covers, posters, brochures, and that kind of thing."

Lindy shot a sharp glance at her niece. "I also do paintings and teach art. It's been lucrative for me."

Roberto spared a quick look at Lindy, then spun the new tire onto the car. "Lindy Morton … I think I might have seen your name on a book cover or perhaps in a magazine. It sounds very familiar."

Lindy admired the tight fit of his jeans as they clung to his thighs and glanced toward her niece. She, too, had her eyes on his backside.

He replaced the bolts and lowered the BMW, pulling out the car jack as it settled on the ground. "Perhaps we might run into each other in Marbella. It's a small town in many ways. Most of the English people stay in the same general area, so you will find many people who speak your language."

Job done, he placed the damaged tire in the well and put the tools away then turned to face her. "You should be okay, but get the tire fixed soon. You don't want to be caught without a spare."

"Yes, you're right. Might I pay you something for your time, Roberto?"

His smile was brief as he glanced at Michelle, who leaned against the truck watching him with obvious interest. "How about you buy me dinner when we meet again in Marbella?"

"But where?" Lindy asked as he started back to his motorcycle.

"No worries. I'll find you." He winked at Michelle, pulled his helmet on, kicked his bike to a start, and rode off.

"Do you think he'll actually find us?" Michelle asked after they'd been back on the road for a few minutes.

"Who knows? He did say Marbella was a small town. There are probably only so many places where tourists congregate. He seemed to be a nice young man."

"He was cute. Those gorgeous eyes and dark hair and—"

"And the tight jeans and leather jacket were sexy." Lindy smiled as the wind blew through her hair, reminding her of a time about thirty years earlier when her passion was a sexy movie star named Johnny Depp rocking a TV series called "21 Jump Street." She'd thought he was the hottest thing she'd ever seen. Guys in leather always looked so damn attractive.

"Yeah, they were. Don't you think he kind of looked like a young Antonio Banderas?" Michelle had a dreamy look on her face as if she was already spinning her own romantic story.

"A little."

Michelle tossed her head, her long ginger-blond hair flowing behind her as the car zipped along. The green scarf holding her hair back flapped in the wind stream, barely clinging. The upturned nose and oval shape of Michelle's face came from her mother, but the dark eyes were from her father's side of the family. So were her tenacity and tendency to overthink things.

"What were you about to say when the tire went flat?" she asked.

"I was saying you might be worrying too much about which college might accept you. You're just starting your senior year in the fall, and there's plenty of time for applications and college considerations. You're an excellent student with high grades and great attributes."

"But colleges aren't like they were when you went, Auntie. Now they expect community service, recommendations from prominent people in your city, plus the high marks, extra-curricular activities, and other stuff. I keep looking at my schedule and trying to think how I'll fit it all in and still have time to study."

It did seem like there was a lot more pressure on the kids these days, Lindy conceded. Every other student would be in the same situation, so they would all be scrambling to get everything done. She didn't know what else to say.

Part of the reason she agreed to bring Michelle on this trip to Spain with her was to give her a chance to relax and see a different part of the world. They'd driven down from Madrid through Andalucía and come out along the Costa del Sol, a place rivaling any Italian coastline for beauty and beaches. She figured the climate and culture here were about as far away from Roanoke, Virginia, as her niece could get.

Once they reached Marbella, Lindy took the BMW to the nearest service station and talked to the owner about repairing the damaged tire.

He pulled it out and examined the cut, muttering under his breath the whole time. Then he pointed to the tear and said, "Look, *señora*. The cut is too big to patch up. You need to take it to the dealer. They can maybe fix, or you can buy a new one."

Lindy thanked him, waited as he put the tire back in the trunk, then she slid back onto the car seat. "I think we'll call the rental company when we get to the resort. They can take care of it."

"How much farther is the place?" Michelle asked.

Lindy checked the navigation unit on the dash. "It's not far now, only a couple of kilometers. It's right on the beach, so we'll see it on the left."

As she drove, she caught glimpses of the Mediterranean Sea between the resorts, hotels, and casinos along the waterfront. A sparkling clear day, not a cloud marred the pale blue sky that highlighted the aquamarine water. "A picture-perfect view," she murmured, itching to capture the varying shades in a painting.

The rambling structure of the Marianna Beach Resort came up on the left, and Lindy turned the car into the entrance, pausing at the gatehouse to advise them she was a guest checking in.

"Pretty fancy," Michelle said as her eyes roamed around the complex of three-story room towers, gardens, and pool areas. Beyond the entryway, a vast expanse of the beach led to the open sea. "Great location. Is this really expensive, Aunt Lindy?"

"It's a vacation resort and part of a condominium exchange. I have three weeks a year in the deal, and I can exchange them for anywhere I want to go. So, we have a week to enjoy here, and then we can go on to other parts of Spain. I imagine we'll run into some of the English-speaking population. Quite a few Brits have retired here or have vacation homes in the sunshine."

"I heard Sean Connery has a home here. Do you think we might see him?"

Lindy laughed. "Maybe, but I wouldn't hold my breath. I believe I read he'd sold it."

She parked the car, and they strolled to reception to check-in. She glanced over as Michelle gaped at the huge lobby with the high ceilings and a giant water fountain in the middle. Spanish tile glistened everywhere — on the floors, on the walls, and around the base of the fountain, screaming affluence. While Lindy cocked a tolerant eyebrow at the girl, her lips twitched up in a smile. She recalled her first experience at a resort hotel in Las Vegas had left her speechless, so she understood her niece's awe. Did her brother never take his family anywhere special? He'd always favored camping and boating, so probably not an upscale resort.

Lindy picked up the room key and directions to their tower then nabbed Michelle and pointed her back to the car. Their suite was on the third floor of 1A, one of the buildings sitting right on the beach, facing the sea. A bellman met them at the unit and carried their luggage upstairs, if you could count loading it onto an elevator as carrying, then he opened the door to the suite with a flourish.

Lindy cast her eyes over the living room area and ran her hand along the back of a full-sized sofa, upholstered in a Spanish mosaic rust, yellow, and red print. Two overstuffed chairs, also rust-colored fabric, flanked it, and she nodded her approval of the color scheme. Lindy admired the heavy oak end tables with ornate brass fittings sitting next to each of the seating choices. As the bellman pulled the floor to ceiling curtains back from the window, her head came up at Michelle's gasp.

"Oh, it's so beautiful! What a spectacular view."

SIGNATURE OF A SOUL

Going to stand beside her, Lindy gazed out and agreed with her niece's assessment. "It is quite wonderful. You can see the curve of the land as it goes toward the south and Gibraltar." She pointed to the long, beach-front coastline. "And look at the varying shades of blue in the sea as it gets deeper and deeper."

She drew Michelle into a one-armed hug, squeezing her shoulders in affection. "I'm glad you agreed to come with me on this trip."

"Thank you for asking me." Michelle returned the hug, but her eyes lingered on the rolling water against the beach.

Turning back from the window, Lindy checked out the rest of the apartment. A dining area with a large wooden table and four chairs sat at the end of the room. Separated from the living room by a wall and an arched opening, a condo-sized kitchen offered all the modern conveniences.

Two bedrooms, a luxurious bathroom between them, were off the entry door side of the living room. As Michelle turned slowly to face the room, Lindy thanked the bellman with a generous tip and dropped onto the couch, happy to stretch her legs out in front of her and enjoy the view. "I think I'm just going to sit here until dinner."

"No," Michelle wailed. "We've got to go down to the beach and walk in the sand, at least. I want to dip my toes in the Mediterranean."

Lindy waved her hand. She was creeping up on forty and had soaked her toes in more sea foam than Michelle even knew existed. "In a little bit, dear. I need to relax for a bit and call the rental company. Why don't you go over to the gift shop near the lobby and get us some bottled waters to put in the refrigerator? Then, we can go down."

With a frown, the girl took the offered money and went on

9

her assigned task. If she knew her niece, Lindy figured it would take her at least an hour to do it. After the girl had gone, she called the car rental office and explained the problem with the car.

"It is no trouble," the representative on the phone said. "You don't worry at all. We'll take care of it." He went on to assure her they would send someone out with a new tire to replace the damaged one and change the spare off the car.

Next, Lindy unpacked her suitcase and changed clothes to something more beach appropriate, a pair of buttercup yellow, Capri-length pants to go wading in the surf. She topped it with a lacy-looking blouse of a slightly lighter shade of the same color.

True to her prediction, Michelle returned about an hour and a half later with a six-pack of bottled water, a six-pack of sodas, and some chips to munch on.

"It's a nice shop, lots of pretty things to attract the *turistas*. And I met a couple of cool boys down there. They'll be at the pool this afternoon. Do you mind if I join them for a while?" She rattled this off as she put the water and soda into the refrigerator.

"I thought you wanted to dip your tootsies in the Mediterranean?" Lindy had pulled out a straw, wide-brimmed sun hat, which she held in her hand.

"I do. But I also want to chat with the guys some more. They've been here three days already and probably have some great suggestions on where we can go."

Lindy gnawed at one end of her sunglasses' earpiece as she listened to her niece. "Let's take a short stroll on the beach, and you can tell me all about them, like where they're from and how old they are. Then, if they sound okay to me, you can go learn more about where they've been."

With a roll of her eyes, Michelle replied, "All right. Fair enough." She folded her jeans up almost to her knees, kicked off her good sandals, and put on a pair of plastic clogs for the beach.

Following the clearly-marked path to the private resort beach, they came to a sandy route with chain-connected stanchions allowing about six feet of walkway across for the short distance to the beach. Ahead the smooth, almost white sand stretched out along the coastline, where many people lounged under umbrellas enjoying the warm afternoon. Lindy glanced back over her shoulder to admire the view toward the mountains. Back toward Malaga, the Sierra Nevada mountains jutted up into the clear sky.

But the fresh, salty scent of the sea beckoned, and Lindy hurried to catch up with her niece, who had strode on ahead and was almost to the water. As the sea washed on the shore, it touched it with light waves, no heavy breakers, or rushing foam. They walked along the edge, feeling the warmth of the sea brush against their skin.

Michelle reached to slip her clogs off, but Lindy touched her hand. "Leave them on. Lots of pebbles along the waterline. Now, tell me about these two boys you met."

"They're cool as ice. Sophomores from Boston University and over here for three weeks before they head back for the new semester. Connor's a linguistics major, speaks four languages, including Spanish, and is studying political science. He plans to go into the diplomatic corps when he graduates. Alan is also a poly-sci major. They're both really smart and kinda cute."

"Ah, there it is. The real reason you want to hang with them." Lindy flashed a smile at her. "They're a little older than you. Do they know you're seventeen?"

"Aunt Lindy!"

"Well, I do have to look out for you, or my brother would have my hide. You can go talk, but nothing else. No going back to their room or anywhere else with them. And you will introduce me when I come to check on you in about thirty minutes."

Michelle's mouth tightened in resignation, but she agreed.

Lindy followed her niece at a discrete distance to get a glimpse of these young men and see which of the several pools they occupied.

Strolling across the patio to another pool, Lindy swayed with grace, her pants clinging seductively to her shape. Always feminine and a very pretty woman, she was used to men noticing her. She found a pair of empty lounge chairs and took the one on the right, stretching her extended frame out, her long legs crossing at the ankles. She pulled out her reader and resumed reading a paranormal romance novel she'd started the previous night.

She'd barely gotten a few minutes into it when a man sat in the chair next to her. She glanced over enough to see the newcomer was much older, silver-haired with a scraggly beard, ruddy cheeks, and bulbous nose, indicating he was a drinker, and he had a beer gut, telling even more of the story. So much for attracting a handsome man to flirt with. Shrugging, she turned back to her book.

A half-hour later, Lindy ambled over to the pool where Michelle held court with the two guys, as well as an older, handsome man, seated at one of the poolside tables. Her slender niece wasn't as curvaceous as Lindy, but she was a beautiful girl, and both of the young men seemed quite charmed by her.

The other man was much too old to be flirting with her niece. Perhaps he was a parent of one of the boys, although Michelle didn't mention anyone else being with them. Two college-age boys wouldn't need parents along.

Michelle held a fruity drink in her hand, and as she spotted her, she waved it in the air like a flag. With a smile, Lindy sashayed over and greeted them.

"Hello, all. I'm Michelle's aunt. You may call me Lindy."

Cutting in before she could embarrass her, Michelle said, "Aunt Lindy, this is Alan..." She motioned to the young man closer to her, a dark blond-haired youth with a light beard just a shade darker than his hair, who was slim and tanned a golden brown. He wore long beachcomber shorts in a bright zigzag pattern that would stand out like a distress flag on any beach. Alan nodded at her and murmured a greeting.

"And this is Connor." Michelle indicated the other young man. This one showed his Irish heritage in the blue eyes and black hair, as well as the handsome jawline. He looked more of a jock than his companion with a hint of a six-pack torso under his shirt, a slim waist, and well-muscled thighs and legs poking out from his more subdued tie-dyed blue swim trunks.

"Pleased to meet you," he said, his voice a pleasant tenor with a Boston accent. Native to the city then, she concluded.

Lindy turned her attention to the other man, who watched her with undisguised interest. Wearing sunglasses and a pleasant, but slightly amused smile, his sandy-brown hair accented his oval face and firm jaw. She estimated he was about her age, maybe a little older. His off-white short-sleeved cotton shirt and light beige slacks showed good fit and quality. A man of considerable means.

"And this gentleman is Colin Hayes," Michelle's voice said

while Lindy seized him up.

"Mister Hayes," she acknowledged with a touch of frost in her tone. She could not approve of him hanging out with an under-aged girl.

"A pleasure, Ms. Morton. Your niece was telling us you're a well-known graphic artist. I probably have a dozen or more books with your cover illustrations." His voice was English, with a proper speech pattern, not showing a sign of the area of England where he grew up, suggesting he had a quality education.

Unlike the boys, he offered his hand, then rose to pull out a chair for her. Good manners were rare these days, and she appreciated it. "I am an artist," she said. "Graphic arts are only part of it. If you've seen my covers, then you know I began by painting them before it became popular to use CGI to create the images. It's merely another skill set in the process, but you need to understand art to do it properly."

Out of the corner of her eye, she saw Alan's eyebrows shoot up.

"Indeed, I do understand. While computers have improved much of the work artists and other creatives do, it is still imperative to know and understand the basics of the work."

In spite of her reservations, Lindy was beginning to warm to this man. "What is it you do, Mr. Hayes?"

He smiled, a dazzling display of even, white teeth. "Nothing so artistic as your work, but I do help the process for others. I'm a television and movie producer, as well as a location scout, which is what I am currently doing."

"So, I gather you're looking for film locations around here?"

He nodded. "Here, in southern Spain, Morocco, and Italy. Possibly, I'll consider other locations, but if I can find what I think the movie needs in these locations, then I can move on to more of the project, such as locking down agreements for the locations and getting filming permits."

"Sounds fascinating. Might I ask how you happened on my niece?"

"It was the other way around, Auntie," Michelle said. She gave Lindy an annoyed glance that suggested she was being rude. "Colin had the table, and we asked if we could join him. At the time, there were no other free ones. He's been a very gracious host." She lifted her drink again in emphasis.

Acknowledging, Lindy said, "Then I must apologize, and thank you for your courtesy."

"I have been remiss as well. Might I get you a cold drink from the bar? Perhaps a Mediterranean Iced Tea? It's very refreshing."

"Sounds delightful. Thank you."

As Colin left to go to the bar, Lindy turned her attention to the two young men. "My niece tells me you've been here a couple of weeks already. What have you seen so far?"

"We were in Barcelona for almost a week," Connor said. "It's a fascinating city. We went to a couple of museums and spent some time on the beach there. Did a little clubbing. Then we took the bus to Valencia and worked our way the rest of the way down the coast."

"We took a sailboat out one day, and I got some beautiful photos of the coast," Alan said. He held up a small camera and shrugged his shoulders. "Digital, I'm afraid."

"Aren't they all now?" Lindy replied. Here they are in Europe, and they're hanging at the beach, she thought. There's so much to see and do, and they're doing something they could have done in Florida.

As if by a signal, the boys shoved their chairs back and got to their feet. Connor spoke for them. "We've gotta get going. We're meeting some friends for dinner. It was nice to meet you both. Michelle, perhaps we'll see you around tomorrow. Be sure to check out the artist's alley in the market."

"I will," Michelle answered, giving them a wave with the almost empty glass as they left.

"Did I scare them off?"

"Maybe. But the guys did have plans for the evening. They'd already told me as much. They met a couple of other students from Boston and made plans to go to a restaurant in the town. Of course, you kind of came on like the high inquisitor. You always put on this genteel southern lady veneer when you're meeting people."

"No, I don't." Lindy regarded her niece with a tolerant smile. "I just wanted them to know you had someone watching out for you. You can never trust these boys on holiday. And sitting down with a stranger? What were you thinking?"

"That we wanted to sit, and this guy was all by himself, and he seemed cool. There were three of us."

"Yes, you and two more strangers joining another stranger."

"You're too suspicious of everyone, Aunt Lindy."

Lindy sighed, thinking of all the differences in the world there were now from when she was a twenty-something traveling across Europe with a friend. "It's a more dangerous world than it used to be, darling. You need to be cautious of everyone, no matter how nice they seem."

"But if you don't ever talk to anyone, how will you get to know them?"

"Good question. I don't know the answer, but I do know

you have to be careful. Now, what was this about an artists' alley?"

"I was wondering if you caught that," Michelle said with a sly look. "There's a street in the market area where artists from all over Spain can display their paintings for sale. I think it's likely Roberto has a stall of his artwork."

"I see. So, you're hoping to meet the handsome Spanish boy again."

"Hey, he changed our tire. If he wanted to rob us, he could have done it easily on the highway." Michelle's eyes narrowed, defying her to deny it.

"You're right. Just don't go imagining any romances. We won't be here very long."

Colin returned with fresh drinks for them all to find the boys gone. "They left?"

Michelle nodded. "Other plans."

He handed Lindy a tall refreshing-looking drink and passed an icy-looking cocktail to Michelle. "And a virgin margarita for the young lady." Then he sat down with a tall drink for himself.

"Tom Collins," Lindy said.

"Yes, indeed. My long-standing drink. So tell me about your work, Lindy." He leaned forward, elbows on his knees, ready to listen.

With his sunglasses still on, Lindy wondered about his eyes. What color they were, what shape? Did he have long eyelashes? He looked handsome, but the eyes were what really showed the spirit and soul of a person.

She'd often talked about her work with strangers, friends, and students, but she didn't want it to sound academic. "Well, Colin, I have always been an artist. From the time I picked up my first crayon and used my bedroom wall for a canvas, I've been drawing, mixing colors, and creating visionary fantasies. Thankfully, I had parents who nurtured my talent rather than stifling it. Given they were both more scientific than artistic, it was extraordinary. I started taking art classes when I was eight, and by the time I was twelve, I was doing commission work for portraits and landscapes. But I loved fantasy art, and for myself, I would create magical images of alien worlds, elf worlds, and spaceships. I displayed my paintings at science fiction conventions where people liked and bought them."

She paused to sip her drink. "I was lucky enough to have an established artist show interest in my work and direct me to an agent who handled book and poster art. By fifteen, I had done my first book cover for a series. One thing led to another, and I began to build a reputation and a demand for my art. After I graduated high school, I went to the Lyme Academy of Fine Art and got my degree, then studied in Paris for two years. By this time, I was well established and in demand for all kinds of custom art. But doing the book covers has always been special. And I love going to conventions still. Yes, there are now more book cover artists than there are ants on a watermelon, but you still need to know what you're doing to create quality work. Do you find something similar in your line of work?"

"Some, yes. Some people are always looking for shortcuts and even come up with brilliant ways to do it, but don't really understand why it has to be a certain way. Look, I have a couple of phone calls to make before it gets too late. Would you ladies honor me by having dinner with me tonight?"

Taken a little off-guard, Lindy nonetheless responded with an affirmative answer for both of them. "We would be delighted."

"Excellent," Colin answered as he got to his feet. "Meet me

in the lobby at seven-thirty, and we can take a cab to the best authentic Spanish restaurant in town." He nodded at them and smiled before he strolled off.

"Thanks for asking me if I wanted to go," Michelle said, sarcasm dripping from her words.

"Of course you want to go. What else would you do? Go looking for more stray young men?"

Michelle's eyes blazed, but her aunt was oblivious as she picked up her reader and her drink glass before starting back to their suite.

Chapter 2

⊗ *Lindy* ⊗

The *Plaza de los Naranjos*, known in English as Orange Tree Square, overflowed with people, mostly tourists, who'd come to the popular city location for dinner, shopping, and maybe a little dancing. A grove of the fragrant citruses lined the central area where white-washed buildings, housing the City Hall, other municipal buildings, restaurants, and small shops, surrounded it. Among the trees and flower beds, tables and chairs covered by orange canopies provided seating for several sidewalk cafes.

As Colin helped Lindy out of the cab, her eyes alighted on the magnificent *Casa del Corregidor*, a Renaissance-style palace, with splendid mustard-colored facades and wrought-iron balconies. "What magnificent," she said, gasping as she spotted the sign over the door. "A restaurant? It's now a restaurant?"

"And a bar and shops. Nothing is sacred these days," Colin told her as she admired the lines of the structure while he turned to assist Michelle. "It was built in 1552 as the mayor's house, but finds new uses in modern Spain." Then he pointed out the *Ermita de Santiago*, or the Hermitage of St. James, which was built before the end of the fifteenth century. "The plaza was actually constructed after these two buildings were erected, then the City Hall came along in 1568."

"This is wonderful," Lindy said. "I must explore it in daylight. I love studying the lines of these old buildings. This would be a delight to paint. Have you ever used it in a movie, Colin?"

"No, but I am looking at it. The problem, of course, is it's always filled with people. It makes filming difficult." He hurried them along to the right side of the square toward the indoor restaurants.

While both women had dressed in cool summer floral dresses, Lindy wore a rose-colored silk shawl wrapped around her shoulders for a little extra warmth. They looked elegant but not too dressy as they rubbed shoulders with girls in tank tops and shorts on the plaza. Although Colin had kept the beige slacks, he sported a casual lightweight short-sleeved cotton shirt.

He led them to a doorway behind one of the open restaurants where a waiter motioned to them to come to the available tables there. As he shook his head at the man, Colin ushered them through the door and up the stairs to the small but elegant restaurant, which overflowed with diners and a waiting line snaked to one side.

"I think we may have a long wait," Lindy said as she looked to see if there were any empty tables.

"Wait here." Colin gave her arm a light touch, then crossed to the host and spoke to him.

Most of the places were set for couples, and the tables were not big enough for three people. But she did glimpse a set-up of two tables together at the side near the balcony where another table for two was positioned.

Colin came back to catch her hand. "Follow me." He led

them to the pushed together tables. "A reservation is a necessity here."

"A man who plans ahead, I like it." Lindy flashed a charming smile at him. Now, in the light slipping through the window in the restaurant, she could see his hazel eyes, a light green shade on the iris rims with golden brown flakes in the middle. His eyes showed so much emotion when he talked animatedly or looked amused, such as now. As he blinked, the silky dark brown lashes covered the base of the lower lid. Very sexy, she decided.

As soon as they were settled, the waiter brought glasses of water with orange slices in them and took their drink order, then advised them of the special of the day, the chef's specialty *paella*. The description of the seafood and chicken extravaganza made her mouth water in anticipation. They discussed it for perhaps a whole thirty seconds before deciding to try it. For *tapas*, Colin suggested the *Tortilla Espanola*, a potato and egg dish, marinated olives, Serrano-ham wrapped plums, and the octopus salad.

Michelle wrinkled her nose at the last suggestion. "Octopus? Really?"

"Trust me, it's delicious."

She shuddered at the prospect but agreed to at least try it.

"You seem very familiar with this area," Lindy said. "Do you come here often?"

He tilted his head charmingly, then said, "My work brings me here at least once a year. I'm not always looking for locations, but sometimes I'm producing a show, and more than a few British actors have homes in this area."

"How exciting," Michelle said. Her interest piqued, her eyes lit up, and she leaned more toward Colin. "Who all lives here?"

He laughed. "Oh, no. I'm not going to name names, young lady. I am sworn to secrecy. But if one's initials started with CF, then maybe you could guess."

Her forehead wrinkled as she thought about it. Then her eyes popped, and she whispered, "Colin Farrell?"

He winked at her, but didn't confirm it, Lindy noticed. "You know Michelle is very interested in theater arts. She's looking at majoring in it next year."

"Are you?" Colin responded, addressing Michelle.

Her smile was shy, but it didn't really hide her confident enthusiasm for the business. "Yes. I've done some acting in school, played the leads in 'Our Town,' and in 'Thoroughly Modern Mille' last year."

"So, you sing and dance also?"

"I do. I'm a triple-threat actress." Her lips tweaked into a smug smile.

He laughed. "I expect you will light up the theaters."

Their *tapas* arrived, and the conversation shifted to the flavors of the food. Michelle took a hesitant stab at the octopus to get a portion on her fork. The pink piece of a tentacle with the suckers still on it made her grimace. Amused, Lindy watched her niece play with it, bringing it almost to her mouth, then stopping before she stabbed a piece herself, popped it between her lips and chewed.

"Quit looking at it and just eat it, Michelle," she advised. "It is a quite pleasing taste, and mostly you will taste the olive oil and seasonings on it."

Encouraged, Michelle did exactly as told, closed her eyes, poked it in her mouth, and chewed. Her face reflected her distaste for the task, but then it changed to surprise when it wasn't as terrible as she thought it would be. "Okay, okay. It wasn't bad. But I don't think I want anymore. I'll have some of the potato things instead."

By the time the *paella* arrived, Lindy and Colin were on their third glass of wine while Michelle was still nursing her non-alcoholic variety. The main dish proved as brilliant as advertised, a delectable concoction of shellfish including clams, prawns, and lobsters plus chicken and ham with a saffron seasoned rice and pasta base with fresh peas in it. Crusty bread, warm from the oven, proved perfect for dipping in the sauce. All talk ceased as they savored the flavors.

Outside on the square, music played loud enough to be heard anywhere in the vicinity as the party geared up for the evening. The nightlife began at nine and went on until the early hours after midnight, or so the waiter informed them.

Colin leaned across the table and said, "Would you like to go to one of the dance clubs?"

"Dancing?" Lindy said. "That would be wonderful. I haven't been out dancing in ages. What do you say, Michelle?"

She looked at her aunt, tolerantly. "I say there will be a lot of drinking, and this under-aged girl will feel somewhat out of place. You two go ahead. I'll take a cab back to the hotel."

"No, no," Colin objected. "There's a great club at the hotel. We'll all go back together. How about it?"

"Perfect," Lindy said.

He was perfect. The right answers, the right food, the right way to treat her. She could easily like this man. But her advice to her niece stood for her also. They could have fun, but it wouldn't do to get serious about anyone they met on a trip abroad.

Back at the resort, Michelle started to say goodnight, but

Lindy interrupted her. "Why don't you come into the club for a while? I'm pretty sure there are sure to be other young people who also aren't old enough to drink, so you might have a good time. If it turns out not, then you can go on to the room, but give it a try. Maybe one of those young men from the pool will be there."

Michelle seemed reluctant but gave in to her aunt's coaxing. "I feel like a third wheel on a bicycle," she muttered.

The club in the hotel was situated in a wing off the lobby that housed various shops, closed now, including a high-end clothing store and an electronics store. But the arcade bustled with about a dozen or more kids playing the colorful and noisy games. Anchoring the end of the wing was the night club called *El Paraiso*, which translated to "the paradise."

As soon as the trio stepped inside, they went from the well-illuminated shopping area to a subtly-lit cavern of neon and candle-wattage lights on the tables that surrounded a dance floor. Several couples were shaking it up to the loud salsa music while many more were sitting it out at the cocktail tables, drinking and chatting. Lindy staked a claim on a table a few layers back from the dance floor and sat at it while Colin borrowed a chair from an empty table and sat next to her, leaving the chair across from them for Michelle. Within a few minutes, a cocktail waitress trotted past, pausing to say she'd be back in a few minutes.

"Do you salsa?" Colin asked. He almost had to shout for Lindy to hear him.

She shook her head, "No. I can samba, but I never learned salsa. Do you?"

"Poorly. But I try."

As promised, the waitress flitted back, took their order, and didn't even blink when Michelle ordered a virgin margarita. Colin told her to run a tab, and she dashed off again. When the music changed to a slower rock beat, Colin offered a hand to Lindy while apologizing to Michelle. Off they went off to the dance floor to join the other gyrating bodies.

"It's been ages since I last went dancing," Lindy told him as she twirled in his hand. "This is a real treat."

"I can't believe a beautiful woman like you isn't out every weekend."

"Too busy with the artwork, designs, and meetings. This trip started as a business meeting, but I'm glad I decided to take some extra time while I was here."

"Something in Spain?" Colin asked.

"No, in Paris. Michelle flew in as I ended my meetings, and we left from there to tour southern France and came on into Spain."

"Sounds like a splendid trip. Where are you heading from here?"

"Well, we plan to stay here for almost a week, then go across to Grenada and then perhaps on to Portugal. I haven't decided yet."

"Oh, definitely see Portugal. It's a beautiful place. I'm glad you'll be here a few more days. Would you care to have dinner with me tomorrow night?"

Lindy noticed the invitation didn't include Michelle. "I'll talk it over with my niece. Since she met those young guys here, she might want to spend the evening by the pool."

The music changed to a slow rhythm, and they eased into an easy-flowing two-step. As Colin pulled her in close to him, Lindy felt the little zing that comes with meeting someone with whom you really connect both intellectually and physically. This man was someone she could forge a relationship with if only they had time. A wishful sighed escaped her lips, and she rested her head on his shoulder.

When they returned to the table, they found their drinks had arrived, but Michelle and her drink were elsewhere. Puzzled, Lindy gazed around the room, eyes searching the dark room until she spotted her niece at a table near the deejay booth talking to a young man who looked familiar and was not either Alan or Connor. If she wasn't mistaken, it appeared their rescuer from earlier had found them.

Chapter 3
⊰ Michelle ⊱

Feeling like an unwanted puppy, Michelle sipped her non-alcoholic drink and decided she wasn't enjoying tagging around after her aunt and Colin. While she appreciated her aunt's efforts to show her around Europe, several of her friends had also traveled over, unescorted. Why couldn't she have come with them?

"Europe's not as safe as it used to be," her father had said. No arguments or reasoning would change his mind. "With the terrorists so close, I don't want you going to Italy or Greece. It's practically in the Middle East's pocket."

"And you think France and Spain are safer?" she'd argued.

"I do. Your aunt knows her way around the continent, and with her connections, you will be much safer than traveling with three other teenagers."

End of discussion, subject closed. It came down to going with her aunt or not going at all. While she loved her aunt, visiting art museums and ancient ruins weren't all she wanted to come to Europe to see and do. If Colin hadn't invited them out to dinner tonight, they probably would have had a meal at one of the hotel restaurants, then watched a movie and gone to bed. She was glad he'd asked them to go clubbing, but honestly, she was hoping to return to the hotel and wander along the beach or even hang at the pool.

Deep in her thoughts, she barely noticed when someone walked up to the table. Glimpsing the snug-fit dark jeans, she only registered it was a man, until he said, "*Senorita* Michelle. *Buenos noches.*"

Her head popped up, and she met his eyes. "Roberto?"

"*Si.* I told you I would find you." His grin was huge and irresistible.

"Come. Come with me. I have a table by the booth, and it is surprisingly quieter there than anywhere else in the room." He held out his hand to her.

Glancing at the other two glasses on the table, Michelle hesitated. "My aunt's drinks…?"

"They will be fine. No one will touch them."

Putting her hand in his, she allowed him to lead her around the back and to the side of the room where the deejay booth filled the corner. Odd as it seemed, it really was quieter right next to the source of the sound than out where she had been sitting. The speakers all faced away from the booth, Roberto explained.

"So, what are your plans for here in Marbella? Go to the beach? Shopping?" Roberto asked. He leaned closer so he wouldn't have to shout it.

"That's up to my aunt. Sure, I'd like to walk along the beach, go into the town, and do a little shopping. But I want to see as much as I can. My aunt likes museums and ruins, so we usually do visit those. This is the first time I've been in a club on this trip. My aunt met an English guy this afternoon, and he took us to dinner and now here. Thank heavens." Michelle felt like she was babbling.

Roberto shot her a knowing look. "*Si.* Your aunt is an artist. Architecture and ancient things interest her. They are potential subjects for a painting. I understand. But you have to have a little fun also, no?"

"Yes!" Michelle laughed. He was very cute, this Spanish boy. "You paint also, so are you interested in those things as well?"

"Of course. But I don't get too carried away. I am young, and I like to have fun." He raised his hands over his head and clapped along with the beat.

"I'd like to see your paintings. Do you have some displayed or for sale here? One of the people I met said there was an artists' alley near the city center. Is it true?"

He shook his head. "Not an alley so much. Just a little group of five artists who display and sell some of their paintings along the sidewalk. It's a couple of blocks toward the hills from the *Plaza de los Naranjas.* If you come by tomorrow, I will show you some of the best I've done. Maybe bring your aunt. But, *un momento...*" He paused and pulled out his smartphone and called up an image. "I have a few pictures of them. Look." He held the phone up to her so she could see.

Michelle squinted at the small image in the darkened club. It appeared to be a street scene in this same area with two older Spanish men drinking wine at an outside café. As near as she could tell, it looked very good. "I like it."

He slid a finger across to the next one, an indoor club and a guitarist on stage, hunched over the instrument with the intensity on his face evident in the painting. Michelle could sense the tension in the body; it done so well. "That's great."

He pushed again, and the image changed to a beach

painting at dusk, the colors amazing and so relaxing. A smile spread across Michelle's lips. "I feel like I could almost step into this one."

Roberto put his phone back in his pocket as he grinned at her. "They are better when you see the real paintings. Try to come tomorrow. I'll be there until two in the afternoon, then *siesta* time."

"I'll see if my aunt is willing. Give me the address."

He swiped a business card from the deejay's booth behind him and jotted the information on the back of it. Michelle tucked it into her little purse that dangled from a chain at her waist and sipped the last of her margarita.

Then the deejay put on a funky rock song, and Roberto did a twirl with his fingers, asking her dance. She nodded, following him to the floor where they broke out into individual steps, but it didn't matter. Everyone was dancing, and no one seemed to be in sync with anyone else. It was rock music.

One dance led to another with a slightly slower beat. Taking Michelle's hands, Roberto taught her a few steps of a *sevillanas* dance, which was kind of a waltz tempo flamenco. She managed to not step on his feet or stumble into anyone before she gave up. "I think I need another drink."

While he went to get her a soft drink, Michelle went back to their table where Roberto had left a reserved marker, and it had, surprisingly, worked. Or maybe no one else wanted to sit next to the booth. Warmed by the crowded club and the dancing, she fanned herself with her hand while she waited. She glimpsed her aunt across the way and wondered if she thought she'd gone back to the room. But then she saw Lindy gaze in her direction and had her answer. Michelle waved her hand a little in acknowledgment.

Roberto returned with a cola drink, and as she sipped it, Michelle chatted with Roberto more about his work and if he sold a lot of paintings.

"Not as much as I would like, but I do okay. I have an agent who handles some sales out of the area for me, and he gets me pretty good prices for my paintings. Just last week, he sold one of my canvases for two hundred fifty euros."

"Is it a good price?"

"Of course. I am not a known artist, so for me, that is very good. Maybe one day, I will earn five hundred per painting, but not yet."

"My aunt makes around fifteen hundred dollars for a book cover, but it is rendered as a digital print. I watched her build a cover once. She did the initial drawing from a sketch with a live model, then added the background sketch before she scanned the whole thing and did the rest of it in an art program. It was fascinating."

"It doesn't seem much like painting if you do it by computer." Roberto frowned as he thought about it. "It's lacking the smell of the paint and the movement of your body in painting. The whole process. I don't know if I would enjoy it as much."

"She says she sometimes misses that part of the creating."

Abruptly, he said, "It's too warm in here. Let's go for a walk on the beach." He stood and offered his hand.

She started to tell him she should advise her aunt but changed her mind. Lindy was occupied with the Englishman, talking animatedly, and they were just going for a short walk.

As they started out of the club, a man about the same age as Roberto caught up with them and said something to Roberto in Spanish. She couldn't understand what they said, but it soon became clear it was an argument. Roberto growled something back to the guy, who was a little smaller and very thin. In return, he fluttered his hands and shouted a response. Roberto waved an arm as if sweeping something away, then held up two fingers and waggled them at the other as his face wore an unhappy scowl.

As they had argued, Michelle had retreated several steps away from this confrontation, fearful it might turn into a fistfight or worse.

The smaller man appeared to capitulate even as he swiped his hand in a wiping-clean gesture, then turned and stalked off. Roberto glared after him before he came to join her. "I am sorry. It was a business matter. That was Arturo, my agent."

"Your agent? And he talks to you like that?" She was surprised, first by the heated argument, then by the youthful look of his agent. He looked like another street kid.

"Ay, he's also a friend. When I started to sell my paintings, he told me he had connections, and he could extend my sales, and it seems he did. So I give him a percentage of any sales he arranges, and we both make money. But sometimes he gets pushy or makes a promise to a client who is unreasonable. Let's go for our walk. I need to calm down."

Although a warm night, the salty scent of the sea blew in on a delicate, cooling breeze. Along the beach, various lights from resorts and clubs cast a glow that reached part-way down the sand. With lights reflecting in the water, no part of the shorefront seemed too dark. The sea lapped across the sand with gently breaking waves and pounded a rhythm mellower than the music they'd left. They held hands as they walked barefoot, each holding their shoes in their unclasped hands.

Breaking the silence, Michelle asked, "Seriously, Roberto, I am curious. How did you know where to find us?"

He laughed, a sensual deep-throated sound. "It was simple deduction. You and your aunt are Americans. Your aunt rented a BMW. So, where would two American ladies who can afford to rent a BMW stay? The logical places are a well-known beach resort such as the Marianna or the Hilton. I figured it would be the Marianna, so I checked out the parking lot and spotted the serviceman changing the tire on the BMW. If I had been wrong, then I would have tried the Hilton tomorrow."

She giggled. "Very clever, *amigo*."

He dropped her hand and curved his arm around her shoulder, urging her closer to him. A little tingle ran through her at the touch of his fingers on her upper arm, and she shivered a little.

He felt it. "Are you chilled?"

"No, not at all." Slipping her arm around his waist, she leaned more against him. "This is nice."

"*Si.*"

They resumed walking, talking quietly as they made their way down the beach. Roberto pointed out the various towns showing like a string of lights along the curve of the beach. He turned her a little toward the direction they'd come. "Back up there, just at the top, is Malaga." He eased her back around again. "And most of this big curve is Marbella, then Estepona with La Linea at the end and beyond is Gibraltar. It is beautiful, is it not?"

"Gorgeous," Michelle said. It took her breath away with the beauty of the lights and the open sea. Somewhere nearby, she heard Spanish music being played, and unexpected love for this place blossomed within her, filling her with warmth. She'd been transported thousands of miles from home to a land of enchantment with foreign sights, food, and music. She was in freaking Spain strolling down the beach with a gorgeous Spanish boy. She loved every moment of this.

And that easily, the whole dull vacation with her aunt turned into the most wonderful evening she'd ever had. Adventure awaited her here, and she would find it.

To cap it off, Roberto dropped his shoes in the sand, then pressed his hand gently against the side of her face and leaned forward to kiss her cheek ever so lightly. Then he shifted to the other one as she eased closer and he pressed his lips against her cheek. His mouth moved to hers, hovered above it for a moment like a butterfly seeking the perfect spot in a flower before he landed another kiss.

Yes, she screamed in her mind. She wrapped her other arm around Roberto's waist and slipped totally into his arms as they continued to kiss. His warm lips tasted of cherry and lime and were pliant against hers. His tongue flicked against her mouth, tasting her lips and seeking an entry point. She hesitated, then yielded, opening her lips enough to allow him to probe.

The tingle she'd felt turned to a surge of electricity down her spine and straight to her pelvis. Wanting turned to desire as she returned his touches and kisses. He pulled his lips away, and reason returned as she recalled they were on a public beach and concluded they were not going to go any further than making out.

She removed her arms and stepped back, signaling an end to this. Her voice was a whisper as she said, "I can't."

"*Lo siento*. I'm sorry." His voice was gentle as he lifted her chin with his knuckles to gaze into her eyes. "Forgive me. You are beautiful, and I like being with you. It was just a kiss."

She nodded, tears at the edges of her eyes as his words

touched her. *Just a kiss*, she thought. *Who is he kidding?* "Being with you is wonderful, Roberto. And I didn't mind the kiss. But we just met, and we're on a public beach." Then she chastised herself because it sounded stupid. "I mean. I really like you, too, but we barely know each other."

"*Si*, it's too soon." He picked up his shoes and turned back toward the resort, offering his arm again. She returned to his side, and they began to stroll back up the beach.

Chapter 4

∝ Lindy ∝

Late morning found Lindy and Michelle exploring the *Plaza de los Naranjos* in more detail than they'd had the opportunity to do the previous night. Lindy studied the lines and architecture of the *Casa del Corregidor*, admiring the beautiful façade and taking photos from various angles as she envisioned them in the painting forming in her mind.

Over breakfast, Michelle had asked her about going to view Roberto's paintings since his stall was just a short distance from the Plaza. At first, Lindy had been a little cross with her about going over to sit with Roberto at the club, but Michelle enjoyed it so much she quickly forgave her, realizing the girl needed to have some fun with someone. Besides, it had given her time alone with Colin. No harm done. Perhaps she should see how skilled an artist the young man was.

After they finished in the Plaza, Michelle led the way, following Roberto's instructions to the narrow street he'd called an alley where several little street shops were set up. As they started up it, looking for Roberto, he spotted them, stepped out into the path, and waved them on the short distance to his display.

Lindy didn't miss the happiness on her niece's face nor the bright smile Roberto gave her. He reached a hand out to Michelle as she got close and pulled her toward the shop. Lindy followed a little behind, then she got her first look at the lovely paintings. There were several street scenes, the kind tourists like to buy to remind them of the vacation spot. And a few more of the beach with the cities and the mountains in the background, again a memorable tourist item. She stopped now and then to peer at the really interesting ones, such as the one with two elderly men under an orange umbrella at a café table playing chess and the elegant one of a beautiful Spanish girl in a white dress sitting in a garden outside a church, her hand just touching a gardenia. These were wonderful. The boy definitely had talent. She was impressed, more than she thought she would be.

"These are very nice, Roberto," she said. "Where did you study art?"

His smile grew bigger. "*Gracias, señora.* I started painting as a child in school, then won an art scholarship in Madrid for two years."

"Well, you have done very well. You should continue to study and learn more, but your technique is quite good. How old are you?"

Out of the corner of her eye, she saw her niece cringe as she asked.

"Nineteen," he answered. "I hope to be able to go back for another year. I live for painting and would like to make it my life's vocation."

Lindy nodded, pleased with his responses. "I'm sure you will. How much is the painting of the two men?"

It wasn't a big canvas, only nine-by-twelve inches, but she

really liked it, liked the character in the men's faces and the mood of the painting. It called out to her, and that was a rare thing.

"It's seventy-five euros," he said. "For you, I will make it sixty euros."

She gave him a sharp look. "Never undervalue your work, young man. I will pay the seventy-five. It is worth it."

He looked surprised but hastened to remove the painting from the hook. "Thank you. I will wrap it for you. I have bubble wrap to protect it." He stepped back to his table and reached below it for the wrap and tape while Lindy continued to look at the paintings.

Michelle looked at her with curiosity as if she couldn't believe she'd just bought a painting.

"It's quite good, Michelle," she said. "I have a place in the sunroom at my condo where it will be a fine focal point."

"I just figured you'd put something of your own there." Michelle picked up a small painting of an Andalusian horse. They'd seen a few when they had driven down from Madrid and crossed the region. It was only a five-by-seven size, but it was beautifully done. Her fingers ran over the paint, feeling the brush strokes.

"Would you like that painting, dear? As a memento of the trip?"Lindy asked.

"Maybe I would."

Lindy turned toward the painter. "Roberto? We'd like the horse painting also."

He looked up to see which one they had in mind. "Oh, that one. It is nice, no? I give it to you. A gift."

"No, no," Lindy objected. "I wish to pay for it. Name the price."

"Thirty euros," he answered. She knew he had deliberately priced it low.

"May I leave these paintings here while I continue shopping in this area?" Lindy asked, not wanting to cart around the bulky-looking bundle Roberto was assembling.

"Of course. It is no problem," Roberto answered, looking up from wrapping tape around the smaller painting. "If you wish, I will bring them to your hotel later this evening. *Siesta* is from one to four, then I work until eight. I can bring them over then."

"I don't want to trouble you."

"I am happy to do it. Perhaps it might be all right for me to invite your niece to dinner if she would like to go?" His smile was charming, and his eyes shone with hope.

Lindy took a moment to glance at Michelle's equally eager face. Her eyebrows rose as she nodded slightly in agreement. What harm would there be in her niece going out with this boy? They'd already gotten acquainted at the club, slipping away on their own. It would also leave her free to enjoy Colin's company alone. "That would be fine then, Roberto. Thank you."

Sometimes when Lindy watched Michelle, she recalled herself as a girl her age, full of energy, joy, and hope as she went to Paris for the first time. She'd been with a group of four girls and a chaperone from her school in North Carolina. It was their senior trip abroad; she was graduating a year ahead of most of her friends and was the youngest one in the group.

They'd come to Paris on a study trip and an introduction to some of the great art. They went to the *Louvre* first to admire the works of some of the greatest artists who had ever lived. Lindy discovered the power of Rembrandt's paintings and the soul searching of Van Gogh. She immersed herself in art that would endure and touch the spirit of those who viewed it for as long as it existed. She wanted to be like the great artists and create something to reach out to people and garner appreciation long after she was gone.

She'd met Etienne at the *Musée d'Orsay*, just a short distance away from the *Louvre*. She and her classmates had wandered down one afternoon to explore some of the nineteenth-century art displayed there. She had been admiring a painting by Monet when he came up beside her to also study the painting, The Cliffs at Etretat, a splendid study of lighting. Etienne was in Paris, up from Lyon, to study art for a semester. A handsome youth with sandy brown hair and blue-green eyes that sparkled like the Mediterranean on a sunny day, he was also a thief, for he soon stole her heart. Even as she knew it was an infatuation, a romance that can only happen when two people with similar interests are thrown together in a romantic setting away from their normal lives, she still fell for his charms. The sexy voice speaking English with a French accent, the twinkle in his eyes when he whispered romantic words in the most romantic language she'd ever heard, and the sweet taste of his lips on her mouth when he kissed her. To a seventeen-year-old, it was intoxicating, more than wine, and she was drunk on the uniqueness of it all. She never wanted those four weeks of her life to end.

When the time came to bid *au revoir*, she was heartbroken, and Etienne vowed to write her. They made a pact; she would return to Paris as soon as she could, and they would study art and make love together. But, of course, it didn't work out that way. He wrote a few times, then she didn't hear from him for over a year. Eventually, another treasured letter came, and she learned he had fallen in love with another girl. She had been shattered.

At the same time, she still recalled them as some of the most beautiful memories of her life. Those magic days in Paris with the dreamiest boy she'd ever known lived within her. They provided a time she could always touch as something so special that for all the pain at the end, it was worth it for the pure joy and happiness of the moments. So, if this Spanish boy could give her niece the same kind of magical memories, how could she deny her the joy?

So long as the girl took precautions and didn't get herself into any trouble. Lindy figured she would need to have a little discussion with Michelle before she went out with Roberto again.

Chapter 5
⊱ Michelle ⊰

Seated on the back of Roberto's motorcycle, Michelle clung to his waist as he shot through the streets from the coast up toward the hills of the city. She was glad she'd had the foresight to dress in jeans and a light shirt. Although the air was still warm, it felt delightful flowing across her face and through her hair as they raced along.

Roberto had brought the paintings as agreed and spoken briefly with her aunt, promising to get her back at a decent hour, which meant not too long after midnight. Aunt Lindy had taken a few minutes to have a "talk" with Michelle about the basics of sexual relationships, the same ones her mother had already covered two years earlier when she first started dating. Mom would have laughed at her aunt, trying to be so responsible about it while she seemed so awkward.

She sometimes wondered why Lindy had never married. She was so pretty and a very sexy-looking woman. She obviously enjoyed the company of men and dressed like an exotic creature to attract them. She was always high fashion in appearance, and it showed. But she'd never maintained a relationship with one for more than a few months, it seemed.

Even her dad wondered why she never settled down with one.

Roberto turned up what looked like an alleyway it was so narrow then stopped the bike near a dimly lit place. She could smell the scents from cooking meats and spices as they wafted out the door.

"This is a family restaurant," Roberto said, offering his hand as she climbed off. "The food is typical Spanish like I would eat at home. You will see. It is very good."

He opened the door preceding her into the entry leading to the stairs. The actual dining area was upstairs while the bottom level provided the family's quarters, he informed her. As they entered, the host greeted Roberto as a friend, making it obvious he frequented the restaurant. The grinning man guided them to a table for two near the window at the front. Their waiter, a friend she suspected, approached as soon as they were seated. Roberto introduced him as Juan, and he executed a little half-bow to her.

"Do you mind if I order for us?" Roberto asked. "I will have them bring the house specialties, and it will be excellent. Trust me."

A little nervously, Michelle nodded her head. She wasn't a big fan of spicy foods, so she hoped there would be something in it she could eat. As it turned out, she needn't have worried. The tapas were a delicious assortment of five delectable dishes with very mild spice except for the one Roberto devoured with glee. The Spanish cured ham rolls were wonderful, the grilled shrimp delightful, and the cheese and olive assortment tasty. By the time the main course of mouth-watering Moroccan lamb chops arrived, Michelle's stomach felt like it would burst and only ate a little, but it tasted divine. For dessert, they brought small slices of an orange almond cake with a tangerine gelato, finishing the meal to perfection.

Throughout the meal, Roberto told her the names of the dishes and how they were made. "My mama makes many of them at home," he said.

"Where does your family live?" she asked.

"Farther back in the hills," he answered. "In one of the small towns away from the big cities where the tourists come. My father works with metal. He welds iron into sculptures."

"So, your artistic ability is inherited."

"A little bit. But he does not paint. Have you an artistic skill?"

"Not in the painting or drawing sense. But I am an actress. Not professional. Not yet, but I'm studying. I want to make it my career."

"An actress? *Bueno*. I bet you are very good, even now."

She blushed a little, hoping the darkness in the room was enough to cover it. Although shy about her intent to make it her profession, she knew she did well with it. "I've been cast in a few plays in school and had the lead in the local theater production of 'Little Women.' I got rave reviews for it."

He flashed a dazzling smile at her. "Then, one day, I may see you in a movie and tell my friends that I knew you."

She shook her head. "No, I hope you will tell your friends that you *know* me. I hope that wherever our paths take us, that we will remain friends." Then she glanced away, afraid she'd revealed too much of how she felt, but she had sensed an extraordinary connection with this boy. Her mother would tell her it was just the setting, and probably her aunt would agree, They may be right, but it didn't lessen the effect any.

He didn't laugh at her, and his voice was passionate when he said, "I would like to always be your friend, Michelle. People come and go in your life, but some are special. I feel that with you, even after such a short time."

"Me, too." She blurted it out, relieved he understood.

"Would you like to see my studio?" he asked. "It's near here, and I can show you a commission painting I am just finishing up."

"I'd be honored," she answered, finishing her coffee.

Roberto's place was a short ride away from the restaurant on a quiet residential street. It turned out it was actually a two-level flat; he used the downstairs living room area for his studio with his sleeping space on the second floor. For a moment, Michelle was taken aback to realize they were at his flat but then chastised herself for being judgmental. He'd brought her here to show her his work. Clearly, he did have a few pieces in progress.

He pulled a large canvas into the light to show her. "This is the commission work. The one Arturo and I fought about last night. It is almost done, but he wanted it sooner than it will be ready."

It was an exquisite piece of art of an elderly Spanish woman with soulful eyes and a whimsical expression tweaking her lips as if she recalled a time of her youth.

Michelle knew her aunt would absolutely adore the piece if even she could see how magnificent it was. "May I take a photo to show my aunt? I swear it won't go anywhere else."

"Of course. I take pictures of all my art since none of it stays with me." He held it up for her to photograph with him in it.

"Tell me about this painting. Did the person who wanted it send you a photo of the woman or an idea of what he wanted?" She studied the countenance a little more. It had a Mona Lisa quality to it in the enigmatic look of the lips and the distant expression of the eyes. Roberto definitely had talent.

"*Si*, he told Arturo what he wanted, but he left the details up to me. He simply said he wanted an old woman outside an adobe casa recalling her youth. Very simple. And he specified the size of the canvas."

"It's an amazing piece of art, Roberto. I think your client will be thrilled with it. Do you know who he is?"

He shook his head. "No, I get the order through Arturo, and he doesn't even know who the client is. It's ordered through a broker in Sevilla who often requests special paintings for clients who do not wish to identify themselves. It's an odd arrangement, but they pay me well for my paintings. I will make almost five hundred Euros off this one."

"That's good then. Show me your other paintings."

The four paintings he was working on were in various stages of painting and drying. He explained how he did the pictures of the town and beaches, which were all very similar. Popular with the tourists, he sold many comparable canvases.

"The ones your aunt bought are more unique," he told her. "I paint those of people in the towns and from my heart. They are a moment of the soul."

He picked up another painting of a raven-haired girl a little older than Michelle, standing in a garden with the mountains in the background. Her hands caressed a rose. Like the old woman, the wistful look on the girl's face called out to her.

"I would like to paint you," he said as he set it back on the easel. "Would you allow me to do it?"

"Me?" Michelle pressed her hand against her chest in surprise.

"You are beautiful, Michelle. I would like to capture your beauty so I can have it forever with me. I would not sell that painting; I would keep it for my own."

"I don't know. How long would it take to do it? Would I need to pose for it? I only have a few days here in Marbella." She was flattered at the suggestion but didn't think she would want to pose for hours.

"Tomorrow, I could get some photos of you in different settings, and I can work from the photos. You would not have to pose, but I would like for you to sit for a quick sketch if you will."

"Okay. That sounds possible. I will see if I can get time away from my aunt tomorrow. I'll call you."

With a plan in mind, they exchanged phone numbers.

Roberto invited her to sit while he got cold drinks for them. As she settled on the loveseat-sized sofa in the room, her eyes followed him back to the small kitchen, as she appraised the place. The flat wasn't big, but it was clean and tidy. His work constituted the primary use of the downstairs area, and the sofa amounted to the only piece of furniture other than a tall barstool. A half-wall separated the kitchen area from it with an opening at the end to allow access. Tiles across the top of the half-wall formed a countertop.

He handed her a fruity drink, and she took a sip, tasting pineapple and orange juices and another flavor suggesting alcohol. "This is good. It has wine in it, doesn't it?"

"Just a little. It's a quick sangria mix. If the wine is a problem, I can get you just the mix, but it does not taste as good." He waited for her answer.

"It's okay. I can drink it. I've had wine at home."

Relieved, he sank onto the sofa beside her and slipped his free hand on top of hers and let it rest there, not moving more than his thumb along the side of her hand.

"Do you often bring girls here?" she asked, a shy tone to her voice. She felt a little foolish, but she also wanted him to know she didn't think she was special for being invited.

He frowned. "No. No, I hardly ever bring anyone here. This is my workplace. My studio. I brought you because I like you very much and because you are interested in what I do. Most girls I meet are not impressed with what I do, and I do not invite them out to dinner or to here. But you understand my passion."

"I see. I didn't mean anything by it. It was just a curiosity." And it still sounded like a line to her. It was pretty much the same as let me show you my etchings. Roberto surely had many girls who were attracted to him. Don't get involved in a romance, her aunt had warned, and she should listen.

His hand slowly began to slide up her arm, rubbing with a delicate touch, just brushing against her skin. His touch was charged with electricity, making her whole body want more. Then he leaned closer to her, his face in front of her, and his eyes gazing into hers as his hand moved up to touch her right temple, tracing his fingers along the edge of her hairline and down to her jaw in a tantalizingly slow crawl. Her breath hitched. Without thought, she tilted her head up so her jaw was a little higher as those searching fingers moved down along to under her chin, then worked their way up to her lower lip. A single finger slid over her lip toward her open mouth, and she captured it inside her moist cave, biting down ever so lightly on it. She tasted sugar on it, sweet and caramel, like brown sugar, as he rubbed the digit against her teeth.

Who would have thought you could stimulate the teeth in such a way? she thought as they almost vibrated with his strokes. She pressed her hand against his chest, feeling the muscles flex beneath his cotton shirt. She heard the short catch in his breath as her fingers roamed over his chest, touching sensitive spots through the material.

His lips moved in toward her, landing on her forehead, then working their way down the right side of her face, skimming with little brushes of kisses toward her mouth where his fingertip now traced the outline of them. She shivered with the anticipation of his lips against hers.

In their closeness, she detected the scents of a mixture of garlic and olives from dinner combined with sage and thyme; she found them stimulating. His skin felt balmy and slightly moist in the evening's warmth. The dampness of her own body from the combined heat of the night and their growing displays of affection left a layer of sweat on her skin.

Michelle felt torn with wanting to go through with this and knowing she should not. She was not untouched as she'd been with a couple of boys at home and had taken precautions, but she knew it was not wise to pursue this with someone she barely knew. Yet, she wanted more of the foreplay, and she desired to touch him, to make him feel as antsy as she did.

His mouth made contact with hers, and all thoughts of resistance vanished. His lips tasted like cherries, limes, and oranges from the sangria, delicious with a tiny kick of barely-bridled passion. His hands cupped the sides of her head as he deepened the kiss. She responded with a low growl of desire and pushed against him as she opened her mouth wider to him.

Roberto's right hand dropped to her blouse to begin undoing the top buttons on it. Then he slipped it inside and cupped her already firm breast within his grasp. Small and compact as they were, she never wore a bra. If it surprised him, he gave no indication, not even a hesitation in his exploration. As his fingers circled and teased, she dropped her head backward with a deep exhale and drew in more air. He moved his mouth slowly down her throat.

Just as his kisses landed on her collarbone, a phone rang. She caught her breath, startled by the sound. For a moment, she thought it was hers, but the ringtone wasn't right. Roberto cursed in Spanish, his voice low as he pulled back from her and answered the call while he sat up.

"Si?" he said, his voice sharp and business-like. He frowned as he listened to the caller, a look of annoyance crossing his face. He rose to his feet to go to the small kitchen to talk, waving a hand at Michelle to indicate she should stay where she was.

She couldn't hear the conversation, but she could see him pacing around the kitchen and could pick up the tone of his voice now and then. He was annoyed, she thought, and his voice came through with a sharp bark of an answer. She guessed this was not good news. Sensing the mood they had started had just vanished, she began buttoning her blouse and went to the bathroom next to the stairs to tidy up a little.

When she came out, Roberto was sitting forward on the sofa with his hands clasped together. He looked up at her and managed a gentle smile. "I am sorry, *carita*. It was business. Arturo again about the painting as if I can make the paint cure any quicker than it does. He should understand that by now. These are not acrylics; they are oils and hand-mixed colors I use. They take time to dry completely before I can continue with the last steps. He wants the painting tomorrow, and I told him it is not possible. If I force it, the paint could crack."

"You're right about it, and he shouldn't try to hurry you," she told him as she sank back to the couch. "I need to get back to my hotel anyway, Roberto. Can you take me? Or I can call for a cab..."

"Of course, I'll take you," he said. He reached an arm around her shoulder to pull her close. "It was good tonight until the phone call. I should turn the annoying thing off at night."

She laughed. "I have the same problem sometimes with people calling me at the most inconvenient time. I'll see you tomorrow, though, one way or another."

He nodded, then reached his other hand across and opened it to reveal an orange paper-wrapped chocolate. "For my *dulce*."

With a girlish laugh, she took it, unwrapped it, and popped the orange-flavored confection into her mouth. Taking her hand, they moseyed to the door where Roberto paused to lock up. She climbed on the back of the motorcycle and wrapped her arms around his waist as he kicked it on. With a quick start, they headed down the hilly road toward the coast.

Briefly, Michelle wondered what her aunt and her father might say about her modeling for a painting. Somehow, she thought Aunt Lindy might approve, but her dad was another whole story.

Chapter 6

෪ Lindy ෨

Colin took Lindy to a restaurant up the beach from the hotel where they could dine by the sea and enjoy the sound of the waves against the shore. Pleased to some extent that Roberto had invited Michelle to dinner, it still nagged at her a little since she needed to be responsible for the girl while they were traveling. She reminded herself she'd traveled in Europe at the same age with less supervision. Their chaperone, a young woman barely five years older than they were, could rarely be found, which meant the girls scurried out and about on their own. Slipping away to spend time with Etienne had been simple.

She brought her attention back to Colin, who had been telling her about his scouting activities for the day, a trip up into the hills above Mijas and looking at possible sets they could use for the film. She listened with fascination as he explained what he looked for in consideration, including easy access for cameras, houses with the right look, and the backgrounds they would be able to use. It took a trained eye and imagination to visualize what the scene would look like through the camera's eye to find just the right spots.

"Isn't there a whole town built for movies near here?" Lindy asked, positive she'd heard of spaghetti westerns being filmed in Spain.

"Oh, yes, there is. Close to Almería. The set at Fort Bravo emulates a western town with Spanish facades, able to fill in for towns in California, New Mexico, Arizona, and Texas during the settlement of the west. Many films have been made there. Unfortunately, it's the wrong look for the movie I'm working on. These days, it pays the bills as a tourist park, but can still be used for films."

"Too bad it's not right for your film. It would simplify your job."

"Simplify, yes, but then it would make me not as necessary to the filming." He laughed. "I enjoy the trips and looking for new and unique locations we can use. I'm going over to Morocco the day after tomorrow to check out a couple of places there." He paused, eyes lighting up. "Listen, why don't you come along with me? We could spend the night and come back on the afternoon ferry the next day."

Taken off guard, Lindy blurted out, "Oh, I couldn't do that. There's Michelle to consider."

"Bring her along, then. It would be good to have your eye looking at the sets as well. As an artist, you would see things I might miss." He smiled encouragingly at her, nodding his head as if it could change her answer.

She considered. "Well, it might give her a different perspective on what life is like in a poorer country than she's used to seeing. Let me discuss it with her tonight, and I'll decide. I'll let you know tomorrow."

"All right, then. Why don't you join me tomorrow? I'm going down to Malaga to check out a couple of places near there. You can see what I do first hand and give me your thoughts." He rested his hand on hers, his fingers rubbing against the back of hers. "We could leave right after breakfast and be back by late afternoon. What do you say?"

Lindy mulled it over for a minute or so. Surely Michelle would be fine on her own for one day. The girl wanted to spend time at the beach, and if she stayed in the hotel area, she should be safe. Smiling, Lindy nodded. "Yes, I'd love it, Colin."

He smiled, bringing a sparkle of joy to his eyes as he leaned forward, planting a gentle kiss on her lips. She closed her eyes, savoring the light touch and delicate taste of the sangria on his mouth. It had been a while since she'd been with a man. Too long.

Holding her hand in his, Colin rose, pulling her up with him, and wrapped an arm around her waist as he guided her out of the restaurant and down to the beach. They strolled along, her head pressed sideways against his shoulder while he leaned his cheek against the top of it.

In some ways, Lindy felt as if she'd known this man for a long time. She felt comfortable, totally at ease, in his arms. The scent of his cologne reminded her of days spent in London and a man, not so different, she'd dated then. Same scent, same easy style. Why had they broken up?

Oh, yes, she remembered. She had a commission in Italy, a painting that would pay a lot of money, but it would take several months. At first, he said he would wait for her. Then as the months stretched and she got another job, the interest began to fade, and he quit waiting for her. Or did she simply cease to care about him? Back then, her focus was on painting, not romance.

She snuggled closer to Colin's side, content to be with him on this magical Spanish night. No doubt about it in her mind. Spain held its own unique enchantment, and she had fallen under its spell. And what was wrong with that?

As they strolled, the waves sloshed against the shore in gentle gurgles. No big breakers rolling in off the Mediterranean Sea tonight. Ahead, lights from the beach resorts reflected crookedly in the water with the gentle rolling. Other couples wandered along, some with bare feet in the surf while others, old and young, just walked hand in hand on a balmy night. Romance lingered in the air as the eastern breeze carried the fresh scent of verbenas and oranges from the plants lining the gardens along the shore.

She inhaled deeply, and Colin squeezed her waist a bit, then turned his head toward her as his mouth sought her lips again. They made contact, and she fell into the embrace as he turned her in his arms while his kisses grew deeper, and her longing increased. Her body felt young again, sparking to the need growing in it as his hands caressed her face, his fingers brushing against her hair. It definitely had been too long.

But they were on a public beach and, while others were also kissing now and then, they weren't exactly making out. As if aware of Lindy's thoughts, Colin pulled back, and a sheepish grin twisted his mouth. "That was more than I expected," he whispered, his British accent making it sound so sexy. "But much less than I want."

"Not here," she said pragmatically.

"Of course not," he agreed. "And not tonight."

With a sigh, he held up his wrist with his watch showing. "It's getting late, and if I'm going to work tomorrow, I need my sleep."

Lindy's laugh came out more like a chortle of relief. She didn't know if she felt quite ready to go to a hotel room with a man she'd only just met, although her body felt ready to party. But she also had Michelle to think about, and she wanted to speak to her before she and Colin left to go scouting in the morning.

Colin walked her back to their beach resort, stopping at the elevator of Lindy's unit. Taking her face in his hand, he kissed her again, his lips lingering a bit, then he murmured, "I will see you in the morning, my dear. Sleep well."

As Lindy opened the door to the room at their condo, she found Michelle had just come home a short time before her and was relaxing on the sofa with a cup of tea.

"Did you have a nice evening, Auntie?"

"Very nice, indeed," Lindy answered. "How about you? Was dinner with your young man good?"

"It was. He took me to a non-tourist restaurant where everyone knew him, and the food was delicious. Then we went to his studio, and Roberto showed me some of his paintings. One he is working on looks amazing. I took a photo of it. Let me show you." She pulled out her phone and called up the photo, handing it to Lindy to see.

Willing to indulge her, Lindy took the camera and looked at the photo. It wasn't very large, but it did look like he'd done a beautiful painting. It was similar to the one she had bought in theme but quite different in expression. As she studied, she sensed something familiar about it, something she'd felt when she'd seen the paintings she'd bought. Every artist has their own style, and this was Roberto's, but it seemed like she'd seen it before.

As she handed the phone back, she said, "It is quite good. A little hard to evaluate in the small image, but it is obviously well done. The expression is excellent. Roberto is quite gifted, I think."

She made herself a cup of tea and sat across from her niece.

"Michelle, would you mind awfully being on your own tomorrow? Colin has asked me to join him on a scouting trip for most of the day, and it does sound like fun. I'd be back before dinner."

Michelle smiled, her eyes lighting up with happiness. "No problem, Auntie. I'm glad you two are getting along so well."

"So, you don't mind?"

With a shake of her head, Michelle replied, "No, of course not. I have things I can do around here."

Sipping her tea, she listened with half an ear as Michelle spoke more about the commissioned painting Roberto was working on and how his agent called him about it. Lindy's mind lingered on Colin and the possibly romantic day she might have with him while looking at various locations. She counted him more fascinating than any man she'd been with in the past five years. Besides, he seemed to have more regard for her talent and work than many men she'd dated. Most just found it mildly interesting, but not something they wanted to discuss in any depth. The idea of including her in their work was out of the question. So, seeing a man who might value her opinion was refreshing.

The idea of spending a couple of days, and a night, with him in Tangiers was exciting, but bringing her niece along would definitely put a damper on the trip, although she would not regret it. She had an obligation to both Michelle and her brother. She promised to take care of her on this trip as Jonathon and Karin, his wife, were so concerned about the safety of their daughter in Europe.

"I have another thing to tell you," she said when Michelle paused for breath in her story. "Colin has invited us to go to Tangiers the day after tomorrow. We'd stay overnight and come back the following afternoon. Doesn't that sound like fun?"

Michelle's eyes widened, and her mouth fell open. "You and me with Colin for over twenty-four hours? You must be joking? In fact, it's kind of weird."

"Why? What makes you think so?" Lindy was stunned at the reaction.

"Auntie, it would really make me a third wheel. The two of you on a romantic little trip with the tag-along, what-can-I-do-with-her niece. How do you see that as a good time for any of us?" Michelle rose to her feet to take her cup back to the kitchenette. Her head was still shaking in denial at the prospect of such a preposterous suggestion.

"We'd have a separate room," Lindy managed to sputter out in defense of the suggestion.

The girl gazed at her from over the counter. "No. This little trip isn't something I want to be involved in. You go ahead with Colin and have a great time. I'll stay here. We have the suite until the weekend, so why shouldn't I just use it while you're gone?"

"That's not an acceptable option," Lindy replied.

"Oh, sure. I can go along being miserable and feeling out of place while the two of you are a couple. Colin doesn't want a teenager tagging along, Aunt Lindy. He wants to spend the time with you. I think you should go and have a good time. Don't worry about me. I'm old enough to take care of myself. I won't do anything outrageous while you're gone. I'll be perfectly safe. There are other teenagers here who may or may not have parents attached, and they are all fine."

Lindy's brow wrinkled into a worried frown as she considered her niece's words. She was right; she was old enough to be on her own for a day and a half. Even chaperoned in Paris,

Lindy had been mostly on her own for all the good the accompanying adult did. If her brother hadn't been so paranoid about this trip, they probably wouldn't even be having this conversation.

With a reluctant sigh, she said, "All right, Michelle. I do want to go with Colin to Morocco, and while I would probably be more comfortable on one level if you came along, I do realize it is an awkward situation for all of us. So, you may stay here. But I want you to check in with me several times during the day, even if it's only a text saying you're fine. You are to stay here at the hotel at night, not go running off with Roberto. You may go into Marbella during the day. Please, please be careful. The world is sometimes wicked."

"I promise I will be careful." Michelle hugged her. "I will be safe here. There's no need to worry."

As Lindy sent her too-happy niece off to bed, she worried if she was doing the right thing. Was she putting her niece at risk to indulge her own happiness? She decided she would put it to the test while she was off with Colin in the Malaga area, then she headed to bed herself.

Chapter 7
✂ Michelle ✂

After a late breakfast in the hotel cafe, Michelle lingered to watch as her aunt and Colin set off in the rental BMW for their excursion to Malaga. She waved one last goodbye as if they were going away for days instead of merely the one day of scouting, then called Roberto.

"I have the whole day to spend with you," she told him, excitement in her voice. "When should I meet you at the Plaza?"

While he was pleased, he told her he couldn't close up the shop before one, so he would head to the *Plaza de los Naranjos* once he was done, and would see her by one-thirty. He instructed her to go to the *Naranjos de Jardin Cafe* across from the city hall and get an outdoor table where he could find her quickly.

A bit disappointed, she returned to the room and dressed in a sleeveless buttercup-yellow dress, a choice she thought would photograph well. She also packed a pair of jeans and a girl-cut t-shirt in her small backpack along with a pale green scarf. She hoped it would suffice for their plan. Excited to be doing this, she hurried out the door, checking to be sure it locked and headed to the hotel lobby where a string of taxis just outside waited for potential fares.

Taking a cab to the plaza, Michelle wandered through the nearby streets, browsing in several shops on the road behind the square to kill time. At one, she found a cute yet practical leather purse that would work well for school in the fall. The pockets looked large enough to carry all her items, except her books, but a just-big-enough side pocket with a zipper would hold her tablet. The price seemed reasonable for leather, and she liked the soft tan color of it. When she spotted a stylish leather wallet, she decided her father would love it and added that to the items she hand-carried. Happy with these purchases, she paid and slipped the shopping bag she'd also bought over her arm before moving on to the next shop.

This one displayed a huge selection of beautiful silk scarves in all colors and designs. She spotted a gorgeous silk blouse in pale green and rose colors and fell in love with it. Long ties at the side crossed to the waist, cinching it in. Michelle couldn't resist and bought it even though it was pricier than she liked. But it would be fantastic for the photos, she was sure. Then she decided to buy a matching long pale green skirt.

By the time she returned to the plaza at almost one-thirty, she had to hunt to find a table near the walkway through the square where Roberto might easily spot her. She spotted one, located just on the edge of the shop's area, and begged the host at the restaurant to let her have it. Settling in, she sent Roberto a text message to let him know she was waiting, then sat back to order an iced tea. She gazed up at the sky, enjoying the high strings of white clouds scattered across it. A light breeze cooled the day a little. She loved it here on the coast, where every day felt like a holiday. She was dreaming about how wonderful it would be to live in Marbella when Roberto walked up behind her.

"*Tan bonito,*" he said in a low, sexy voice, and a grin spread across her face.

She turned, springing from her chair to throw her arms around his neck as he kissed her briefly.

Once they sat, the waiter brought menus for them, and they chatted as they made their choices. Since she wasn't too hungry after a large breakfast, she ordered a small salad while Roberto went for a sandwich. Then she showed him the blouse she'd just bought.

"Is this perfect?" she asked. "I just fell in love with it as soon as I spotted it. What do you think?"

"The color is splendid," he said as he felt the material. "Fine quality as well. I wish for you to wear it in the pictures. Will you?"

She grinned. "I knew you would. I got the skirt as well."

"We can take several with you in this as well as what you're wearing now. Did you bring jeans also?" He eyed her backpack.

"I did."

"Excellent. There is a garden near here where I would like to take a few shots of you, then we can go up into the hills for more photos. I have a couple of places in my mind. So you put the jeans on when we go on my bike."

She nodded. "I like the plan."

As she ate, she kept glancing at his face, seeing those movie-star good looks and wondering why he wasn't someone's steady boyfriend at the very least. He was young, yes, but it would seem he could have his pick of the local girls. "So, have you gone out with many tourists?" Michelle knew it sounded like she was fishing, which she was, but she was curious.

"No. A couple now and then have caught my eye, but I do not go looking for them. I liked you when I first talked to you. If you had not intrigued me then, I would not have come looking for you. But I think you are different from most of the girls who come here for the summer."

She laughed. "Oh, I came looking for sun, sea, and fun like all the rest. But I was saddled with my aunt, and that put a damper on the plan."

"But you don't come here like the spoiled American girl or the diva who expects people to jump to her command. We get a lot of those. And I don't like a girl who throws herself at me. You're a little, how do you say, bashful?" As he said it, she blushed a shade, proving his point, and he grinned.

A few blocks from the Plaza, a small, private garden, lush with beautiful flowers and flowing water fountains, hid behind a tall wall. The owners of the house knew Roberto and welcomed them both as friends when they arrived to do the pictures. The lady, who Roberto introduced as Señora Navarro, showed Michelle to the bathroom to freshen her makeup and hair before she went out to the garden where Roberto had already chosen several spots to stage the photos.

Michelle admired a stunning wrought-iron bench set among some birds-of-paradise plants. Situated where the decorative stucco wall with elegant arches in the background met the edge of a surrounding hillside, the area imbued an air of solitude. Roberto showed her where he wanted her to sit and encouraged her to strike a few different poses and expressions.

Taking a deep breath, she pretended it was a fashion photoshoot, moving her neck to a sexy angle, then turning her head a different direction and swinging her hair around. Roberto took photo after photo as she changed positions, then he came over and sat beside her.

"Michelle, let's try for more emotion in this. I want you to look like your lover has just left you for another woman. I want to see the sorrow and loss in your face."

She thought about it for a moment, then had the inspiration for it as she imagined saying goodbye to Roberto after a night of passion fulfilled all her fantasies, knowing she would never see him again. Her eyes held the wistful pain of separation as her mouth remembered the last touch of his lips. She carried the emotions through several changes while Roberto shouted encouragement as he took many photos.

Then he suggested she change into the green and rose blouse and matching skirt, so she retreated to the dressing room. Slipping out of the yellow dress, she pulled on the green skirt, then paused to put her hair up. She liked the look with just three hairpins holding her long hair in a sophisticated twist, so she left it up and pulled on her blouse, leaving the top button open and tying the ends into a sexy square knot at the left hip. She adjusted her makeup to bring out her eyes a little more.

As she returned to the garden, Roberto stared at her, taking in the more sophisticated look. "*Que bonita.* You are gorgeous. So elegant. A man would be a fool to leave you."

She glowed with the praise, barely whispering, "Thank you."

Within the garden, sat an exquisite gazebo—Roberto called it a *mirador*—in the middle of a mirror lake surrounded by gardens. The view created pure enchantment. Kneeling, the skirt flowing around her, she gazed into the water where her reflection showed. Across from her, Roberto took pictures, moving around for different views as she changed her position slowly. He came into the gazebo and took more photos as she shifted her poses even more.

After she'd exhausted nearly every pose she could manage and pulled a variety of expressions, he asked her to remove just one hairpin letting part of her hair fall in a wave over her shoulder, then he took those photos. At his request, she released the rest of her hair and shook it out, and he continued to photograph her. They moved to other parts of the garden where he took even more photos. She figured he must have taken over a hundred at this point.

"Enough," he said. "I think I have inspiration for many more paintings from here. Change into your jeans, and we'll go up above the city." He gave her a quick hug as she went back to the house to change. This had been amazing, and if she was lucky, he might give her a few shots to add to her portfolio.

As she came back, she saw their hostess had brought out a pitcher of lemonade. Roberto sat under a canopy sipping a glass while he thumbed through the images on his camera.

"*Por favor*, for you, enjoy a *limonada*," Señora Navarro said as she offered a glass. "You have been working hard. You need a break."

Roberto didn't seem to be in a hurry, so she accepted it and sat next to him to try to peer over his shoulder to glimpse the photos. The angle wasn't clear enough for her to see the detail and colors, but he seemed to be pleased with the results.

"Can I see them?" she asked.

He looked up. "Of course, but they aren't very big on the screen. Once I can put them on a computer, you will see the detail better."

She nodded and took the offered camera. He showed her which button to push to advance the displayed images. She worked her way through photo after photo of herself in so many poses with shots ranging from full length to mid-length to close-up. She made mental notes of her preferred shots.

As she handed the camera back, she said, "They look fabulous. Might I have copies of some of them?"

"Naturally, I thought you would want copies, so I will copy the best ones for you and put them on a thumb drive. Okay?"

"Perfect."

She beamed with a radiant smile, so he lifted the camera up to grab another quick photo. Then he indicated they needed to get going. It was almost four o'clock already, and he wanted to get into the hills before it got too late. Sunset occurred around nine at this time of year, but too many shadows would be more challenging to photograph around, he explained.

In many ways, the hills and mountains of Marbella were comparable to those of the Los Angeles area, except more vegetation seemed to grow naturally in the dry ground. Even though it was mid-summer, many plants and shrubs spread across the hillsides like multi-colored throw rugs. As the winding roads snaked above the town, they cascaded through condominiums, houses, and elegant residential areas. The higher up the hillside, the better the view and the finer the houses. Likewise, Michelle felt sure the price tags ascended equally. They went by a palatial-looking villa with its generous balconies facing the Mediterranean Sea. Purported to be a family residence, it resembled a grand hotel it was so enormous

Maybe someday I'll be a multi-million-dollar movie star and be able to afford one of these places overlooking the world, Michelle thought. It would be a wild fantasy come to fruition if it were to happen. Even if the odds were stacked against it, fate never concerned itself with statistics. She kept telling herself that, and with the right connections, she might have a better than average chance.

Roberto leaned left to swing the bike around another corner, and ahead of them, a small grated road branched off and left the houses behind as it climbed up the hillside toward a particularly green-looking gully area. As they neared it, he pulled the motorcycle to a stop and kicked the stand down, then climbed off.

Michelle slid off the back, her eyes tracking down toward the sea. Below them, the whole of the Marbella to Gibraltar coastline shone in the afternoon light. Houses, in uneven rows and circles, and blocks of white and tan buildings marched down to the coastal road where the resorts and clubs took over. In various areas, little patches of green and color splashes stood out as the parks, gardens, and squares.

Roberto caught her arm and led her to a trail leading down into the gully area. She paused, hearing the gurgle of running water as it leaped from level to level down the hill.

"A stream?" she asked.

"*Si.* A little creek runs most of the summer as the snowfall from the highest elevations melts. In the spring, it is fuller and rushes down to a reservoir above the city. Now it just makes a slow journey, and these plants in this gully benefit from the water."

The further into the crevice they went, the lusher the vegetation. Even gorgeous wildflowers bloomed. Lavender grew in patches of sun, and Michelle could detect the scent mixed with the sweetness of rosemary plants. Tall bushes of all sorts, including a few wild olive trees, grew in abundance. Bright yellow flowers stood out on bushes of hardy broom. When they reached the stream, Roberto pulled her along toward a place where there was a break in the tall trees, and a splash of light burst through, giving it an otherworldly look.

"Here," he said. "I want you to pose here."

Nearby, a bird-of-paradise flower bloomed, and Michelle decided to play with it for a photo. She got nose to beak with it, so to speak, and Roberto took the pictures from several angles. Using a small opening between bushes as a dressing room, she slipped out of her tee-shirt and put the green blouse and skirt back on, twisted her hair to a side bun, and posed with it again for a different look.

Roberto pulled some of the purple lavender flowers and laced them in her hair, then got photos of her caressing the bush that had donated the ornaments. She stood in the stream in her bare feet, lifting the skirt to keep it from getting wet. Roberto teased her, calling her a Spanish diva, and they laughed.

In no time it seemed, three hours had fled while they chased the sunlight and took photos. As they finished, Roberto joined her for a shot, squeezing up against her and wrapping his free arm around her waist while she turned to lay her head against his shoulder, and he snapped the picture with a remote.

When Michelle gazed at the photo, it looked incredibly beautiful and romantic. She felt like a different person with him, like a wild, exotic butterfly flirting with a dynamic dragonfly. As he looked over her shoulder, he turned her face toward him and kissed her, his lips sweet with the taste of lemons and sugar still. She turned into his arms, and they drank deeply of each other's lips.

He reluctantly pulled away, looking at the darkening sky and told her to change clothes so they could get down to the town before dark. After she hurriedly changed into her jeans, he began to pick their way back to his motorcycle.

"Are you hungry?" he asked, stepping over some succulent

plants carpeting the ground.

"Famished," she answered.

"Then we'll go to the best seafood place in the area."

Michelle got her third text message of the day from Lindy as she and Roberto were going into a little café near Roberto's studio. She paused to read the note with an update from her aunt. They were stopping for dinner, then they would be on their way back to Marbella, arriving in about two hours. She sent a quick acknowledgment, telling them to take their time. She knew this was a test and wanted to reassure her aunt she would be fine if she went to Tangier with Colin the next day.

Roberto raised a questioning eyebrow as she replied and tucked her phone back in her pocket. "My aunt is just checking on me. She may go on an overnight trip with Colin tomorrow, and I asked to stay here, so she's deciding still. It's not like I haven't been anywhere on my own before. My mom and dad aren't as protective as Aunt Lindy."

He nodded as they followed a waiter to the table. "She just feels responsible. Has she had any children of her own?"

"No. She never married, and she's led a pretty independent life. She's like an Auntie Mame character, a bit wild and eccentric. But I think she's afraid of my father."

They sat, and the waiter spoke to Roberto in Spanish, then switched to English when he realized she didn't follow what he was saying. "Pardon, miss. Our special tonight is steamed prawns with saffron-infused rice and fresh asparagus. We also have *paella* with clams, lobster, and chicken, also in a saffron sauce."

Even though it remained an expensive spice, it appeared saffron was the seasoning of Spain, but to be fair, *paella* was the national dish, and it was delicious. Nonetheless, she decided to go with the prawns. Roberto ordered a white wine to go with it. She was underage, but they didn't card her, so she accepted the poured glass.

"Just one," she told Roberto with an impish look.

"Of course," he agreed.

"So, did you work on the commissioned painting today?" she asked. He hadn't said anything, and so far, it seemed Arturo had not called him again.

He winced as if it was a sore subject. "A little bit, but there is something that bothers me about the eyes, and I want to fix it. Arturo wants it by tomorrow evening, so when I go home tonight, I'll try to get it done. If I am satisfied, then maybe he can take it. I hate being rushed. You cannot do your best work with someone setting deadlines on it."

"Then, you need to stand by your convictions."

The waiter delivered a plate of *tapas* and Michelle selected a ham and olive roll. "It's your name and reputation that you're building."

"You are right." He saluted her with the wine and took a sip before eating a piece of fried squid.

As Michelle looked around the dark café with candles on the tables and a guitarist playing in the background, she thought this all seemed surreal. Was she really here in a little local restaurant in Spain with a handsome, charming native artist talking about his work? Was he really so interested in her that he took her photos, many times, and wanted to paint her? Did he find her beautiful or just interesting-looking? Most of all, was she falling for him? It was not a good idea, and she knew it.

Chapter 8

∽ Lindy ∾

As Lindy rushed to pack a few things in her smaller bag, she questioned her sanity again. She shouldn't be leaving Michelle here alone and running off with Colin for an overnight trip. If she'd been here on her own, it would be an entirely different matter, but what kind of example was this to set for an impressionable young girl?

Colin wasn't like any of the flings she'd had over the years, and she really felt there was a connection with him. Their day exploring Malaga and surrounds had been fantastic. They'd looked at the settings and seen them through different yet similar eyes—she, from the view of an artist and he, from the lens of a film camera. They'd compared notes, each pointing out something the other might not have noticed and finding different perspectives in the observations. She'd felt more stimulated creatively than she had in quite some time, and she found herself anxious to sketch an image or two to pursue when she had time. She snapped dozens of photos she could revisit for inspiration while he did the same to analyze later to determine which locations he would ultimately use for the movie.

Michelle might have found the day dull and even tedious had she been along, but Lindy reveled in the beauty and possibilities. She suspected the Tangier trip would be equally as wonderful and quite probably, even more tedious for her niece if she forced Michelle to come with them. The girl had gotten along fine while they were off in Malaga. She'd even dined with Roberto, who, it seemed, was a fine young man as well as a kindred spirit.

She turned to her niece, who sat at the kitchen counter, sipping an orange tea while she got everything ready to go. "I'm almost set. Are you sure you're okay with this?"

"Yes, I'll be just hunky-dory, Auntie. I've been home alone many times, and this place is secure with limited access and security guards. I promise I won't go wandering around the town alone after dark, and I'll text you every six or eight hours, or you can do the same. Go and have a great time with Colin." She flashed a conspiratorial smile at Lindy.

"All right, then. I'm off. You have the hotel name and number in Tangier in case the cell phone doesn't work." She pulled Michelle into a tight embrace. "Be safe, darling, and call me if there are any problems."

Michelle kissed her cheek. "I will. Not stop worrying and go!"

Colin waited by his rental car, a gray Ford Escort, which he told Lindy was better to take to Gibraltar than the BMW. Even then, he'd told her he was leaving it at the ferry dock in Algeciras rather than taking it to Morocco. Once they were there, he'd hire a taxi to drive them around. She agreed it sounded like a good plan.

She'd been to Morocco many years earlier with a tour group, and it wasn't entirely safe. No matter how exotic or romantic it might seem, it was still a third world country and part of a different culture that wasn't entirely friendly toward the western world. Not as risky as going to Iraq or Iran, Colin assured her, but they did need to be cautious and alert. While

Tangier was a tourist location, and they encouraged filming as much as any city looking for the revenue, it also was a city of thieves, smugglers, drug runners, and kidnappers.

"So, why are we going there?" Lindy asked, a touch of humor in her voice, as he explained all this on the drive to the ferry.

"It's a unique filming spot. The Kasbah would be perfect for about four scenes, and at least one shot at the seawall."

They took the mid-morning ferry from Algeciras, or more specifically, the east side of Tarifa on the Rio de la Miel where the port was located, crossing the Straits of Gibraltar to land in Tangier just after noon. The new Tangier-Med port had opened in recent years, and it deposited them about forty kilometers away from the city.

After they cleared customs, Colin flagged down a taxicab and struck a deal with the driver to be exclusive to them for the next thirty or so hours until they caught the late afternoon ferry back the following day. He gave him the hotel address in Tangier, a medium-sized European-owned place in mid-town. Constructed in the Moroccan-style with beautiful arches and intricate design work, the building surrounded a huge square garden with a fountain and beds filled with blooming flowers.

As they checked into their room, Lindy delighted in the light and airy space and the squatting queen-sized bed with a canopy and silk curtains. Arched windows showed etched designs around the frames. Light blue and gold silk-brocade curtains hung from the ceiling and just brushed the floor. She crossed to push them back from a window.

"It's wonderful," Lindy said as she peered toward the gardens and the café beyond. "It's like a little oasis in the town."

"It is quite nice, isn't it?" Colin answered. He came to gaze over her shoulder and slid his arms around her waist to give her a squeeze. Leaning forward a little, he nibbled at her neck, and she giggled like a schoolgirl.

"Are you getting hungry?" Lindy asked.

"Yes, but it could wait a little while."

He kissed just below her left ear, then down a little, following her jawline.

"No, it can't." Her voice sounded wistful, yet firm. "Don't you have an appointment in an hour and a half?"

He sighed. "Yes. Let's grab a quick lunch at the café, then head over to the director's office."

As soon as they finished dining, they left the hotel and found their cab waited for them as agreed. Colin cracked a little smile as he told her he hadn't been entirely sure their driver had understood, so he was relieved.

An office building near the kasbah housed the director's office. The older-looking building surprised them with a modern interior. Taking the elevator to the third floor, they located the office. Jarrah Samaha, the official in charge of filming in Tangier and the first person a scout should visit, greeted them warmly. A modern businessman, he dressed in white slacks and a white *kurta,* or long-sleeved shirt, that came almost to his knees, and he wore a white cotton *talib* rounded hat on his head.

Although Lindy had dressed in loose-fitting white slacks and a long-sleeved shirt and had put her hair into a tight bun, wrapping a blue scarf around it, she worried her clothing wasn't conservative enough. Samaha gave her an approving smile and a little nod, but it was clear he was interested in only what Colin had to say. She stepped back out of the way and stood against the wall, gazing out the window toward the city, appearing not to listen to the conversation.

Colin explained what he needed for the film, asked about *Kasbah* and *medina* film spots, and a location near the seawall he had used before on another project. Samaha assured him he had several shops in the medina that would fit the bill and offered to show them to him.

As if she weren't there at all, he led the way to the door. Colin fell into step with him, signaling to Lindy to come with them. She hurried to catch up but kept a step or two behind. The entrance to the *kasbah* was a couple of blocks away, and they walked briskly toward it. Lindy's ankle turned a little on the cobblestones, and she stumbled. She shouldn't have worn the chunky heels, she decided. The ends were just the right thickness to catch the cracks, so she'd have to be careful.

An outdoor market, the *medina* or central town, featured stalls, food markets, and buildings selling all kinds of wares such as pots, skillets, clothing, silks, shoes, and even meat shops where hundreds of people browsed, purchased clothes and other goods, then shopped for dinner.

Lindy was jostled as she tried to follow Colin; however, between the crowd and her attempts to avoid any missteps, she was losing contact with him. She stumbled again and almost fell, but a man caught her arm, steadying her. He wore one of the long robes and a turban on his head, and sunglasses covered his eyes. Nodding politely, she thanked him and stepped away to continue, but he held onto her arm.

"Are you lost?" he asked, his English marked by a strong accent, more Spanish than Middle Eastern.

"No. My friend is ahead and probably looking for me now. Please excuse me."

"I will help you find him." He kept hold of her arm and began walking with her in the direction she'd been going.

Lindy's mind raced with worry since she knew that in the past, sometimes women were abducted in the area surrounding the *medina*. Was this man just trying to help her, or was he going to lead her away from the crowd where someone might respond if she screamed?

She balked, stepping back as he tried to pull her. "No. I will call him, and he'll come back for me."

"Is not necessary." He pulled again at her arm.

"Let me go. Now. Or I will scream." She jerked her head away, and he grabbed for her, his hand sliding around her neck, pinching it as he tried to grip her.

As he turned her face toward him, he looked at her, eyes hidden behind the glasses, but a hard line on lips. "I try to help you, so you come with me." He started to reach inside his robe.

Her first thought was he had a gun or a knife. She jerked hard and kicked at him, pulling her arm away from him and started to run. The path through the crowd proved difficult with so many people and so little open room, but she went as fast as she could. She was afraid it wouldn't be fast enough, and she screamed Colin's name as loud as she could.

She cut through a vegetable market where there was a little more space than on the main walk, then ran back out into it, still yelling for Colin. Behind her, she could hear the man pursuing her, yelling for her to wait.

Her heel caught again, then snapped off, and she tumbled to the ground, landing on her right knee and twisting her ankle. Struggling to get to her feet, she was startled when hands grabbed her again. She tried to turn to fight off the man only to find a woman attempting to help her up and then, just behind the lady, Colin coming toward her.

"Thank you," she sobbed to the woman, her emotions suddenly overwhelmed by escaping what she was sure was an abduction. Then Colin stood beside her, reaching to pull her into his arms.

"Lindy? What happened? I turned around, and you weren't there."

"My ankle. I think I twisted it. Shoe broke. A man was chasing me." She spat it all out at once and turned into his embrace.

Alarm showing on his face, she saw Colin look around the crowd, then shake his head. She followed his eyes and couldn't spot the man who'd grabbed her. So many men wore robes and head coverings. It could have been any of them, but more likely he faded into the crowd when he saw help coming.

Colin put his arm around her waist to help her walk, and she limped along, the pressure on her knee, causing it to hurt, and her ankle twinged with each step. They tried this for about fifteen feet before Colin picked her up and carried her the rest of the way to a café located another fifty feet or so down the alleyway. He set her at the table and sent the waiter to get a towel and ice for her ankle, then ordered a cooling tea for both of them.

Colin excused himself for a few minutes, pulling out his phone as he went to a quieter area. While he was gone, she sent a text message to Michelle, checking to see if everything was all right in Marbella. She didn't tell her about her twisted ankle, not eager to reveal she'd been in trouble. As she waited for a response, the waiter returned with a bucket filled with cold water and a little ice, along with a towel for her ankle. Dipping the cloth, she wrapped it around her injury rather than sticking her foot in the bucket.

The tea had arrived by the time Colin came back and sat down across from her. He glanced at the bucket of water and the wrapped ankle and gave her a reassuring smile.

"That's better then, isn't it? Not quite what I expected."

"Me, either," she replied, then her phone beeped with the text message from Michelle. All fine there, and she sighed in relief. "I'm sorry to interrupt your scouting. Are you going back to join Mr. Samaha again?"

"In a little bit. He's gone ahead to talk to the owner of a shop I might use. But our taxi is on his way here, so I'm going to send you back to the hotel to ice and rest your ankle and knee." He caught her hand and squeezed it.

"Oh, no. That's not necessary. Maybe I could just wait here for you. I should be safe if I'm near the waiters, don't you think?" She wanted to put on a brave show for him, but she was nervous about being left alone.

"Probably, but I'd feel better if you were safe in our room. I'll be a couple of hours yet, so you might as well be comfortable."

She put on a disappointed look, but said, "Yes, you're probably right. Thank you for being so understanding."

He lifted her hand and kissed the back of it.

As he'd said, the taxi came to the nearest side street to the *kasbah*, and Colin carried her to it rather than having her hopping through the street. He helped her into the back seat and told the driver to take her back to the hotel, then he leaned in and pressed a tender kiss to her lips.

"The hotel manager will help you get to our room. I'll see you as soon as I'm done here, darling."

Lindy caught his hand, squeezing it with affection as she

gave him another apologetic look. He'd called her darling for the first time, and she was moved by it. It had been a very long time since she'd had such tender feelings for anyone. She felt a few tears slipping to the edges of her eyes and looked away as the taxi moved into traffic.

Back in the room, the shock of the afternoon began to wear off, and Lindy felt tired. She didn't know if the stranger in the *medina* was really trying to assist her or abduct her, but she couldn't help feeling it was the latter, or he would have let go of her arm when she asked. But she would never know. She was just grateful for the help she'd gotten, and Colin coming back for her. No doubt, it didn't help his meeting with the director any as she was inconsequential in Samaha's eyes. She would have to make it up to her man with something special.

Her ankle was swollen and turning a little black and blue, but she didn't think it was too bad. She'd been soaking it since she got back in the room, and it was feeling better already. Her knee had a bruise and a scrape, but nothing too serious. She'd cleaned it and put ice on it also. She had to laugh at herself. She'd been worried about Michelle, and here she was the one who'd gotten into trouble and hurt.

* * *

Colin arrived about three hours after she'd returned to the hotel and appeared to be in a buoyant mood, so she guessed the rest of his inspection went well.

"You're pretty chipper," she said.

"I am. The hardest part of my work here is done, which was haggling with the three shop owners and Samaha on agreed pricing within the film's budget. But we've got it sorted, and I am still a little lower than projected, so it's good." He set his camera on the end table and went into the bathroom to wash his hands.

"Great! Does that complete all you came to do?"

Lindy had wrapped her ankle in a stretch bandage now and was able to hobble around on it, but still set it on a footstool while she sat.

"I still need to go out to the edge of the town where the seawall is and look for an open location there. If the property is owned by the town, I just need to arrange for permits and pay a little kickback to the clerk. It's the way it tends to work in places like this. How's the ankle?"

"Better. It's only a little twist, and it should be okay to walk on tomorrow so long as I keep it wrapped. I am really sorry. I should have worn flats to go to the *kasbah*. I don't know what I was thinking."

He came over and stood behind the cushioned chair, where she sat and started rubbing her shoulders. "Don't worry about it. These things happen. I'm just glad you weren't hurt worse."

"Me, too. That man frightened me, Colin. All the stories of kidnapping and white slavery went through my mind."

"Unfortunately, I didn't see him, and the street was so crowded. But it would be unusual for a kidnapper to try to grab someone in the middle of a crowd when they're obviously unwilling."

His hands worked magic on her shoulder and neck muscles as she closed her eyes and relaxed a little more. "He said he was trying to help me, but he grabbed my arm and wouldn't let go. I don't know what he thought he was doing."

"Maybe he was trying to maneuver you to a place where he could rob you. Thievery is quite common here, even more than in Europe." Colin paused in his massage as he thought about it.

"Don't stop that," she instructed as she placed her right hand on his and rubbed the top. "But I wasn't even carrying my purse. I have a few euros and my passport tucked into a bra pouch, so what did he think he would steal?"

Colin tapped her left ear with his unencumbered hand. "Maybe those sapphire earrings you're wearing, darling. He might have thought they would be worth quite a bit."

She caught her breath, and her other hand went to her throat, where a gold chain normally held the matching sapphire and diamond drop. "My necklace! It's gone. That must have been what he was after. He grabbed me, and while I struggled, he somehow got the clasp loose or broke it to get it. I didn't even notice."

Colin came around to look at her throat, not to see if the necklace was missing, but if there were any signs of bruising on her neck where the thief might have pulled it off her. "We'll have to report this to the police."

She shook her head, and her emotions plummeted. "No, it's insured. The police won't be able to find the man on the poor description I can give. Let it go."

Applying logic, Colin knelt and encouraged her. "The insurance company won't pay if you don't file a report. It's a formality, and they all pretty much figure you won't see it again. Unless it's unique, engraved, or there's something to distinguish it if it shows up on the market, it's gone."

"Oh damn, you're right. No, it's just a necklace, a pretty bauble someone gave me, but worth about two thousand dollars with the earrings. I should have taken them off before we started on this trip, but I didn't think about it."

"We'll visit the police station in the morning," Colin said.

"It won't take long to file the report, then we can go on out to check out the sea road."

"Very well," she agreed. "I'll get changed for dinner."

"We don't have to," he answered as she hobbled toward the bathroom.

In the end, Lindy insisted they go down to the café rather than eating in the room. With leaning on Colin's arm, she was able to walk the short distance to the elevator, then to the restaurant. They ordered from the menu and chatted as they ate. Colin described the shops he'd settled on. One sold copper pots and pans with samples of their wares hanging from hooks and making a great display.

"I also picked a shop that sells silk clothing, beautiful kaftans, and traditional clothing as well. It will be very colorful in the film, and a great spot for the movie leads to meet and do some business. I think the director will be pleased with the choices. I'm going to send him the images when we go back to the room. I wish you could have seen them and given me your input."

"I wish I had, as well. Will you show me the photos?"

"Yes, I think I can hook the camera up to the television in the room so you can see them." He finished his couscous with lamb and shoved his plate aside.

They looked over the dessert menu and ordered *M'hanncha*, also called a snake cake, which turned out to be a delightful pastry of figs rolled in filo dough. Complemented with strong Moroccan coffee, they indulged in the tasty treat.

"Except for my unfortunate accident, this has been a really lovely day," Lindy said as she sipped the hot beverage.

"It was," he agreed. "I am sorry about your ankle and the

theft, though. I should have noticed you were wearing the jewelry and said something."

"It isn't your fault. I knew better."

He offered his arm to help her back to their room. As she took it, she considered what might happen now. They had one bed in the place, and she knew he wanted to make love with her. She wanted him as much as he wanted her. She watched as his broad-shouldered, muscular body moved ahead of her to the door and speculated on how sexy he would look naked.

Excusing herself, Lindy went to the bathroom to freshen up and covertly check her text messages. Nothing from Michelle. Several hours had passed since she'd last contacted her. Mildly concerned, she sent a note asking how her evening had gone. While she changed into her negligee and brushed out her hair, she waited for a response, but nothing came through. Lindy figured she was probably out with Roberto, and she'd get a message a little later.

When she returned to the room, she found the lights turned down low, and Colin already in the bed, covers pulled up to his waist, and a pillow propped behind him. She stopped in the doorway and leaned against it, taking a sexy pose with an arm raised while the other pulled her lightweight robe back to reveal her long, slender legs. Her short and very revealing nude-colored nightgown barely covered her torso. She kept her right leg to the back, so the bandages on her knee and ankle were scarcely noticeable. Puckering her lips into a Marilyn Monroe full-lipped smile, she lowered her eyelids to a drowsy, yet seductive look.

Her heart raced as she took in the sight of her Englishman. His broad chest rippled with firm muscles while a thin line of light brown hair tracked down the middle, leaving the lightly tanned pectorals gleaming with the sheen of oil. He, too, freshened up, she noted, pleased and excited by the prospect. Beside the bed, a bottle of wine chilled in an ice bucket. He held a glass of it in his hand, then raised it toward her. His mouth tipped up in a close-mouthed smile, a clear invitation to join him.

With a slow, sensuous strut made a little less effective by her slight limp, she closed the distance between the doorframe and the bed. She slipped into the bed next to Colin as he poured another glass and passed it to her.

"To you, my dear Lindy. The best part of this whole trip. May this be the start of a long and lasting relationship." Colin held up his glass in a toast to her.

"And to you," she answered as she tapped her glass against his. "The man who makes my blood race in delight."

They drank, then she set the glass on the bedside table as he put his on the other side next to the ice bucket. Turning back to her, he reached across to place his hand under her chin, lifting it toward his mouth as he moved closer. Her skin savored the touch of his slightly chilled fingers, and she half-closed her eyes as she anticipated the kiss. Without thought, she placed her right hand on his chest, running her fingers down the middle, just lightly skimming the hairs, feeling the slightly coarse texture of them, and noting how they seemed to pulse to her contact.

The delicate scent of almond reached her as his lips and body moved even closer until his mouth closed over hers in a polite, gentle kiss that began to grow deeper as she responded to it. He released, then came in again for another firmer and more passion-filled taste of her, his lips pressing hard against hers. She wrapped both arms around his middle, pulling him into her as her breasts pushed against his chest in their closeness. She could feel his pulse under her hands as his breath caught.

Her left hand slipped below the sheet and pushed down farther, running over his hip to slide across his smoothly muscled thigh. He felt like smooth marble, a work of art. She wanted to see him, to admire the perfect lines of his body. She brought her left leg up and used her foot to push the sheet almost off the bed.

In response, Colin eased back a little on the lip lock, broke it, and kissed her lightly again as he slipped the sheer robe off her shoulders, revealing the thin straps holding her shortie nightgown up. Then he slid those slowly off first the left shoulder, then the right until they slipped off, and the gown dropped to her waist, revealing her still firm and aroused assets. His teeth bit down with a gentle nip as his lips pulled at her skin. A gasp escaped from her throat, and she fought back a deep, animal-like moan as he repeated the kissing, pulling cycle.

Fire spread through her body, igniting a need she hadn't felt in many years. She burned with a flame no one had fanned to an inferno since Estaban had first sparked it. How could just his touch do this? Dear heavens, could she stand the full onslaught of his passion?

As she moved to take him in her hands, he caught them and pulled them over her head, positioning his body over hers so he could move against her. Her gown was nothing more than a belt of fabric around her waist as he'd worked it up with slow rocking movements as he continued to kiss her from her mouth to her stomach in a spiraling line of moist, delicious kisses.

She fell into the passion, feeling only the electric tingle of his mouth, fingers, and skin pressed against hers in a symphony of need and desire lifting her from her own skin to soar in ecstasy. Oh, God, she gasped in silence, what had been in the drink? Was this all the released passion she had denied for so long?

Moisture warmed her between her legs, and she felt the growing pressure against her body as Colin's needs also responded to their fervor. With a firm, but still delicate touch, he moved his hand down to slide between her legs to prepare her. Her body squirmed under him, demanding more, and she gasped and cried out, "Please, now. Now!"

His mouth closed over hers as he entered her with a short thrust, then a deeper one as he began a slow rocking nearly driving her over the edge, but didn't take her completely. He released her hands to shift his hands to cup her rear, then lift as he started the passionate drive that brought her to the brink, then flung her into the abyss. She clung to him like a monkey to a coconut palm in a hurricane. Her body rocked with the storm as it burst across them both.

Colin slipped his arms across her side, just under her ribs, sending a tingle of sensation through Lindy as he snuggled her closer to him. His chin rested against her shoulder, with his lips close to her ear as he whispered, "You are absolutely stunning, darling."

She shifted her left arm back to slide across his hips, giving her hand the freedom to caress the firmness of his well-muscled posterior. It felt like smooth marble to her touch, but much warmer. "You're pretty sensational yourself, lover," she answered. "Your ex-wife was a fool."

He chuckled then showered the back of her neck with little kisses.

Relaxed and sated, her eyes half-closed as she pressed even

closer to him as if she might meld with him. He had half-pulled the sheets back up the bed, although they were still warm from their exertion. They had made love with more exhilaration and passion than she'd ever experienced, even with the fabled Esteban. Dreamily, she closed her eyes as he rubbed her shoulders, and somehow, she drifted off to sleep in the middle of it.

Awaking a few hours later to a still-dark room, Lindy was no longer wrapped in Colin's arms, but he remained close to her, although turned onto his left side with his back curved to her. A tiny smile touched her lips as she thought about running her finger up the line of his spine but then decided more sleep sounded better than another round of sex. *You're getting old, girl,* she told herself. *A younger me would go for it.*

She glanced at the clock to see the time. Four-eighteen. Had Michelle texted her back? She reached for the phone and didn't see any notice of a new message. Thinking it might have gone to a folder, she displayed the recent texts, but nothing from her since early afternoon. A concerned look wrinkled her brow as she considered this. Perhaps she hadn't gotten the message for some reason, or maybe Michelle couldn't send one from her phone. She sent another text asking her to contact her, then set it back on the nightstand. If she didn't have anything by morning, she'd call her.

She rolled back toward Colin, pulled the light blanket up a little higher, and slipped an arm over his waist as she cuddled closer.

Chapter 9
Michelle

Wearing a barely-there white bikini, Michelle sat on a wooden box and tried to look provocative as she held a pose while Roberto sketched. The position grew more uncomfortable the longer she held it as her left leg bent while her heel pressed against the box, and her right leg stretched out in front of her. Posed with her left arm behind her for support, she tilted her head toward the artist. A pair of standing lights illuminated the work area of the studio, casting a warm glow on her body.

"Are you almost done, Roberto? I can't hold this much longer. My leg is starting to cramp." She didn't want to sound wimpy, but the calf muscle in her left leg sent little twinges of pain up her nerves.

"*Un momento.* Another moment only," he said, looking up from his sketchpad to give her a reassuring smile.

His fingers made quick, sure strokes as his pencil scratched across the rough paper to create a well-executed framework of the girl. He told her he wanted to capture all the key elements to make working on the painted canvas easier, even though he had taken many photos for reference. This was the fourth sketch he'd done of her in this position as he moved to different angles around the room.

The moment stretched to several moments, and Michelle

gritted her teeth, then moved her leg. "That's it. *Finito*. I have to move." They'd been at it for almost two hours, and this was the third pose she'd done for him. She bent forward to rub at her leg as she rocked her foot back and forth on the floor to try to loosen the cramped muscle.

"It's good. I have what need and the pictures." He set the tablet down and crossed the room to her, where he pulled her to her feet and helped her limp across the room to the sofa.

"And this is why I have no desire to do modeling for a living. Too much posing," Michelle complained.

Conceding she was playing this up more than it actually hurt, she allowed his assistance and sank onto one end. Roberto dropped down at the other end and lifted her leg into his lap, then began massaging the tight muscle. His strong fingers worked the knot as he pressed and squeezed against her calf.

Feeling the tendons start to relax, she closed her eyes as the cramping eased. "Ah, you could keep doing that for hours."

"You know, I think it was a fortunate incident your aunt had the flat tire. Otherwise, I would not have been animated by you."

She blinked at him, trying to figure out what he meant. "You mean I inspire you or something like that?"

"*Si*. You are my muse."

She laughed at the earnestness in his voice and replied, "Hardly, although I may amuse you."

Stretching her arms above her, she let her eyes drift shut again and tilted her head back against the cushion, exposing her long neck. Roberto swooped in like a hawk, planting a pecking kiss in the pulsing hollow at the base of her throat. Her eyes flew open as he worked his way, tiny kiss after tiny kiss, up her throat, then landing with a plunge to her open mouth.

Oh, my, what a tantalizing feeling, she thought, but she should not allow it. Not yet.

As he skimmed his hand over her stomach, he brushed against a ticklish spot under her ribs, and Michelle broke the kiss with giggling. His eyes twinkled in amusement as he gloated,

"Ah, ticklish!" Then he began searching for more sensitive spots, running his hands over places where she might react.

Michelle squirmed under him, trying to retaliate by finding a place where he might react as well. Alas, he had the advantage with her being nearly naked, and they were soon a jumble of arms and legs, laughing and cursing as they slid to the floor.

"You're wicked!" Michelle wiped at the tears of laughter running down her cheeks.

Robert sat back, braced on his elbows pressed to the floor behind him. "Guilty, *carita*." He gazed at her with a look of admiration in his eyes and said in a low, sexy voice, "You are *maravilloso*. So beautiful and spirited."

She blushed. "And you are so full of it."

"What?" He acted innocent, pressing a hand against his heart and looking wounded.

"You know, *amigo*. I'm hungry. I'm going to go change while you find dinner for us." She started up the stairs to his bedroom, where she'd left her clothes in the larger bathroom. Glancing back, she caught him watching her; his expression was amused and adorable.

She popped into the bathroom to freshen up and change into her cut-off jeans and a cropped tank top. Her aunt would probably have a cow if she knew she was riding around on the back of Roberto's motorcycle in such a skimpy outfit, but so many girls her age were wearing them here, and while Auntie's away, little Michie will stray… a little. Grabbing her drawstring bag from the floor, she wrapped it around her arm.

Bounding down the stairs, she caught Roberto studying the commissioned painting Arturo was so anxious to receive. He seemed pleased although he'd said there was something a little off in the eyes, but he would need more time to correct it. He doubted Arturo would let him have it.

"Well, to my non-expert eye, it looks fine," she said. She hugged him as he turned to pick up the sketchpad to hand it to her.

"Take a look," he said, "while I go clean up a little."

She nodded and sat on the stool where he'd perched while drawing. Her eyes grew in astonishment as she turned the pages and realized the number of sketches he'd done of each pose. Of course, she was aware he had moved around the room, just as he'd done with the camera with each pose, but she didn't realize he was doing four and five sketches of each new position. The book held dozens of pencil drawings, capturing her body, her face, and her hair in a minimal number of lines and curves. What she didn't know about art could probably fill several volumes, but she did know when someone had outstanding talent. If Aunt Lindy would help him, Roberto could become a famous artist sooner.

Roberto came back down, ready to go out for the evening. Michelle grinned at him, noting he looked dressier than she did.

"I hope you don't have something fancy in mind. I could go back to the hotel and change?"

"No, you are fine as you are. It's a small café, then we go to a dance club where locals go. Nothing dressy." He held out a hand. "What do you think of the sketches?"

"They're amazing. I didn't realize you did so many."

She climbed on the back of his bike, and they were off again to a café not far from the town, a quiet, family-run place. Their dinner was simple but filled with delicious flavors.

While they ate, Roberto's phone buzzed, and he excused himself to take the call. Watching his expressions shift and his free hand clenching and waving, Michelle guessed the intense conversation involved Arturo calling about the painting again. From the annoyed frown on Roberto's face, she could surmise Arturo didn't want to wait any longer for it.

When he returned to the table, she said, "He won't wait another day or two, huh?"

"No. He needs it tomorrow. No excuses, he says. So it goes to him as it is. Little flaws and all."

While he sounded resigned to it, she also picked up on the disappointment. "I know you would rather it be perfect, but there are times you just can't do any more."

"Let's go dance off some aggression. We don't want your leg to cramp again, and the exercise will help."

The club was smaller and darker than the one at the hotel, but it was full of young people drinking, dancing, and making out in the corners. In fact, a bit of smooching was happening on the dance floor, as well. A few neon lights blinked in and out above the bar, and six people perched on stools in front of it. The dance floor was about a ten-foot-by-ten-foot wooden square with a dozen or so small tables surrounding it. People danced close to each other, making it a tight squeeze to get between them to even get to the floor.

Serious about coming to dance, Roberto led her out and began to bop to the rhythm. Mostly, upbeat rock music and free-form dancing kept them moving, but now and then it slowed down for a simple two-step or something in the Latin line that she fumbled as best she could. Michelle welcomed a break to sit and drink her cold cherry limeade for a half hour or so. Then he pulled her back to the floor for another four dances. Or was it five? She was losing count when she realized it was after midnight, and she hadn't checked for a text from her aunt.

She found a table and sat to pull out her phone, her fingers searching in the handbag for it and coming up empty. She started taking everything out of it and couldn't believe it when it was empty, and the phone wasn't there.

"Oh, damn. Aunt Lindy is going to go nuts if I don't get a text back to her soon," she said as Roberto watched her reload the bag with her wallet, lipstick, compact, address book, sunglasses, and a toothbrush. He raised an eyebrow at the last item.

"You never know when you need one," she told him and dumped it into the bag. "My phone must have fallen out at your place."

"You can use mine." He pulled it out to offer it to her.

"I don't remember Lindy's number. It's in my phone, and I never memorized it." She felt dumb.

He nodded. "Then let's go back to the studio. You can get the phone, make the call, and then I'll take you home."

"Thanks, amigo. You're the best." Her smile lit up her eyes.

In less than fifteen minutes, they'd made the quick ride back to the studio. Roberto stopped at the door, pointed to the slightly opened edge, and caught her arm to hold her back. "Stay here," he told Michelle in a barely audible whisper. He reached for a brick beside the door, then shoved it open and stepped inside.

Michelle waited with her body pressed against the outside wall trying to stay out of the way if someone should come bounding out. Unconsciously holding her breath in case someone might hear her, she waited and worried. A light came on in the room, and she heard Roberto shout in Spanish. It didn't sound polite. Then it sounded like he ran upstairs, silence for a few minutes then steps coming back down.

"You can come in, Michelle," he called to her.

She pushed through the door and stopped in shock. The studio looked like a tornado had gone through. Paintings and palates dumped on the floor, a couple of stands broken. Someone had made a total mess of it. Roberto straightened up the tipped-over sofa and dropped onto the arm of it to survey the mess.

"Is upstairs—?"

"No, it's just down here. Nothing was touched upstairs." His voice was flat.

"Why? Is anything missing?" She looked around, trying to see familiar paintings in the mess. Where was the sketchbook? What about the computer? Was it secure?

"I think so. If I am not mistaken, the commissioned painting is gone. I don't see it under any of the ones scattered around. And I think one of the other better ones is gone, the dancer outside a club taking a break. And maybe more. Until I do an inventory, I don't know what else might be stolen."

"I'm so sorry. But it makes no sense. Who would take them?"

He shook his head. "I can only think of one person. Arturo. He is the only one who was concerned about the commission painting. The other, I don't know."

"Why would he take it? You were giving it to him tomorrow."

* * *

Michelle stood behind Roberto while he demanded to know if Arturo had his paintings, and the smaller man denied it in both English and Spanish. Still shaking his head, Arturo opened the door to the bedroom and switched on a lamp so they could see nothing was hidden. Roberto stepped into the room, but Michelle stopped just inside the door. Even the closet, holding about a dozen hangers of clothing, was merely an open alcove in the room with nothing hidden in it. A single bed sat in the middle with a lamp on a little nightstand next to it. A short dresser occupied the entry wall, and a computer tablet sat on it, which appeared to be all Arturo used for handling his business.

Judging from the look of consternation crunching his confused face, she would say he was telling the truth. Weasel-looking or no, he didn't look like he had the nerve to steal anything, and the apartment reflected a poor person's home.

"The commission painting is gone," Roberto told him in English for her sake.

Arturo looked stricken. "¿Qué? ¿Está tomado?"

"Yes. That one and at least one other painting I was doing for the gallery downtown. The best pieces. There may be more. I have not been through everything yet."

Arturo sank onto the bed, the shock still on his face. "*Este es terrible, amigo.*" Then he recalled Michelle and switched to English. "My client— *Our* client is expecting delivery this week. What can I tell him?"

Roberto shrugged. "The truth. It's been stolen. I can recreate it, but it will take at least two weeks."

Arturo looked like he might cry. "The commission I get on it is my rent money. I was counting on it."

Sitting on the bed, Roberto dropped a hand on his friend's

shoulder. "I am sorry. I can loan you some to tide you over. I have another painting you might sell to someone for more cash. I will give it to you."

Michelle saw the tears in Arturo's eyes as Roberto talked to him and stepped away from the doorway, leaving the two friends to their privacy. She felt like an intruder, and this was between them. Going back to the kitchen, she opened her bag and pulled out her wallet. She slipped two twenty-euro notes onto the counter where Arturo could find them. She was a soft touch, and maybe it would buy the scrawny-looking guy some food. Hell, it might even be enough to pay the rent on this hovel.

She stood near the door in the living room, waiting nervously, when Roberto hurried out, leaving Arturo behind. He caught her hand and rubbed the back soothingly. "I am sorry for dragging you along. I was so angry."

"I know. It's okay. But now, we need to report the break-in. You have valuable paintings missing."

"*Si.* Arturo will contact our client and see if he will wait for the painting. It was a good commission, and I would be unhappy to lose it. But it is what it is, no?"

Roberto called the police to report the theft while he climbed back on the bike. He thought maybe they would need to go by the police station and file the report, but an officer said he would come out to investigate and take his statement there. They barely made it back to the studio before a police car pulled up in the narrow road and parked. Roberto greeted the officer and opened the door to allow him in.

The place was still a mess, nothing new added to the piles, and nothing picked up. Roberto explained the whole situation to the officer, a middle-aged man with a pleasant smile and a bushy mustache who kept eyeing Michelle with a twinkle in his eye.

The officer took both their statements and handed Roberto a form to complete for the insurance company. Using his phone, he took about ten photos of the mess. "Do you have any photos of the missing paintings?" he asked Roberto in Spanish.

"I think I do," he answered, his eyes going to his computer. "If they didn't destroy any files on my computer."

"Good. You send them to this email at the station," the officer said and handed him a business card. Then, he said he would send someone over to test for fingerprints and to not touch anything until he was done.

Roberto tossed the form on the kitchen counter. "Like I have insurance to cover my losses. To them, it would be just canvases and paint, nothing of any real value. I am a street artist. How you say it? A dime a dozen?"

Michelle nodded. "Yeah. Only you aren't just a street artist. The painting was worth quite a bit."

"But I can't prove it to them." He grabbed a beer and offered her a cola before they dropped onto the sofa to wait for the forensics person to arrive. Well into the early hours of the morning, the tension and excitement of the night took a toll on both of them. Michelle yawned and sipped the cold drink.

"So you and Arturo were friends from school?"

He laughed. "No, Arturo is from here. I went to school near Malaga. I met him when I first moved here. He tried to be an artist, but he wasn't so good. So instead, he decided to become an agent and try to sell art to shop owners or hotels for a commission. It worked okay, then he started getting orders from a few private clients, and a few sales a year keeps him in his apartment."

"I see." Michelle thought for a few minutes. "Arturo has

more than one private client who requests paintings, you say?"

He nodded.

"I know it's probably a long shot, but is it possible any of the other private clients might have resorted to stealing paintings?"

Roberto frowned as he thought about it. "I don't see why one would. They request them through Arturo, and it is only a few weeks at most before I have it done."

The knock at the door halted the conversation, although Michelle continued to think about a possible motive for stealing them. The forensic officer came in, talked to Roberto for a few minutes, then began taking more photographs of the crime scene while she and Roberto watched with interest from their perch on the sofa.

He used a hand-light to shine on the paintings, easels, and the scattered palates. His head swayed back and forth as he gazed at each item. "Only one set of prints on these," he told Roberto. "They are probably yours unless the *señorita* touched them?"

"No. She picked up the sketchbook but didn't touch any of the paintings," he answered.

The expert detected fingerprints on the computer and camera as well, but still only the one set. He asked Roberto for his phone and pointed the light at it as well. "The prints look the same as the others, but I will scan and run them to be sure. I think your burglar used gloves. You say the only area disturbed was the downstairs?"

"Yes. Nothing looked out of place upstairs, and the only things I have of any value are here. Mostly the paintings, my computer, and the camera. I am not a famous artist, so I don't see why he took the paintings. The computer or the camera would have been worth much more." Roberto gazed at the piles of paintings on the floor with resignation.

"It is *extraño*," the tech agreed. "But who knows what the burglar wanted? Maybe it was a troublemaker or someone who wanted to create a problem for you. Up to the detectives to figure out." He packed up his things and headed for the door. "Do not disturb anything down here until you hear from the department. They may want to take another look. I don't think there is any more evidence here."

Half-asleep by this point, Michelle had stretched out on the sofa. Through nearly closed eyes, she watched as Roberto walked with the tech to the door. She barely saw Roberto nod as he showed him out the door, closed it, and put the safety lock on.

She was out like a tripped circuit breaker before he turned again.

Chapter 10

cs Lindy ฌ

Lindy woke late in the morning to an empty bed. She turned to look at the clock and saw it was almost eleven. Snapping to her senses, she reached for her phone to see if she had any messages. When she saw one, she expected it to be from Michelle but was disappointed it came from Colin. She didn't even read it, skipping over it to see if she had missed one from Michelle, but there was nothing.

Anxiety hit her, and she called Michelle's mobile phone. It rang and rang and rang as she let it go for at least fifteen rings before giving up. She wasn't answering her phone. Lindy hurried to the bathroom to take care of necessities then took a quick shower to wake up and wash the scent of the night off her before she returned to her phone.

She called the hotel in Marbella, had them ring their room, and waited as she hoped for an answer. The hotel operator came back on to tell her no one was picking up. She asked if she might page Michelle in the hotel, suggesting she may be at lunch. The operator put her through to the main desk, and Lindy went through the whole request again. There was a delay and recorded music while the clerk presumably paged her niece in the restaurant and the lobby. Lindy fidgeted, panic growing in her as she feared something might have happened to Michelle.

The clerk came back on. "I'm sorry, señora. She does not answer the page. Both keys to your room are checked in, so it appears she is not in the hotel or the room right now. You can try again later."

"Wait," she said before he hung up. "Could you please put a message in her box to call her aunt?"

"Of course," he said, his voice calm and agreeable as if nothing was out of order while she imagined the worst.

She hung up and sat on the side of the bed, feeling numb. This was the worst possible situation. She was in another damn country while her niece was missing in Spain. Her brother would hang her out with the wash to dry if he learned about it. If she didn't find the girl, it would be worse. Why wasn't she answering her phone?

And where the hell was Colin? At last, she called up his message and read it. He hadn't wanted to disturb her when he woke to go check out the sea road. He expected to be back by one and told her to go ahead and order breakfast or lunch in for herself. They had a three-twenty ferry back to Algeciras.

"No!" she cried the word aloud. "Oh, no. I have to get back to Spain now." Shaking with worry and agitation, she called Colin's phone and waited for him to answer. At first, she thought she wasn't going to have any more luck with him than with Michelle, but then he picked up on the fifth ring.

"Colin, Michelle is missing," she blurted into the phone, her voice a tone sharp with her worry.

"Missing? What happened?" he asked. His voice was concerned but not panicked. Of course, she wasn't his niece.

"She hasn't gotten back to me since yesterday afternoon, and she's not answering her phone. She's not picking up at the hotel. I'm afraid something terrible has happened."

"Now it might not be bad," Colin said, trying to be reasonable. "Do you have the boy's phone number? The artist?"

"Roberto? No, I don't. Oh, I should have gotten it before we left. I am such a dope." Her voice cracked as she hovered on the edge of tears.

"Don't panic. It may be nothing. She may have a dead battery, or she dropped the phone, and it's not working, or she accidentally turned it off."

"I guess it's possible. She has been bouncing all around with it, and it's her third one this year." He was making sense, but it didn't reassure her. "Are you coming back yet?"

"I have one more location to check out, and then I'll head back. It won't be long. Get some food and a coffee, and try not to worry." He sounded so reasonable as he said it, but as soon as she hung up, the anxiety and guilt set in again. What was she thinking? She should never have brought Michelle to Europe at all.

Coffee and a breakfast roll arrived via room service, and Lindy signed the bill in between nervous glances at the clock. Where was Colin? She sipped at the coffee, but couldn't eat the roll. She called Michelle again and sent text messages. She paced back and forth, barely noticing the twinges in her still-sore ankle. She'd packed her overnight bag, ready to leave for the ferry as soon as possible. They needed to get back to Marbella quickly.

By the time Colin opened the door, she was a frenetic hurricane of worry.

"I still can't reach her," she told him. "We have to get back as soon as we can. I need to find her."

Colin pulled her in his arms, offering comfort while he tried to contain her frantic hand motions. "Just calm down. You can't do anything right now, and I need you to settle down so we can discuss this logically, darling."

"Logically? My niece is missing! My responsibility. I shouldn't have left her there alone. I was an idiot to do it. What was I thinking?"

"You're not an idiot." He picked up on the last thing she said. "Lindy, she is seventeen, not a little girl. And she's a smart girl."

"Seventeen-year-old, smart-ass girls get abducted and killed, too, you know." Her voice was angry when she ripped herself out of his hold. "She may have been in an accident on the damn motorcycle or went out into the sea and drowned, or who knows what?"

Colin held up a hand with his index finger in the air as if to warn her. "Listen to yourself. You're creating scenarios that haven't happened and worrying about what if's. Until we learn something, this is doing no good. Just sit down, drink some water and wait, and I'll try to at least alleviate some of your fears, okay?"

She glared at him, feeling like he was trying to pacify her when she was being ripped apart with her worries. Nonetheless, she dropped to the chair in the room, poured a glass of orange-infused water, and sipped it.

Colin pulled out his smartphone, looked up a number, and dialed. Whoever he called, he spoke to them in Spanish as he asked a few questions and waited for answers. He didn't sound alarmed, but Lindy's anxiety grew as he talked. "*Si, muchas gracias,*" he said, then gave out his phone number, which even her limited Spanish recognized.

He sat down on the bed and addressed her calmly. "I just spoke to the police in Marbella. Michelle has not been involved in an accident or drowning; however, she was on a police report from early this morning as a witness to a break-in at Roberto Aponte's studio. She was fine. The kids were not there at the time. Now, my guess is she spent the rest of the night at Roberto's, and she hasn't returned to the hotel yet."

"Oh, my Lord," Lindy said, her southern accent stronger than ever. "They're sure she's all right?"

He nodded. "Yes. I gave them my phone number in case they have any more information. She probably misplaced her phone or forgot to call you in all the excitement of the break-in."

Relieved, Lindy felt tears of relief start down her cheeks and reached for a tissue to wipe them off. "I am sorry I yelled at you. All I could do was think of the worst situation. I was so afraid."

Colin came to her, pulled her to her feet, and into his arms, then rocked her back and forth as she cried against his shoulder.

In spite of Lindy's efforts to hurry Colin along, they still arrived at the port only a little earlier than originally planned, so they took the ferry they had expected to take. Lindy was calmer now. Even though she still didn't connect with Michelle when she tried calling while waiting for the ferry, she was comforted by knowing the police had Colin's phone number. If something happened, they would call.

Now she was more angry with her niece for not keeping in contact as she'd told her to do. This was the last time on this trip she was going to allow her to do anything by herself. She was fearful of talking to her brother until she had the whole story, although she'd received a text from him just asking how it was going.

They had a sandwich from the snack bar, and Colin showed her some of the photos he'd taken through his tablet. The sites he'd chosen were great, and she was sorry she hadn't actually been with him for either the kasbah shops or the sea road. That certainly hadn't worked out the way she hoped it would. But she'd enjoyed the evening on Saturday and was happy to know he was an understanding man.

"You really are quite something, Colin Haines," she said as they sat on the deck watching the coast of Spain come closer. "I meant it when I said your ex-wife was a fool and not just for the sexual reason. I don't know what I would have done if you hadn't taken charge today. I don't usually fall apart in a crisis situation, but Michelle is my responsibility, and I feel like I failed."

"Likewise, even if you do keep me on my toes." As his broad smile spread, his eyes twinkled. "Is this a good time to point out that if you hadn't met me, you wouldn't have been in Morocco?"

"No, don't apply logic to it. Meeting you is one of the great perks of this trip. I hope we can remain friends after we go our separate ways."

"I'm counting on it, Melinda Morton."

She took off her sunglasses, biting the end piece as she studied his face. Not many people knew her full name. "You've known who I am all along, haven't you?"

"Not entirely. When you said your name was Lindy Morton, it rang a bell, but I didn't put it together right away. Eventually, it connected. I have seen your work often. It's usually just signed L. Morton, I believe. I admit I did Google you and found the full name in your bio."

"Damn Internet. Nothing is secret anymore."

He caught her hand and squeezed. "Nope. Miss Melinda Morton, born in Charleston, South Carolina to two mathematicians and was a child prodigy as an artist."

"I suppose you know my birth date as well, so you know how old I am. Honestly, nothing is sacred." She frowned at the thought.

"I do indeed and frankly, my dear, I truly do not give a damn."

They both laughed, lightening the moment. She was growing fonder of him by the days, but she wasn't sure it was a good thing.

The boat docked a little late, and it seemed to take a long time to get off and through Spanish customs.

While Lindy waited, she heard a ping from her phone and checked to see a text alert from Michelle, but there was nothing in the message. Had it been sent accidentally? She tried calling again but still no answer.

Once they reclaimed Colin's car, they were on their way northeast to get back to the hotel. Worry set in again after the false alarm phone call, then it was replaced with annoyance. She growled when Colin said anything for the last thirty kilometers into Marbella.

As soon as they arrived at the hotel, Lindy checked at the front desk to find Michelle's key wasn't in the slot, meaning she was either in the room or, most likely, on the hotel property, since the standard convention was to check the key at the desk if you're leaving the property. She and Colin went to her suite but didn't find Michelle, although her purse sat on the counter in the kitchenette.

"She's probably at the pool or on the beach," Colin said.

"I hope. Why isn't the girl answering her phone?" Lindy dialed the number again, and they heard a faint ring coming from Michelle's bedroom. Lindy opened the door and spotted the phone on the bedside table, plugged in and charging. She frowned, threw up her hands in exasperation, and picked up the phone. It showed about fifty-percent charged. "Well, this explains the lack of an answer. She didn't keep it charged and apparently hasn't been anywhere near it while it has been recharging."

Following the course of better wisdom, Colin remained silent, shaking his head in sympathy for Lindy's plight with her niece.

"Thanks for putting up with me today." She came back to his side to give him a hug. "I have just been worried about her. Just wait until I find her. I'm going to head down to the pool area to look. There's no need for you to come along with me." She couldn't see him wasting more of his time with her problem, and she knew he had some people to contact about the locations.

"You're sure?" he asked, a look of concern on his face.

She nodded. "Yes. If I can't find her, I'll let you know."

"Okay. Will I see you for dinner?"

"Looking forward to it. I'll call you later." She walked out the door with him and down to the elevator. Thankfully, her ankle didn't bother her much, and the elastic wrap on it was keeping it comfortable, but she would have words, along with a few limps on it, for Michelle when she found her.

The pool area, which encompassed three pools, teemed with a moderately large crowd of tanned bodies of all shapes and sizes. Lindy worked her way to the verandah above to see if she could spot Michelle's more pale body among the people. She walked slowly along it, squinting into the sun in spite of her sunglasses. Only beginning its long descent toward the mountains, it promised quite a few hours until the late sunset.

Despair crept up on her. How would she spot Michelle in all these sun-seekers? Then she spotted a young woman lying face down on one of the loungers so her backside could tan. It looked like Michelle, although she couldn't be certain until she got closer. She elbowed her way down the steps, weaving through the lounge chairs and tables. Her ankle was beginning to bother her some, and she cursed Michelle roundly in her mind.

She was almost to her when the girl turned toward her. Same color hair and light skin, but it wasn't Michelle. Lindy's spirits dropped as she continued on by the lounger and continued to search. She came to the end, then took the path toward the beach. She fretted about walking much more than she'd wanted to do, and the sand wasn't proving any easier for her sore ankle to handle.

She came to the end of the path to the beach, then turned to gaze to the south where a few umbrellas formed shelters against the sun. Under the third one, she spotted Michelle, who was sprawled on a towel and reading. She stalked up to her, ankle protesting every step.

"You were supposed to check in every few hours," she said, the anger seeping into her voice even though she had wanted to keep calm.

Michelle's head popped up from the book in surprise. "Aunt Lindy?" She sat up straight, her eyes wide and lips turned down in shame. "I'm sorry. I misplaced my phone, and I didn't find it until this afternoon, then it had run out of juice. So I brought it back here and plugged it in. It's still charging."

"I saw," Lindy answered. "I was very worried about you. I imagined all kinds of scenarios happening. Why didn't you use another phone to call me?"

She looked down. "I didn't have your number. It was on my phone, and I don't have it memorized."

"Oh, for cripes sake!" Lindy's voice took on the deeper southern drawl it gained when she was annoyed. What did these young people use for brains? "Let's go back to the room now. My ankle's killing me, and I want to get off this sand."

"What's wrong with your ankle?" Michelle hurried to obey, gathering up the towel, her sunhat, and beach bag.

"It's a long damn story, but the upshot was I twisted it in the casbah." She set off limping a little ahead of her niece but called back over her shoulder. "You *do know* the phone works while it's charging, don't you?"

While relieved to find Michelle and know she was okay, Lindy seethed with fury that the girl hadn't kept in touch as she'd promised to do. Losing her phone was not unusual, especially for her niece, who seemed to lose or break them on a fairly frequent basis. But to not have noted her number in an address book or her tablet or to have had the sense to call the hotel in Tangier was just plain annoying. Now, her ankle really ached by the time they got back to the room and put Lindy in a real snit.

Michelle darted into her room as soon as they got there, and Lindy presumed it was to avoid a tongue-lashing. That might be the wisest move the girl had made.

She hobbled to the bathroom to get a towel then went to the refrigerator for ice before crashing on the sofa. She propped her injured leg up and removed the bandage. Making an ice pack, she wrapped it around her ankle the best she could. Then she leaned back and closed her eyes to wait for the throbbing to stop. She almost drifted off until she heard Michelle come out of her bedroom. Opening an eye, she noted the girl was dressed in jean shorts and a t-shirt top tied at the waist.

"I hope you're not planning on going out," she said.

"Because you are grounded."

Michelle plopped in the chair across from her like a dropped anvil, her shoulders slumped. "I said I was sorry. Jeez, my phone was missing, then dead. How was I to call? I was with Roberto. He was doing some sketches of me, then we went to dinner and after—"

"And did you spend the night with him? I called here, and your key was in the box, but no one answered in the room."

Michelle's gaze dropped to the floor. She said nothing.

"Did you think I wouldn't try to contact you? That I wouldn't be concerned about what might have happened to you when you didn't check in, and you weren't here? I trusted you, and you betrayed my trust." Lindy's face reflected the anger she felt as her eyebrows angled in toward her nose, and her lips spread into a tough-looking line. "No, you are not going out again tonight or tomorrow night, or for the whole time we're still here."

"But Roberto—"

"No, but anything. I said you're grounded, and I mean it." Lindy was not in the mood for any excuses or arguments. "You may call him and tell him you're grounded from going out."

"Can he come here?" Michelle asked in a meek voice with a touch of whine in it.

"Not tonight. Maybe tomorrow."

Undisguised anger in her face, Michelle jumped to her feet, went to her bedroom, and shut the door with unnecessary force.

Lindy shot a glare in her direction and shook her head. No help for it. She picked up the hotel phone and called Colin's room. "Hello, handsome. I found Michelle, and she is fine. But I irritated my ankle again with all the walking I had to do. She was on the beach, and that didn't help it any. I'm afraid I am not up to going out to dinner tonight."

A smile blossomed on her face when he suggested they have dinner in her room. "That sounds perfect. We have a dining table here, so why not use it? In about an hour?"

He readily agreed, settling the issue. She wasn't sure if Michelle would join them or continue to sulk in her room, but they would order enough food for her. While she remembered how unjust her parents sometimes seemed when she was Michelle's age, she also knew that she had to be firm. The girl broke her agreement and quite probably spent the night with Roberto. If they did anything, she could only hope that they used protection. At times like this, she wasn't sure how well she actually knew her niece.

Chapter 11
෴ *Michelle* ෴

Devastated by her aunt's reaction, Michelle called Roberto to tell him she couldn't meet him. While she expounded on the unfairness of it, she nonetheless would obey her aunt's directive. He commiserated with her and agreed with her decision.

"She's your aunt, and her word is the final one in this," he said, being more reasonable than she.

"I'm not a child. I've traveled places alone or with girlfriends. I can take care of myself, but she treats me like a child. I thought this would be more fun, two freewheeling women on an adventure." Anger fueled her words as she felt her aunt didn't let her explain and was being unreasonable.

"That may be true, *carita*. But to her, you are still a young girl who needs protecting. She left you on your own for her own reasons, and she probably feels guilty about it when you didn't do as you promised."

"Maybe, but she won't even listen to me," she sighed with exaggeration. "Is there any news on the break-in?"

"No. Nothing. I heard from Arturo, and the client has canceled the deal. He doesn't want to wait any longer for the painting, so it's a lost commission for both of us."

"I am sorry, Roberto." She knew it meant a lot to him and even more to Arturo.

"It's okay. There will be others. I helped Arturo out, and

he'll find other work."

They talked for another twenty minutes before Michelle felt ready to say goodbye, telling him she hoped her aunt would allow them to see each other again before they moved on to the next city on their tour. It proved a painful reminder that this friendship was only temporary, and she might never see him again, although he swore he would keep in touch.

After she hung up, she copied down her aunt's cell phone number from the phone and put it into her tablet. If she'd done it before, she would have been able to call her from the tablet. She'd been stupid, and now she was paying the price for it. No matter what Roberto said, she still felt like her aunt was seeing her as a little girl rather than an almost adult. She tried to look at it from Lindy's view. Given her father's fears of her traveling in Europe, maybe it was easy to see why her aunt was overly cautious.

When Lindy knocked on her door and called her for dinner, she almost didn't respond. Then she was going to tell her she wasn't hungry, but she was. And if she was going to reconcile with her aunt, then having Colin at the dinner table could mean she had a buffer. Her aunt might be more reasonable.

She popped into the bathroom to wash her face and run a brush through her hair as she formulated her game plan. Satisfied she looked presentable, she stepped through the door and into the dining area with a hint of trepidation. Her aunt glanced up and nodded toward the chair at her left. A dinner plate was already set up, and dishes of food sat on the table. It looked as if she and Colin had ordered a family-style meal.

Taking the indicated seat, Michelle sat and took a calming breath. "I am so sorry, Aunt Lindy. I didn't intend to cause you any worry, and you're right, I should have made a note of your phone number. I hope you can forgive me." She spoke in a soft, contrite voice, trying to sound as sincere as possible.

"Of course, I forgive you, Michelle. I had just put more faith in you to be responsible and do as I'd asked. I also blame myself. I should never have left you alone here."

"Oh, no. Nothing bad happened to me. Although there were some problems for Roberto and it's part of the reason I didn't find my phone sooner." Michelle put on her most imploring expression, willing her aunt to believe her.

"Problems? What happened with Roberto? Why did you spend the night there?" Lindy's tone was sharp, and her eyes narrowed in concern and worry. Michelle could tell she was thinking about the worst scenario possible in her mind; her niece slept with the street artist.

"It's not what you're thinking. Roberto did some sketches of me, then we went out to dinner. When we came back, his studio had been broken into, and paintings were stolen. By the time the police came, and the reports were filed, I was so tired I slept on his downstairs sofa alone."

Lindy's brow wrinkled in a perplexed look as she listened. If she was relieved at Michelle's words, it didn't touch her face. After a few moments, she asked, "Someone stole his paintings?"

"Only a few of them. The one commission piece he was almost done with and two other paintings similar to the ones you bought. Others, like the street scenes and the seascapes, were scattered around the studio. Whoever it was made a mess, but the only things missing were those unique paintings."

"What made those special?" Colin asked, sitting forward in interest. "Why would someone want to steal them?"

"They were not the kind he normally sells to tourists," Michelle answered. "One was a dancer taking a break, and another was a pair of old men playing chess in the square."

"The character studies, "Lindy noted. "The ones that really show Roberto's talent. They caught my eye when we were at his stall." She appeared thoughtful as she turned to Colin. "I bought two of them. Let me show you."

Sliding her chair back, she rose and limped to her bedroom. She returned in a minute with the two wrapped packages. In a flash, Colin was beside her, taking the paintings and offering his arm to help her back to the table.

With a twinge of guilt, Michelle realized the trek in the sand searching for her hadn't done her aunt's sprained ankle any good. But still thinking about the paintings, Michelle sprang from her seat. "Be right back," she said and dashed to her bedroom.

Her phone was still plugged in, but it was almost fully charged. She snatched it loose and returned to the dining area as she pressed the symbol for the photo application. "I took photos of some of the paintings in the studio before we went out to dinner. I can show you the stolen ones."

Colin had already unwrapped the paintings her aunt had bought and was studying them with interest. Like Lindy, he seemed to know a lot about art and was noting the brushstrokes and detailing as well as the style. "These are very good and show a real flair in his strokes, a unique hand in the execution. At the same time, they look familiar. Was he copying another artist's work?"

"No. I thought the same thing, and I asked him," Lindy replied. "He said this is his own style, although he has copied the greats in the past. Many art students take a stab at it in order to learn."

Colin turned to Michelle and took the offered smartphone

with its small screen to look at the photos she'd taken. He studied each of them a few moments before handing the phone to Lindy. Like Colin, she peered closely at each picture, increasing the size on them as she looked at the strokes.

"Yes, these strokes are like the ones on the paintings I bought. Definitely the same artist, and I would say his own style. But there is a sense of familiarity in the paintings, and I can't place what it is. Maybe it's the subject matter more than the detail."

Lindy flipped the pictures back a few farther and pulled up one of the sketches of Michelle. She studied it, then called up another. She looked up at her niece. "He's done a remarkable job with the sketches of you. Why was he doing them?"

Michelle dropped her gaze to the table for a heartbeat or two. Was her aunt censuring her images or just worried how Roberto might use them? She looked up and smiled a little, showing confidence. "I was modeling for him, so he has the form for future paintings. He won't be using my face, but my body. More like the shape of my body, although he promised he would do a painting of me."

"So, you were an artist's model." Lindy's voice held a touch of amusement.

"I've done it before," she answered. "Roberto also took some amazing photos of me, and I'm going to include a couple in my actor's portfolio."

"Ah, he's also a photographer," her aunt commented. "But then many artists like to work from a photo these days."

Colin held up one of the paintings again, studying it as they talked. "Lindy, would you mind I took this painting with me? I'd like to show it to a friend who is an art expert and get his opinion."

"Opinion of what?" Michelle asked, her eyebrows arching in a quizzical look with a downturn of her mouth. If he thought Roberto was copying another artist, she would be angry.

"Just the quality of the painting," he assured her. "Like your aunt, I see familiarity in the work itself. Nothing to worry about, but perhaps his style is similar to another artist I've seen. Even so, this is a beautiful piece of art, and I'd like my friend's appraisal."

Lindy nodded her agreement. "Go ahead and take it. When will you be coming back?"

"Back?" Michelle's gaze flicked from her aunt to Colin. He was leaving?

"I have to check a couple of locations in Italy, but it will only be a few days. I'll catch up with you when I get back and return the painting then."

Discussion over, Michelle cleaned up the dining table, then retreated to her bedroom so Colin and Lindy could have time together before he left the next morning. She liked Colin and was pleased to see the sparkle in her aunt's eyes when she was with him.

She dropped onto the bed, opened her phone to a social media page, and caught up with her friends back home as well as the ones having a great time in Rome. She still wished she could have gone with them, but then she wouldn't have met Roberto, and that made her very happy.

Heaving a wistful sigh, she hoped her aunt would relent and let her see Roberto before they left to go to the next city.

Chapter 12
✂ Lindy ✄

As Lindy watched Michelle finish up the dishes, she reflected on her concerns of the past twenty-four hours and felt somewhat abashed she had thought the worst of her niece. Was she over-protective? Lindy had been in Europe on her own at about the same age as Michelle, and here the girl was saddled with her aunt, who was only a little younger than her father. She knew her brother's worries about his daughter being alone over here were real. Europe's countries did not offer the same safety as they did when she was young.

But much of it hadn't changed. It was mostly the radicals she needed to worry about. One could not deny the troubles in the Middle East had extended past their borders, and any of the European countries were at risk. If it seemed Rome was a risky spot, was Spain, with its strong Arabic influence, any less? Many Muslims lived here, as well.

"A penny for them," Colin said, his voice quiet, but curious.

She glanced at him as she realized she'd drifted off in her own thoughts and quite forgotten he was in the room.

"Just thinking about how much the world has changed since I was Michelle's age. And it's not all good."

"That's very true," he said. "Everything seems to be at a faster pace these days. Danger is much closer than it used to be.

Even for you."

Her laugh came out a little brittle. "Indeed, it is. I don't know what I would have done if you hadn't been there in the market. I've never been attacked before."

"As lovely as it is to hear your praise, the fact is you wouldn't have been in trouble if I hadn't talked you into coming along with me."

As she saw the guilty look on his face, Lindy responded with a warm smile. "I loved being with you, Colin. You do know how to show a woman a unique time. I could have done without the sprained ankle, but to be honest, it was just a bit exciting to be robbed and almost abducted. It will be a great story I can tell at a convention or a party."

"In that case," he replied as he reached across and caught her hand, "I was happy to oblige." He lifted her hand to his lips and kissed the back of it with a flourish.

Touched by the action, Lindy tried to recall the last time a man had made such a romantic gesture. Perhaps there had been one early in her career when she was at a convention, and a fan had reached out in playful affection, but it was not like this. The touch of his lips against her sensitive skin sent a thrill through her, reminding her of the burning connection between them.

She lifted her eyes to him with desire in them, and he pulled her to her feet. Wrapping his arms around her, he pulled her close and hummed a little bit of a waltz as he glided her around the room, ending at the sofa near the windows where he dipped her dramatically and planted a kiss in his best movie scene fashion. Lindy barely contained the snort of a laugh trying to escape, but a glance at his sincerely intense face took care of that moment, and she melted into his embrace as she raised her arms to circle his neck.

He lowered her to the sofa and slid down beside her, their lips still locked in an ever-deepening kiss. Her arms shifted to help support her body. As his fingers pressed tenderly against her cheeks, she brought her left hand to his shoulder and began easing it across to the front of his shirt where he'd left the first button undone.

She helped the next along, and the one after it until the last had slipped out of its assigned hole. Allowing her fingers to explore, they roamed over Colin's chest in a slow, gentle crawl as they outlined the curves of his muscles and the dips between them.

At the same time, Colin's mouth slid away from hers and began traveling south over her chin and down her throat in flutters of delicate kisses, making her stomach dip and quiver. She pulled in a deep intake of breath as she shivered internally. His mouth found her collarbone as he nipped his way across it, and his hand slipped down to slide under her silky tank top where he could caress the top of one breast.

Just as Colin's other hand slipped under the straps, Lindy heard noises from Michelle's room and the door opening. She swatted Colin's hand away at the same time he starting straightening up. By the time Michelle stepped through the door, they were sitting side-by-side on the sofa, with their clothes mostly straightened, although Colin's shirt was held closed by his left hand, and one of Lindy's straps was still off her shoulder.

But Michelle didn't even look their way, just slipped across into the bathroom.

"Maybe we shouldn't do this here," Lindy said in a soft voice.

"I was thinking the same thing," he replied and ran his

other hand through his hair. "I should get to bed anyway to get started early in the morning."

"Me, too," Lindy replied, feeling a ping of disappointment.

He rose to his feet and buttoned his shirt partway while Lindy straightened her top the rest of the way as she got up. While Michelle was still in the bathroom, she walked with him to the door and paused there.

"So, goodnight," she said with a sad turn of her lips. "We can meet at the café in the hotel for breakfast if you have time?"

"I'll make time," he answered, pulling her into his arms for another kiss. "Say seven?" At her nod, he stepped through the door.

Wistfully, her eyes followed his retreating figure down the short hallway, past the elevator to the stairs, where he bounced down them with a youthful step. If her ankle hadn't been so sore, she would have followed him right then. Instead, she turned in the doorway and shut the door behind her, a sigh of longing marking the moment.

Wearing dark green linen slacks and a breezy apricot-colored short-sleeved blouse, Lindy walked with Colin to his car, which was already loaded with his suitcase and the wrapped painting he was borrowing. He had her phone number as well as the phone number and address in Sevilla where she and Michelle would be heading next.

"If something comes up, and I can't catch up with you in Sevilla, then I'll ship the painting back there or on to your address in London if you prefer," he said as he turned to her, taking her hands in his.

She nodded. "The London address would probably be better, but I do hope we meet up in Sevilla." His work would take precedence, she reminded herself, but she was not ready to break this relationship, not when it was just starting, and there was so much promise. It's a rare meeting that brings a stranger into your life who seems so exciting, charming, and wonderful, and it had been a long time since she'd felt so optimistic. No, she didn't want to see it end. Not now and not like this.

"Me, too." He smiled, and his eyes twinkled as he hugged her close. "I want to see you again soon, Lindy. So I will be in touch, and we'll connect. I promise."

"I'll hold you to it," she replied as he kissed her, one last sweet kiss, leaving her breathless, before he got in the car, waved, and drove off toward the airport in Malaga.

"So, he's on his way," Michelle said as she came up behind Lindy. She'd not come down for breakfast, but it appeared she had made it in time to see the farewell scene.

"He is." She turned to face Michelle. The girl looked happier today, even though she probably still resented the restrictions she'd placed on her. With a sigh, she thought she would likely relent. Her niece hadn't done anything too bad except worry her. She was young and having a good time with a handsome boy. Would she have done anything differently herself at the same age? To be honest, didn't she run off on a whim with an enticing gentleman herself?

"Have you eaten yet?"

Michelle nodded, "I had some fruit. How's the ankle?"

"Still a little sore, but much better."

"You never told me what happened." Michelle opened the door to the lobby for her.

"It's a..." Lindy paused as she walked gingerly through the opening. "...complicated story. Let's just say I tripped on the cobblestones in the Kasbah and twisted it."

The younger woman winced in sympathy. "Those uneven surfaces will nail you every time."

"True enough. It's not the first time I've taken a tumble on uneven pavement, as they say in Britain. I once fell flat on my face in a stumble just outside the National Theater when I went to see 'The Tempest' in London. Got a black eye from it and attracted more attention than I wanted. One of the paparazzi got a photo of it. Great headline in the Daily News the next day, 'Well-known American artist falls for the Bard.'"

"Oh, no!" Michelle laughed.

" 'Fraid so. It's the price of even a small amount of fame, my dear." She tilted her head toward the coffee bar in the lobby. "Let's grab a decent cup of coffee and decide what we'll do today."

Over a caramel cinnamon latte, Lindy asked Michelle to tell her again about the robbery and what was taken. As Michelle went over the details again, Lindy made a note or two in her tablet and frowned a little. "It just doesn't make sense, Michelle. The paintings aren't high value, and I doubt Roberto has anything in his place worth stealing. The most valuable item would have been the commission painting, and it's only of value to the person who was buying it. Why would anyone take it? Although there's still something niggling at me about his paintings, I can't pin it down. What do you say we go talk to your young man this afternoon and see if we can get any more clues?"

Michelle's face burst with a big grin. "Really? That would be awesome. He has a flash drive for me with the photos he took of me on it so I can get it and show them to you. The few I've seen are really beautiful. Wait until you see."

Lindy laughed. "I'm sure they are." All was forgiven, and

everything was back to normal. Except for the puzzle of the stolen paintings.

After a relaxing morning by the pool and gazing out at the Mediterranean, Lindy and Michelle went into town and shopped a bit, ate a fresh garden salad at one of the outdoor cafes, then made their way to the street where Roberto's stall sat at the curbside. To Lindy's surprise, several people crowded into the small space to view the paintings as Roberto packaged up one of the smaller paintings into a neatly tied bundle for a plump middle-aged woman in beige cargo pedal pushers and a tied t-shirt top. A large raffia skimmer hat and sunglasses completed the American-abroad look.

When he looked up from his task, he saw Michelle, flashed a smile, and held up a finger to indicate to wait. Then he handed the package to the woman who grinned happily, thanked him, then turned to her husband, an equally plump, round-faced man, also wearing a hat against the hot afternoon sun. Together, they ambled off down the street with their souvenir of Spain.

They could do worse, Lindy thought. At least Roberto's paintings were well-executed and might be worth something someday. But this number of people buying even surprised her. Following two more sales of pleasant-looking Spanish street scenes, the customers thinned and began moving down the street.

His last customer, a young woman clutching a larger canvas of a young male Spanish dancer, handed the painting to him and hurriedly dug in her purse for her money. She glanced down the street, anxiety evident in her eyes. Roberto counted out her change and put the painting in a bag, then started to wrap it, but she shook her head.

"No, it's okay. The bag is good enough. I'll pack it later."

She snatched the bag, then slinging her purse up over her shoulder, started on a quick walk, almost running after the other people.

"That was quite a group," Lindy said as they stepped into the shade of the overhang of the booth.

Roberto put the last money away, then stood to hug Michelle. "Yes. They were from a tour group. A friend of mine is the guide and pointed them to me. She embellished my importance by telling them about the robbery. I guess if I am great enough to steal from, then they must buy one of my paintings."

"You're kidding," Michelle gasped out. "They're buying because you were robbed."

"So it would appear. I usually get a few who stop by and make one or two sales from the tourist groups, but today, there were a dozen buying. Maybe theft is good for my business."

"Or maybe your friend is very good at PR," Lindy said. She was studying a canvas of an old man dozing on a park bench with the setting sun breaking through the trees behind him. It was exquisite with the lightness of the shading, giving it an ethereal quality. The odd sense of familiarity touched her again like she had seen this kind of painting before. Picking it up, she handed it to Roberto. "I'd like to buy this one. It wasn't here a few days ago, was it?"

"No, I just finished it last night. It's old Manuelo, who used to work at the bank until he retired a few years ago. Now he siestas in the park until dark then goes out to party. It's how he fights being lonely. These are his sunset years."

"You captured it well. Michelle and I were talking about the robbery, and I was wondering if you had any idea why anyone would steal your paintings?"

A thoughtful frown wrinkled his forehead, but he shook his head. "It puzzles me, too. I am only a street artist, and you can see my paintings aren't valued that highly. I get about five-hundred euros for the commission paintings when I get them, but they are large canvases and lots of paint, so they are worth a little more."

"Tell me about the stolen one. Michelle showed me a photo she took of it."

"It was a little less than a meter tall and half that in width, so a tall painting, done in oils, which take longer to dry. I was almost done and pushing the customer to wait until it dried before I delivered."

"Was the size requested by the client?"

"*Si*. The size, subject, and dominant colors of the painting. I have done work for this client several times, and always, the request is very specific."

Odd, Lindy thought, but then amended her perception since it wasn't too unlike doing a book cover painting where the size, colors, and subject matter might be pre-determined by the publisher. Still, there was something peculiar about this whole deal. "Have you ever met this client?"

Roberto finished wrapping the painting she'd just purchased, setting it on the small table he used for a desk. He glanced up at her. "No. I don't even know his name. Arturo, my agent, deals with him. He gets the request by email with the details of what the client wants. When the painting is complete, I turn it over to Arturo, and he meets with a courier who receives it, gives Arturo the money, and then delivers it to the client."

Even Michelle's forehead wrinkled with frown lines at this. Lindy pursed her lips as she thought about the strange arrangement. "That's a curious way to conduct the business, don't you think?"

Roberto shrugged. "He pays well and on completion of the project. He told Arturo he wishes privacy and not to disclose any information about himself. Perhaps he is a celebrity, and he fears I might try to promote myself by advertising I have created paintings for him."

She thought about his words for a bit before she said, "Maybe you're right, but it still seems peculiar. I think you need to find a real agent. Arturo is a friend, but he's not much of an agent, is he?"

"No, you are right. He is a friend, and he helps me out with the sales."

"How did Arturo connect with this client initially?" Michelle asked, voicing the question Lindy was about to ask.

Roberto reached to a pottery bowl behind him and pulled out two business cards, handing one to each of them. "I usually give my customers a card with their paintings with my name and information and an email address to contact me if they wish more paintings. Arturo handles the email. I get requests every now and then for paintings, so we figured this secret client must have purchased a painting from here or the hotel where I sometimes display."

Lindy studied the card for a few moments, noting he had designed it well using a pastel painting for the background. Character studies, portraits, urban and pastoral paintings; commission work accepted, it read. Clever marketing. She may not have been giving Roberto enough credit in the business department. She didn't think to include a business card with every painting or even have them available on her vendor tables until her newly-acquired agent when she was twenty-two had instructed her to do it.

She tucked the card into her purse and gave Roberto an approving smile. Reaching for her package, she said, "Good job on this. And thank you for answering my questions. But right now, my ankle is aching. I think a session in one of the spas this afternoon is most appealing, so I am going back to the hotel. Why don't you come by this evening and we'll have dinner?"

She saw her niece's face alter to a disappointed look and added, "If you wish to visit longer with Roberto, Michelle, you may do so. Just let me know if anything delays you."

"Thank you," Michelle said in a soft voice as her eyes lit up with joy.

As Lindy took her purchase and made her way cautiously to the corner to get a taxi, she felt content inside. She had forgiven the girl, and all was well again. She felt certain she could trust Michelle not to screw it up.

Chapter 13
ೞ Michelle ೞ

As the hawk flies, Seville was situated pretty much the same distance from Marbella as the A397 road went, but Michelle guessed the bird could traverse the mountain passages on wind currents much faster than she and her aunt made the drive across the winding one-hundred-sixteen miles cutting through the mountains. Traffic near the historical city of Ronda delayed them nearly thirty minutes as they'd arrived at an unexpectedly busy time for repair work on the highway.

Unlike the coastal route where the Mediterranean was an almost constant vista, this pass featured a steady view of Spanish fir trees and scrub bushes alongside the road as it wound between the mountain peaks. Near the city, the road began a gradual climb taking take them above the deep ravine cut by the Guadalevin River to form the cliffs of Ronda's foundation. Higher up, she could look across the valley from the elevated view, and the trees gave way to more barren land alongside them. Close to the city, a few olive tree farms began to sprinkle the open countryside between stands of fir trees.

"Ronda is an ancient place, and there are cave paintings nearby from the Neolithic era," Lindy said as she navigated a turn off the main highway. "Let's stop for coffee and a snack, then take a little time to admire the city while I tell you more about it."

"It looks old." Michelle noted the ancient-looking buildings in the central part of the city. The main influences of southern Spain were evident in the architecture here; Roman and Moorish. The buildings looked ornate and elegant, but most of them wore the clean look of care with whitewashed, plastered walls and regal wrought iron.

"It is old," her aunt answered as she looked for a place to park near the cliff and the shopping area. Spotting an open spot, she maneuvered the car into it, backing up, easing in, pulling forward, then repeating a few times to get it wedged into the almost too small opening.

As Michelle slipped out the door while keeping an eye on the oncoming traffic, she spotted a familiar logo for an American fast food place. "We could always get coffee there," she said as she came around the car and pointed to the place.

Lindy followed her gesture, then frowned. "And we could get some better coffee or cocoa at this nice pastry shop a short walk away."

She turned away from the icon and strolled toward a store with a pleasant green awning over the window. A painted sign on the salmon-colored wall declared it as Café Constanza.

The delectable fragrances of oranges, cloves, cinnamon, and other spices greeted them as they entered. At once, a middle-aged Spanish woman, with high cheekbones and an aristocratic manner, welcomed them warmly, gesturing to a table near the window. The shop appeared clean with modern furnishings and equipment although the exterior wore the appearance of at least ten centuries earlier. While the menu had many familiar items on it, from ham sandwiches to tortillas and a wide assortment of pastries, they both yielded to the scents filling the café and ordered the orange almond cake along with cinnamon cocoa.

As soon as they'd given their order, Michelle checked her smartphone, hoping for a text from Roberto. Even though they'd exchanged a quick goodbye before she and her aunt had left this morning, she still hoped he would stay in touch often. *Pausing for coffee in Ronda*, she keyed in and sent it.

"Missing him already?" Lindy asked.

She nodded. "Aren't you missing Colin?"

"I am, but this is nothing more than a holiday romance, sweetie. You can't get too serious about anyone you meet while traveling. Although I think Colin should have checked Ronda out during his scouting. This is a spectacular place."

"Is that why you never married?" Michelle asked, seeing an opportunity to ask about her single status.

"Something like it. I've met a lot of men in various cities in the world, but the fellow you meet on the road rarely ends up the same when you get into a domestic situation. Even Colin. He's charming, romantic, and seems very exciting. But he's also divorced; that tells me he probably isn't all of those things at home. We all play parts when we're traveling. Now, I could be wrong, and he may have just not had the right wife, but in some ways, it's better to never find out. At least, you still have a wonderful, although bittersweet memory of the affair."

"That sounds sad, Aunt Lindy. If you never take any chances, you'll never find real happiness."

Lindy wiped the pastry flakes off her lips with a napkin and regarded her niece for a few moments. "True, maybe, but you also don't have the pain and heartache of a terrible breakup. Of feeling like your soul has been ripped from your body, and it will never be whole again."

"Wow, that breakup must have been a dozy," Michelle

mumbled.

Her aunt frowned at her, then pulled out her wallet to pay for their treats. "We'd best get back on the road if we want to get to Sevilla before evening."

As they waited, she noticed Lindy stared at one of the paintings on the wall behind her. She turned to look at it. Even she could see the resemblance in style to Roberto's work. "It kind of looks like something Roberto did," she said.

"I was thinking the same thing." Her aunt got to her feet and moved closer to look at the painting. It was of a child and his mother on the seashore as they strolled barefoot along the beach.

Turning to the woman who had greeted them, she asked, "I am very interested in this painting. I see it's unsigned, but can you tell me who the artist is?"

She glanced at the canvas on the wall. "It is quite charming, is it not? But as to the artist's name, no, I am sorry. I don't know who painted it. I bought it a few years ago on a trip to Marbella. It was done by a street artist, I believe. At least, it was for sale in a stall there."

"I see. It is a very nice painting. It reminds me of an artist who lives there. Perhaps it was the same one. His name is Roberto?"

The woman smiled but shook her head. "I'm sorry, I just don't know."

"By any chance, would it be for sale?"

"No, señora. I don't sell the paintings."

"I see. I would be willing to give you three-hundred euros for it."

Her eyes widened. "Three hundred? Well, perhaps..."

Michelle gaped in surprise. What was her aunt doing?

Maybe it was Roberto's work, and maybe it wasn't, but paying three hundred for an unsigned painting by an unknown artist?

As the woman removed the painting from the wall, Lindy pulled out the cash and handed it to the owner, who smiled, and no doubt considered it a great sale.

Lindy deposited the painting in the back seat as she indicated Michelle should get in. "Sevilla awaits."

"Why?" Michelle asked. "Why that painting?"

Lindy started the car and began easing it out of the tight parking space. "I'm playing a hunch, dear. I'm pretty sure it's one of Roberto's paintings, and I'm curious why it isn't signed."

"But three-hundred euros for a hunch?" Michelle dropped her head against the back of the seat. She couldn't follow her aunt's thinking on this one.

They arrived in Sevilla in the middle of late afternoon traffic, the main road leading in being backed up, but the area shone splendidly in the golden sunlight. Like many Spanish cities, it shared a mix of modern and medieval architecture. Most of the towns in southern Spain had been influenced by Moorish architecture as the workers came in from across the Straits of Gibraltar. The resulting designs decorated the elegant archways with lacelike facades typical of Arabia.

"Further north, around Segovia and toward Barcelona, you don't see these open arches and intricate walls," Lindy told her. "The north had more of the European influence from the Romans and the Greeks. But wait until you see the Alcazar here in town. It is exquisite."

Her aunt exited off the highway, turning into a narrower street toward the central part of town. Michelle was glad she wasn't driving, but the other drivers still made her jump with their near misses and honking horns. She breathed a sigh of relief as Lindy pulled the car into the parking area for the Hotel El Greco, an older-looking but well-maintained place near the central plaza of the city. Leave it to her aunt to find one named for Spain's well-known artist.

Inside, the hotel had a charming old-world elegance, although the elevator to their floor was rather small and slow. Michelle thought it must have been installed shortly after the machinery was designed and hadn't been replaced since then.

Whatever failings the elevator may have had, the room itself more than compensated. While it was only a single bedroom, the two large twin beds were comfortable and modern, as were the dressing table and wardrobe. Like the lobby downstairs, arched facades formed the frame for the large windows facing the plaza. Being on the fifth floor gave them a decent view, without too many impediments, toward the city center and the cathedral there.

"It's beautiful," Michelle said as she gazed at the magnificent architecture of the city. With the Arabian decoration so prominent on the buildings, it resembled a fairy tale city in many ways. Yet, the cathedral was massive, and she couldn't wait to go exploring the downtown area.

She glanced at her aunt, who had started to unpack her clothes and was hanging her dresses in the wardrobe. "Can we go to the plaza tonight? It looks so beautiful, and it's a lovely evening."

"I don't see why not. We should have a few more hours of light, and the plaza is beautiful at sunset." Lindy put a few folded items into a drawer, pulled out her bathroom items, then zipped the suitcase closed again. She turned to face Michelle. "And there are several excellent restaurants along the streets."

"Let's go now," Michelle said, her grin stretching her face wide and her eyes twinkling.

"Don't you want to unpack a little?"

"It can wait." She grabbed her purse and reached for her aunt's hand. "Let's go now."

With a laugh, Lindy picked up her purse as Michelle pulled her toward the door.

The *Plaza de España* was about a fifteen-minute walk from the hotel, and although quite a few people were on the streets, Michelle navigated a way through them with ease. Before she left home, she'd looked at the things to do in Seville, and had seen photos of the plaza with all the city tiles so she couldn't wait to see them in reality.

Spain and Portugal were famous for their colorful tiles. Even at the hotel and along the street, many doorways and walls were decorated with brightly colored ceramic tiles. *One day,* Michelle promised herself, *I am going to have a Spanish-style house with a tiled entryway with colorful designs made just for me.*

A few people stood around gazing at the tiles, but many more just crossed the plaza, leaving it fairly open for Michelle and her aunt to get close and really look at them. Excited, Michelle pointed to the tiled bench for Segovia, a splendidly beautiful three-sided bench with turquoise, burgundy, and gold heraldic-looking images crafted into them with the back tile being the entry aches to the medieval city. Then, there was one for Malaga with different shades of blue, green, and a scene with knights on horseback.

She grinned as she turned to her aunt. "This is so beautiful! So many tiles all over the plaza." She spun around in a slow circle taking in the gigantic plaza with the magnificent portico and fountains.

With a smile, her aunt pointed out the colors and the significance of the details on the tiles. The Plaza wasn't too many years old, having been built in 1929 for a Spanish-American exhibition. In terms of Europe, even the tiles were considered recent additions. Still, they were so beautiful that Michelle wanted a photo of every single one of them.

As Michelle noticed Lindy standing back and watching, she also caught the proud smile on her aunt's face. Perhaps she was pleased her niece saw the beauty and workmanship in these pieces of art, Michelle conceded. After all, she hadn't given much of an indication she might be inspired by anything like it.

With more tiles than she had imagined, Michelle was glad she'd brought her camera rather than just relying on her phone. She hoped she had enough battery power to get all of them and still have some left. She knelt to take another photo, and someone bumped her, nearly knocking her off balance and to the ground.

"Oh, pardon," a man's voice said, and the pardon part sounded more French than Spanish.

Michelle looked up to see a thirty-something man bending toward her, reaching out a hand to help to her feet. He said something in Spanish and at her blank look, changed to English.

"I am so sorry, *mam'selle*. I was distracted by my phone and didn't see you. Are you all right?"

She nodded, "Yes, I'm fine. I guess I was kind of in the way. I was taking photos…"

"Of course. The tiles are magnificent. You're a tourist, yes? It's to be expected."

Just then, Lindy came up. "Are you okay, Michelle?"

"Yes, it was just a bump. I didn't even fall."

The man turned to address her aunt. "I apologize, ma'am. I didn't see your daughter."

"Niece," Lindy corrected automatically.

As they talked, Michelle looked him over. Slim, very attractive, about her aunt's age and dressed in a cool blue shirt with a beige linen jacket. As he smiled, lines on his face crinkled into a very charming face. His narrow nose pushed in a little at the top, and his gray eyes sparkled as he spoke.

"I am Alain Marchant," he said. "I have a villa near here, although my main home is in Paris."

"Delighted. My name is Lindy, and you stumbled over Michelle."

"My pleasure to meet you both. I am not normally clumsy. But it is good to see someone with an appreciation for the art found in the city."

"Indeed. I take it you are among those."

"Yes, of course. I am not just a collector of fine art, but I am also an art dealer."

Michelle watched her aunt's right eyebrow arch, and a small smile played at her lips. This felt like a repeat of the meeting with Colin.

"Really? Do you have a gallery?"

"Yes, in Paris. I show many different artists there."

"Such as?"

As he named off several different artists, Michelle tuned him out and resumed taking photos. On a whim, she turned and snapped one of her aunt with Marchant. They were almost the same height, with her aunt being just a bit shorter, although she was wearing a slight heel.

"Perhaps you and your niece would like to join me for dinner?" Marchant said. Michelle turned to look, shaking her head at her aunt.

"Unfortunately, not tonight," Lindy declined. "We already have plans."

"Perhaps tomorrow at my villa?" he persisted. "I can have my driver bring you at seven. I insist. I hadn't realized you are an artist, but now I recall your name. I would love to converse with you, and perhaps I may persuade you to display a few pieces at my gallery. What do you say?"

Michelle saw the hesitation in Lindy's eyes, but then the smile. "Yes, that would be lovely. Seven o'clock then." She offered him her hand, and he bent and kissed the back of it.

Michelle's eyes popped wide. He kissed her hand! She should have taken a photo of that.

Marchant smiled at her, then went on about his business, walking away quickly with his attention back on the phone in his hand.

"Dinner? Really?"

"I know, Michelle, but it could mean business for me. If he really is an art dealer ..." She paused to flick the business card in her hand, then continued, "... I might be able to sell a few paintings."

"Well, I'm not too enthused."

"It's only dinner," Lindy said. "And it gives us a chance to see his villa. Maybe it's spectacular."

Michelle looked away, her thoughts on Roberto, and she wished he were here with her. "So, what's on the agenda for tomorrow?"

"Two big things, my dear niece. We'll go to the Cathedral, which is magnificent and houses a tomb for Columbus. And we'll visit the Alcazar. That alone is the whole afternoon. Wait until you see it."

As the sun cast its last rays on the plaza, Michelle turned to get a photo of the fountain with the fading streams of light on it. Then the street lights began coming on, and they walked toward a restaurant where her aunt proclaimed, "They have the best food in Seville."

Located in a well-tended area of the city, Alain Marchant's villa ranked with several large homes per block dominating the neighborhood. From the exterior, it looked like a fairly simple stucco, although big, square house with elegant wrought iron covering the arched windows and door entrance. Instead of the butler Michelle expected, a short, plump housekeeper greeted them with a big smile.

"Welcome. Please come in." Her English was very good, with only a slight accent. "Señor Marchant will be down in a few minutes. You may wait in the main room if you please."

She motioned them to the large living room on the right-hand side of the entry hall. Double doors, set inside a huge decorative oak wood arch with carved leaves and acorns on it, swung open to the inside where plump, comfortable-looking sofas and chairs sat on top of the luxurious carpeting. Paintings decorated the walls, and a few sculptures accented the room's warm colors of creamy yellow, light brown, and gold.

Turing in a circle, Michelle's gaze caught the large glass doors that opened onto a traditional-style central courtyard with numerous arches surrounding it. Lush gardens and shrubs, a fountain, patio, and grass beckoned the family to enjoy the outdoors.

Michelle sat on the loveseat facing the room's entrance while Lindy went over to examine one of the paintings. After a few moments, she moved on to another, then a sculpture next to the wall. Michelle just took in the overall effect of the room, beginning with the high ceilings, trimmed with oak panels with more carvings in them. They suggested Marchant had a great deal of money and spent lavishly on the furnishings of this place.

Assuming dinner would be dressy, Michelle had chosen a light green sleeveless summer A-line dress to flatter her model-slim figure. She wore green sling-back heels, which were comfortable and fashionable. Overall, she felt it gave her a look of innocence to charm and warn their host.

On the other hand, her aunt had dressed with sophistication in mind. Michelle envied the dark blue cocktail dress that hugged Lindy's curves and highlighted her assets to perfection. Flower patterned black nylons covered her long legs, and open-toed, high-heeled sandals completed the look. Around her neck, she wore a double strand of pearls with matching earrings easily visible as she'd pulled her hair up into an elegant French twist. Michelle admitted her aunt was a stunning woman and admired her taste in clothing and accessories. As she raised her left arm to touch the finish of a vase, her petite watch glistened with three twisted-pearl strands catching the light. One day, Michelle vowed, she would be as worldly as Lindy.

As Lindy shifted to another painting, Alain strode into the room, words of welcome pouring out before he even passed the entry.

"I am so pleased you've accepted my dinner invitation. I hope you do not mind, but I have invited a friend of mine to join us. Jose Cárdenas is an art collector, and I mentioned to him I was having the amazing Melinda Morton and her beautiful niece over for dinner. Well, you know, he practically begged to meet you."

Lindy smiled, and her right eyebrow raised just a little, an indicator to Michelle that she was not totally pleased with this turn. But she said, "Well, it would be hard to say no to a fan of my work. I didn't know I had many outside the world of science fiction and fantasy fandom."

Marchant approached her, glancing at the painting she had been perusing. "Of course. Not all of your work has been book covers and fantasy canvases. You have done some excellent character studies and light illusion pieces garnering high praise in certain quarters."

"A few," she conceded and turned away from the painting. "But even those were done in preparation for doing a fantasy project."

Alain went to the ice bucket and decanter set out on a side table along with glasses. "Might I offer you sangria before dinner? I even have a virgin version if your niece is not—"

"I would love a glass of sangria," Michelle said. "I'm legal in Spain, I believe." Her coquettish glance and sharp look challenged Lindy to dispute it.

Marchant glanced toward her aunt, who gave a brief nod of approval.

Alain dropped ice cubes into the glasses, poured the wine beverage, then topped each glass with sugar encrusted mint leaves and a fresh orange slice. Smiling, he handed a glass to Lindy, then Michelle, before raising his glass in a toast. "To fortuitous meetings. May they lead to good friendships and prosperous partnerships."

He sat on the sofa at an angle to her while Lindy took the other end, far enough away to be out of touching distance and close enough for easy conversation.

As they drank, Michelle thought it was an odd toast, but

maybe not from Alain's view. Her aunt could become a client if she chose to sell some paintings through him. It occurred to her she didn't know that much about Lindy's business other than she created book covers, mostly science fiction and fantasy, although she knew she'd done a few contemporary romance covers. But she never thought she actually painted canvases. The skill was a dying art in the book cover business, but obviously, people still bought real, original paintings to decorate their homes and offices.

She had been excited by Roberto's artwork but hadn't given much thought to what her aunt did for a living. She admitted she hadn't credited her aunt with the talent this art dealer now raved about. She'd never seen an actual painting her aunt had done, only the book covers.

As the doorbell chimed, a shortened version of "Ode to Joy" with just the first two bars, Alain set his drink on the low table and pushed to his feet. "I believe that's Jose now. Please excuse me."

Michelle glanced a little nervously at Lindy as Alain went to greet his other guest. She hadn't counted on more people being at dinner, and she wasn't comfortable with the idea. Her Spanish was almost non-existent, so she hoped the newcomer spoke English. She could hear Alain speak to him in Spanish as the conversation drifted in as they approached.

Soon, he showed the newcomer into the room and introduced him to the ladies, in English. "Jose, *amigo*. This lovely lady," he paused to motion to Lindy, "is Melinda Morton, a very celebrated artist from the United States. And the other equally beautiful young lady is her niece, Michelle."

He said her name with the French pronunciation, which made her tingle a little because it sounded so elegant, so foreign.

"My pleasure, ladies," Cárdenas replied with a friendly smile. A little taller than Alain, he appeared to be a little younger also, although a few strands of silvery gray showed at the temples of his almost black hair. A few laugh lines crinkled the edges of his eyes, and she couldn't help but notice the long, thick eyelashes; any woman would envy those.

Lindy rose to her feet to accept the offered hand he thrust toward her, and Michelle noticed he shook it gently, not pumping like some men did. Then he brushed his other hand over the top before he released it as if to add emphasis to the moment.

"I am delighted my good friend invited me this evening. I am very familiar with your work. Believe it or not, I read science fiction novels, and your covers have drawn me to some books I've greatly enjoyed. But I have also seen some of your early paintings and love your style," he said, the words flowing out with enthusiasm.

If this had been a convention, Michelle might have called him a fanboy.

Lindy was courteous, thanking him for the praise and asking him about the books he had read. "Oh, that's an excellent one," she said when he mentioned a cover. "I also read most of the books I illustrate. It helps me to capture the main characters or the setting if I can find the perfect scene in the novel."

Alain poured a sangria for Jose as they talked and handed it to him with a slight smirk. "So, you have something in common. Excellent. But I believe dinner is ready for us, so if you follow me, I will show you to the dining room."

They crossed the hall to the first door on the right, which he pushed open, revealing an elegant dining hall behind it. The table looked large enough to easily seat twenty people, but only the far end of it was set up for the four of them. Excess chairs had been removed to rest along the wall, and the remaining ones were spaced to give each of them plenty of elbow space. A cream-colored lace tablecloth covered a solid red one and called attention to the matching cream with red-accents china that gleamed under the six-armed chandelier.

Michelle caught her breath at the sheer opulence of the whole room. Wooden arches framed beautiful murals of the Spanish countryside. Wrought iron sconces featured globe lights, not turned on at the moment, but they looked beautiful. She had never been in a room so rich-feeling, and she felt like a country bumpkin. Her family was not poor, but they didn't have this kind of luxury.

Lindy also admired the murals and the dainty china statues positioned across the sideboard. Unlike Michelle, her aunt appeared very comfortable in this setting. Again, Michelle realized how little she actually knew about her aunt and her success in the world.

Once they were seated, Alain rang a bell at the side of his plate, and a gentleman appeared with a bottle of wine in his hands.

"This is an excellent chardonnay from a winery I partially own here in Spain. It would be my privilege to share it with you all tonight."

"We are honored," Lindy answered and gave him a nod of thanks.

Once the wine was poured, the serving-man left and returned with the appetizer course, grilled shrimp on lettuce leaves with green grapes. As they ate, conversation slowed quite a bit, but Alain asked Lindy several questions about her work and if she had a project at the moment.

"I have one in the planning stages," she replied. "I don't do as many covers as I used to do. There are many more artists in the field, and the techniques have changed considerably. I still prefer to paint the images rather than relying on computers to fill in my colors and simulate brush strokes."

"I concur with your assessment," Jose said and raised his wine glass to her. "While there are many beautiful images created on the computer, they lack the heart of having the artist actually apply the paint. I guess that is why I am an art collector. I see the soul in the painting."

Lindy returned the sentiment with a slight, enigmatic smile.

The next course arrived, a rack of lamb surrounded by roasted new potatoes, baby carrots, and kohlrabi. When she didn't think about what she was eating, Michelle had to admit the meat tasted amazing and was so tender it practically fell off the bones. She just wasn't keen on eating baby anything. Well, except for the potatoes and the carrots. Mostly she stayed silent during the meal and listened to the three-way conversation around her. When it came to discussing art, the only thing she knew was what she liked, and the little she'd learned in a few short days with Roberto.

After dinner, they retired to the living room again, where Alain started to pour glasses of brandy.

"None for me," Michelle said. "I think I've had enough to drink for the evening. Would you have any lemon water, by chance?"

He nodded. "I am sure we do. I often enjoy it in the afternoon."

After he handed the brandy to Lindy and Jose, he left the room to get the water for her. *No bell in here*, Michelle concluded.

"So, Jose, tell me about your art collection," Lindy said and started the man off on another conversation about his art and how much he enjoyed looking at the paintings. "In fact, I am expecting to pick up a painting tonight, so we can ask Alain about it when he returns."

"I am back." Alain swept into the room with a glass of the requested beverage. "And did I hear your comment about your new painting?"

"I did. Do you have it yet?"

"There was a delay, and it has not arrived yet. I am sorry. But I will have it tomorrow, I believe."

"Bad luck. I had hoped I might show it to Melinda. It's by a well-known Basque artist, who took the art scene by storm over the past five years."

Michelle watched as Lindy's eyebrows went up. "Really? Who might that be?"

"Pablo de Sintra," Alain answered. "He is an old man whose paintings began to be very popular in just a short time. He paints mostly character studies, and he has magnificent use of lighting and color. I have one in my small gallery here. Would you like to see?"

"Absolutely," Lindy replied.

Setting his brandy glass on the coffee table, Alain motioned for them to join him. They left their drinks and followed him to the room next to the dining room. When he turned on the lights, they saw a gallery the size of a small room in the Louvre, which displayed about forty paintings of various sizes. Scattered through it, several cases highlighted small sculptures illuminated by soft base lighting.

"Wow, this is amazing," Michelle said as she took in the full scope of the room.

"You have quite a collection here," Lindy agreed.

"Yes, there are many excellent paintings. Feel free to look around. But first, allow me to show you the de Sintra."

"Yes, please," Jose interjected as Lindy nodded.

Alain took the lead again as they crossed to the other side of the room, Michelle trailing up the rear, to a medium-sized painting on the wall. As with all the paintings, an overhanging light illuminated the canvas to its best advantage. Even she could see the merits of the wonderful study of a young woman hanging clothes on a line in a yard. Behind her, two children played in the front of the back door of a whitewashed house. The colors were vibrant, and the composition very pleasing to the eye.

In fact, Michelle thought it looked really familiar. Roberto's paintings had a similar look. She noticed her aunt stepping closer to study the canvas, watching as her eyes dropped to the signature at the lower right-hand side for several moments.

"I believe I've seen his work before," Lindy said. "As I look at it, I recall an exhibit in a New York gallery that featured his paintings. It was about three years ago. I went to see what all the fuss was about. He is very talented. You are fortunate to be getting one of his paintings, Jose."

He nodded. "Yes, I believe so. Although I confess, I would love to have one of your paintings. While the book covers are plentiful, the actual paintings seem to be somewhat rare."

"True. I agree," Alain said. "But I hope to convince her to make some available through my gallery. Shall I keep you in mind if she allows me to market a few?"

"Of course. I meant what I said."

"It's a possibility," Lindy said. "But one we need to discuss another time. For now, I want to look at a few of these paintings, then Michelle and I need to be getting home. We have a busy day planned for tomorrow."

"Ah, what is on the agenda?" Cárdenas asked.

"We're going to Italica to look around and perhaps do a little sketching."

"Excellent choice. Might I offer my services as a guide? I know quite a bit about the history." Jose's eyebrows rose in a hopeful expression.

"It's very kind of you to offer," Lindy said, easing the rejection with a smile, "but I have other arrangements."

"Another time then."

Lindy shifted her attention to another one of the paintings that had caught her eye. A realistic-looking scene by a Spanish painter, Antonio Lopez Garcia, whose work she admired. In fact, she had one hanging in her home in London.

About fifteen minutes later, Alain called for his car to take them back to their hotel, and they bid the two gentlemen a good night. Once they'd climbed in, Alain leaned through the window to Lindy and said, "I would like to see you again to discuss marketing the paintings more. Perhaps I might meet you for dinner tomorrow night?"

Michelle blinked, wondering if he was trying to do business with her aunt or trying for a romantic liaison. She relaxed a little when Lindy replied, "I am not sure what time we will be back or if I will feel up to it after a day among the ruins. Call me about five, and I'll let you know." She slipped a business card into his hand with her cell phone number on it.

Alain gave a brief nod before he stepped back from the car to allow it to leave. Michelle kept an eye on him as they pulled away, then turned to her aunt and asked in a low voice, "What was that about? Do you want to meet with him again?"

"I may," she whispered back. "But I'm going to check

Marchant out before I do any business with him. We'll talk about it tomorrow."

Chapter 14
❧ Lindy ❧

Lindy swung the car into a slot in the parking area at Italica and reached for her sun hat as Michelle tucked her phone into the fanny pack she wore at her right hip. Since the Roman ruins were situated only nine kilometers from Seville, they hadn't felt rushed to get there and had lingered over their rooftop breakfast. They didn't talk much during the drive, although Lindy thought quite a bit about the previous evening's events.

She'd looked up Marchant's gallery on the internet when they'd gotten back to the hotel, and he seemed legitimate. His gallery displayed and sold work by a wide range of artists. Still, she wasn't certain her particular art would be comfortable in the setting. He was the sole distributor for works by several European artists, including Pablo de Sintra. In fact, Marchant had discovered the Basque artist living in relative poverty in a town near the Portuguese city rather than in it. He took the city name as his artistic moniker because Alain had suggested it and now signed his paintings in that way.

If she placed a canvas or two with Marchant, she did not wish to sign an exclusive agreement with him, so the details would need to be discussed as would any commission he might receive from the sale. She had shown her work many times, but she rarely placed them for sale in a gallery. In the early days, she would display the book cover art at conventions and would sometimes sell them from there to the fans who willingly bid the cost up to a very nice amount although not close to what she might get from a collector these days. Perhaps even Señor Cardenas might be willing to fork over several thousand to have the cover painting for a favorite book. Money, however, was not a motivation for her placing a painting with Marchant. Several non-book related paintings she'd done had received critical acclaim when she'd displayed them, and she wondered if they would draw more interest to her work.

She loved doing the book covers, but as she'd said, the business had slowed some in recent years. She worked mostly for two or three larger publishing houses, but so many writers were publishing books now, and digitally-created covers were plentiful. For as many writers as they were, it seemed an equal number of artists were providing covers at very reasonable fees. Perhaps she was becoming a dinosaur in the business with wanting to continue to paint the covers. And it wasn't because she didn't know how to use the new tools of the trade; it was a matter of preference. Sooner or later, she might have to switch to using the computer.

Putting a few paintings with Marchant might give her an indication if there would be an outlet for her paintings in the legitimate art world. She wanted to check him out further, though and would have her business manager check into his background more. If nothing else, she'd learned to be cautious over the years.

The other thing that troubled her a little was the painting by Pablo de Sintra, which bore a strong resemblance to Roberto's paintings in style, color, and brush strokes. She found it curious Roberto would imitate de Sintra's style so closely in his own work. Had Michelle noticed?

Her niece had spent the time over breakfast catching up with her friends, keying in messages nimbly with her three-fingered typing on the tiny keyboard on her phone. *Young people,* Lindy thought. *They can't be out of touch for any length of time these days.*

Now, as they got out of the car, Michelle turned to her aunt and asked, "You know, we didn't talk much last night after the party, but you looked at the painting closely, didn't you? Did you notice anything about it?"

Lindy nodded, "I did. What about you?"

"I thought it resembled Roberto's style. Does that mean he's copying this Pablo-guy?"

"Either copying very well or something else is going on."

"What do you mean?"

Lindy began walking toward the entry to the ruins, and Michelle fell into step beside her. "I mean the style is so much like Roberto's that I can't really tell the difference. The brush strokes, the color mix, the subject matter – it's all the same as his. There would be no reason for him to duplicate the style so completely it's virtually impossible to tell the difference."

"Are you saying that the painting was actually Roberto's? Or is Roberto really Pablo?"

Lindy shrugged. "All I can really say without an expert analysis is the painting styles are so similar they could be by the same artist or one extremely good forger. But neither option makes sense."

"I can ask Roberto if that specific painting is his," Michelle replied, her voice sounding a little tense.

"It would help if we had a photo and could send it to him. Just describing it might not trigger a memory for him, but if he could see it..."

"I do." She pulled out her phone again and tapped on the screen. "I took a picture with my phone while you were looking at it. I think it's clear enough for you to see most of the canvas." She held the phone up to show Lindy.

Taking the phone from her, Lindy enlarged the image a little and smiled. "Yes, I think it's good enough for him to recall. Send it to him and ask if he painted it, but don't say anything about Pablo de Sintra. I don't want to stir up a hornet's nest if there's no meat at the table."

Michelle nodded, then tapped in a quick note to Roberto, attached the photo, and sent it as Lindy paid the entry fees for the grounds.

Entering, Michelle and Lindy paused to gaze over the beautiful, yet dry-looking landscape of the ancient Roman city. Near the entry, a beautiful garden with flowers, bushes, and trees beckoned them, and they responded, turning into the nearest pathway to go in. Meandering through, they peered at the various beds of flowers and made their way to the town where the base stones and pillars outlined what had once been houses. Within the destroyed walls, the marble mosaic floors drew their eyes as so many of them had different beautiful and unique patterns within the designs.

Michelle took pictures at almost everyone as they paused to study them for a few minutes. "It's like a museum," she said as she lined up a shot with three open, marble-floored rooms in a row. "So much beauty in an ancient city. Who would have thought?"

"Well, Rome was an advanced civilization. Look at the streets here and even the channels for their plumbing. Rome in the first century was quite modern in many respects, and Italica was built by Romans at the beginning of the third century,"

Lindy stated before she paused to look at the guidebook she'd brought. "Hadrian, the emperor who built the wall in England, was born here, as were two other emperors."

Michelle squinted at her as she pushed her sunhat up a little. "Didn't you tell that man last night that you had arranged a guide for today?"

Lindy held up her book. "I did. So, I fudged a little, but all we need to know is in here." She tapped the cover. "For instance, over here is the House of Birds, so-called because of the birds worked into the mosaic on the floor."

Michelle followed her into the first of the many rooms that made up the house, all of them now just an outline in stone but with much of the floor mosaics still in place.

"This would have been an aristocrat's home. It even had this *peristylum* – that's this little patio area – with a well in it to provide water." She led on through the ruins while she glanced at the layout in the book. "Ah, and back here is a *triclinium* with two patios, one on each side. This one—" She paused to point at the one on her left. "—had a fountain while the other had a pool."

Michelle's lip skewed up on the side. "Getting pretty free with those fancy words, aren't you?"

Lindy laughed. "They're in the guidebook. I don't speak Latin. At least, not much."

"So, all of this belonged to Rome at the time?" Michelle asked, waving her arm to indicate the whole area.

"Yes, Spain was under Roman rule then. They were a conquering nation, but generally, they brought some good improvements with them, like the aqueducts, roads, dams, and bridges. Even the amphitheater. Like the Greeks, they were great creators."

"How did the world fall so far behind?" Michelle asked. "I mean, the Middle Ages were dim."

Lindy shrugged. It was a good question, but she didn't have an answer. "Let's head over to the amphitheater. This is a very good representation of their construction skill as much of it is still standing."

As they walked through the main *vomitorium,* or entryway, to the coliseum, Lindy marveled at the size of it. She'd been to Italica many years earlier, but it hadn't been as excavated as it was now. They stepped through into the semi-circular two-story building, getting their first look at the central arena.

Michelle gasped. "Omigod, it's the dragon pit!" She jumped up and down a couple of times. "I can't believe it. I have to get pictures!" She lifted her camera and took a photo right then.

"Excuse me," Lindy said. "The dragon pit? What are you talking about?"

"*Game of Thrones.* Aunt Lindy, this was used in the television series. Didn't you recognize it?"

Lindy's face clouded with puzzlement. "Uh, no, I don't watch the show."

"What?!" Michelle's eyebrows lifted almost to her hairline in shock. "You don't watch it? You've got to be kidding."

Her niece rolled her eyes then pointed to the central part of the arena where huge openings in the ground formed the pits where animals were kept for the games. "This is where Jon Snow came to talk with Cersei, and the dragons came bringing Daenerys." She looked around the area and pointed to a section of the wall. "Over there is where the dragon climbed down to let Daenerys climb off. They covered those pits with a stage to make the meeting spot. Can I go down to the stage area behind it?"

Lindy nodded. "Of course." She waited as Michelle hurried to the arena and climbed up to the stage overlooking the pits. Well, at least, she'd found something that truly impressed the girl. She strolled over, noting all the work done to excavate the theater.

Michelle walked out on the stage and made a slow turn, waving her arms at the tiers of seating around the entire arena. "It must seat thousands, auntie."

Lindy consulted her guide book. ""It can seat twenty-five thousand people. Many of the dignitaries from nearby came for the events, but I don't know if anyone knows if it was ever filled. The whole town barely had a population of eight thousand, so it certainly exceeded the needs of the town. But even in the third century, Seville was a larger city, and doubtless, it attracted visitors from there."

Michelle marched to where she perceived center stage to be and struck a pose as she pretended to play to the most important audience, where the Roman senators might sit with the local *head honcho*. "Take a photo of me here, please, Aunt Lindy. I want to send it to my theater friends and joke about playing a huge outdoor theater."

Laughing, Lindy framed the photo to get a close up of her niece with the seats and pillars rising behind her lending their antiquity and stateliness to the image. Liking what she saw, she encouraged Michelle to do a few performance poses and snapped several more photos as the girl obliged.

As she thumbed through the images with her niece peering over her shoulder, Lindy saw what Roberto had seen in her — a naturally graceful young woman who looked beautiful on film. It would be easy to paint her in a variety of settings and poses. If she made it as a film actress, she would likely photograph well.

Her natural beauty shined, and when she wore make-up, she looked stunning.

"Oh, I love those, auntie. Might I put a few in my portfolio along with the ones from the Alcazar yesterday and the ones from the fountain?"

"That's some portfolio you're going to have. Of course, you can have them. But I'm sure there will be many more photos to come on this trip. Many places in Spain are picturesque, and the light is wonderful with the color of the stones here. I've done paintings of Italica from my first visit here in 1989. Much of the excavation we see now wasn't even started then, not until 2001. So it's like seeing it for the first time in many ways. Perhaps I'll do more paintings, and you might make a fitting subject for one if you don't mind me painting you in a Roman tunic to give it a romance cover look."

"Seriously?" Michelle's eyes widened, and a huge smile lit up her face. "You'd put me on a book cover?"

"Well, it wouldn't look exactly like you, but you and most of your friends could probably see the resemblance."

"So long as it isn't distorted like the French painter did."

"You mean Picasso? He was a Spanish painter, dear. In fact, he was from Malaga, where we were a few days ago. His style of art is called 'cubism,' and he was one of the creators of it. But no, I don't do it. I prefer something more realistic, especially when painting book covers."

"Then it would be cool. But I have one request."

Lindy lifted an eyebrow as if to say, what?

"Could you put a dragon in the painting?"

"A dragon? I don't believe I've ever done one before. Maybe this won't be a romance ..."

"Sure, it could. He could be a dragon shifter who's madly in love with the maiden."

"Maybe." Lindy grinned then pointed toward the entry plaza where towering cypress trees stood, along with a couple of pillars and a fine example of the colorful mosaics so popular in the Mediterranean countries. "Let's go over, and I'll take a few photos of you in various poses. One of those will serve as the basis for the painting."

As if parting from an unseen audience, Lindy watched Michelle give a little bow to the seats and prance out to the courtyard area. Just as she started to lean against one of the broken columns, her phone played a cheery little tune, and she whipped it out of her pocket to answer.

Lindy shook her head and looked away, checking out the sun's position and making notes on her own phone as to the angle, the colors, and depth of the shadows while she waited for Michelle to finish. She wanted to include some of the tiles in the painting, so she photographed several of them, and turned her attention to the column itself, getting a detailed shot of the base and the top of it so she would have a clear image for the work.

Call finished, Michelle hung up then came up to her. "That was Roberto. He does recall the painting. It was a special order he did a few years ago. He'd only been selling a few paintings then, and a man asked him if he could do a custom painting for him. He said it was one of his first commission jobs."

Lindy frowned. "Did he say if his client requested a specific style?"

"No, and I didn't think to ask since you didn't want me to say anything about Pablo de Sinatra."

"Sintra, not Sinatra. One's a city, and the other's a singer. It's all right. The resemblance could be a coincidence, but I still want to check on it. Now, stand over by that column, lean against it, and look wistfully toward the statue across the way."

A dozen photographs later, they located a café in the nearby town of Santiponce and ordered *café con leche,* the Spanish version of *café au lait,* and a basket of pastries to tide them over until dinner.

While Michelle prattled on about what Roberto was doing, Lindy thought about the painting and the best way to check it out. She had a few contacts, but she thought Colin might have better ones. She regretted not getting his cell phone number or any of the places where she might reach him in Italy. Perhaps the production company he was working for might tell her. What was the name of it? She closed her eyes and tried to recall what he'd said. The name of it danced right at the edge of her memory, almost there, but not quite. *It will come to me soon if I just don't fret about it.*

"Omigod, he's on his way here," Michelle's excited voice cut through her thoughts.

"What?"

"Roberto. He's coming to Seville to see me… us. Maybe he's curious about the painting. Or he just misses me, but he left a couple of hours ago."

"Well, that's a surprise," Lindy replied, not sure what to say. Did the question about the painting trigger his response? They would find out soon enough.

Chapter 15
❧ Michelle ❧

Michelle and Lindy had almost arrived back in Seville when Lindy's phone rang a little after five p.m. At her indication, Michelle answered it, knowing her aunt expected a call from Alain and was not surprised to hear his voice although he sounded both off guard and pleased she picked up the call.

"Can you hold just a few moments? My aunt is pulling the car off the road so she can talk to you." She listened as he told her again how pleased he was she'd come to dinner the previous night, and he hoped she and her aunt would allow him to take them to an excellent restaurant tonight.

"I can't make it tonight myself. I have other plans this evening, but here's my aunt." She handed the phone to Lindy as soon as the car was safely stopped on the shoulder.

Although Lindy put a smile in her voice, she wasn't as sure about the dinner plans as she told him, "We won't be back in Seville for about another thirty minutes, and we are expecting a friend. So it would be almost eight before I would be free to go out. Is that too late?"

She waited as he spoke, arching an eyebrow at Michelle, then said, "All right. Yes, fine. I'll meet you in the lobby of the hotel at eight-thirty."

"You could have gone sooner," Michelle said when Lindy clicked the phone off and tucked it back into the pocket of her handbag.

"I'm hoping Roberto is here before I go out. I have a couple of questions for him, and I want to know what you two will be doing." Lindy pulled the car back into traffic.

"Honestly, don't you trust me?" Michelle sounded offended.

"Of course, I do. But you're in a foreign country, and in a city that you, and possibly Roberto, are neither one familiar with, so I would like to know what your plans are before I go out for the evening. And you'd better make sure your phone is charged."

Michelle shot an annoyed look at her aunt, but she did have a point or two. She didn't know what Roberto had in mind, and she was as surprised as her aunt with his decision to come to Seville. Nonetheless, she was excited to see him. She wondered what questions Lindy had in mind for him, but she thought they had something to do with the painting. Although she wasn't saying much about it, she knew Lindy had suspicions about the piece and who actually painted it. For herself, she had faith Roberto didn't copy anyone's art style, but the painting was a mystery.

They pulled into the hotel parking about five-forty-five and went into the lobby. As they checked for their room key, the concierge told them a young man was waiting for them in the hotel lounge.

"Already?" Michelle asked. "He's here already?"

"He must have left Marbella before he called you back," Lindy said.

They turned to the lounge, as the place called the bar, and

went in. Roberto spotted them as soon as they entered and jumped to his feet to come to meet them.

"Let's go up to our room so we can talk," Lindy suggested.

"*Si*," Roberto agreed. He had gotten a glass of wine, which he picked up to take with him, but he paused to ask them, "Would you like wine or some other drink?"

Michelle shook her head as Lindy went on ahead to the elevator. As it clunked to the fourth floor, Michelle asked Roberto about the trip over, and he admitted he'd left before noon.

Once they were in the room, Lindy grabbed a bottle of water, twisted the top off, and sat in the chair at the little round table by the window. Then she turned to Roberto and asked, "Why did you decide to come on such short notice? Did it have to do with the painting?"

He took a seat on the edge of the bed and sipped at his wine. "Yes and no. My curiosity was aroused when I saw the painting in the photo. It was one of the first ones I did when I started selling my work in Marbella. I remembered it because it was a special request. But also, I wanted to deliver a small picture I had done for a friend here, and it gave me an excuse to see Michelle as well."

"Tell me, were you trying to duplicate another artist's style when you painted it? In fact, are you copying a well-known artist now?"

Eyebrows shooting up, Roberto looked utterly shocked at the suggestion. Even Michelle's eyes shot wide with alarm when her aunt flat out asked the question. He spoke up at once. "No, I do not copy any other artists. My style is my own. Why do you ask?"

"You're positive you painted the canvas in the photo

Michelle sent?"

"Of course, I am. I recall painting it very clearly."

"Have you ever heard of an artist called Pablo de Sintra?"

He shook his head. "No, I don't think so. He is not one I am familiar with."

"He's become a name in the art world in the past five years. His first art gained attention about the time you did the painting we saw last night. The canvas hangs in the home of an art dealer here in Seville, and it is signed by Pablo de Sintra." Lindy stared at him intently, waiting for his reaction.

Michelle's eyes darted to him, anger and embarrassment that her aunt would even ask the question making her cheeks blush.

"What?! No, I am sure it is my painting. If anyone else could have one that matches it, then that person copied me. No one could have come up with the same scene and the same model since she is my cousin." Roberto's voice held a touch of anger, and he waved his right hand to indicate a negative, but he remained calm as he spoke. Deep concern showed in his dark eyes. "You say an art dealer has it on display at his home?"

"Yes, a Frenchman named Alain Marchant. Have you heard the name before?" Lindy replied.

Roberto's eyebrows pulled together as he thought. "The name is familiar, but I have never met him. I am sure. Can you describe him?"

"He's about five-foot-nine, medium build, on the thin side. He has an oval face, with more of a point at the chin. His eyes are gray, not too wide, and narrow set. He has an average length Roman nose. But I can do better than describe him." She held up her phone to display a photo of Marchant from the gallery web site.

Roberto took the photo and studied the image, then shook his head. "I don't recall ever seeing him. If he had bought a painting from me, I would have remembered." He frowned as he continued to look. The photo was one of three on the webpage. He pointed to the one next to him. "This man, the light-haired one, I have seen him before, but I don't recall where."

Lindy took the phone and studied the other man's face. "Lovell Clavier is the gallery's business manager. Did you study in Paris at any time where you might have encountered him?"

"I was there for a couple of months, but I don't recall seeing him. I am at a loss. All I know is the painting is one of mine." He slumped back on the bed.

"I had to ask you," Lindy said, "because I suspect something is not right. It's possible Pablo de Sintra saw your painting and duplicated it. If this was an early painting of his also, he might have just copied the style. But I want to check into it more. Don't concern yourself until we learn more."

"You made it sound like an accusation," Michelle interjected, the irritation in her voice sounding bitter. She felt her aunt could have handled it better.

"No, no, it's all right," Roberto said, holding out his right hand to Michelle. "I'm not offended. It was a fair question, and now there is a puzzle why my painting bears another man's name. Perhaps I should be flattered if someone has copied one of my pieces and claimed it. It means I am good, no?" He laughed a little, and Michelle returned the smile.

"You're right. It's a puzzle. Perhaps I can learn more about it from Marchant without revealing anything. So, what are your plans for the evening?" Lindy relaxed back in the chair as she asked.

Roberto's expression brightened as he replied, "I know a couple of nice, typical Spanish food restaurants here in the area. And with your permission, I would like to take Michelle to a flamenco club to see some amazing dancers."

"Sounds delightful. Don't stay out too late. I know the clubs stay open into the early hours, but please get her back by midnight. Are you staying at the hotel, Roberto?"

"No, my cousin lives here, so I will be staying there tonight and going back home tomorrow."

"Then maybe you can stop by here for breakfast in the morning," Lindy suggested.

"Yes, I would like that," he replied, then stood and picked up his wine glass. "I'm going to return this to the bar, and I'll wait for you down there, Michelle."

She nodded. "It will take me about fifteen minutes to get ready." She walked with him to the room door and said in a low voice, "I'm sorry my aunt sounded like an inquisitioner. I never thought for a moment "

"It's okay. She is just trying to understand as am I. I am sure we will find a good answer." He gave her a quick kiss, setting her heart quivering, then turned to go to the elevator.

Michelle whirled back around and glared at her aunt. "You made it sound like he was a forger."

"Nonsense. A forger would have signed the original artist's name on the painting. No, if it's a copy of Roberto's painting, which is duplicated very well, and signed by another artist, then it is theft. But it could be an unintentional one if the artist copied it for practice and didn't intend to sell it. If Marchant saw it and wanted it for his own gallery, then it would be a private transaction, and so long as he doesn't sell it, there would be no crime involved."

"Sounds complicated."

"It is, which is why I want to learn more about the situation. Now go get ready." Lindy opened her tablet and began searching the web.

Michelle pulled out a pretty yellow and red floral dress and headed to the bathroom, then came back out to grab a pair of slacks and a yellow fiesta blouse as she remembered she would be on the back of Roberto's motorcycle. When she came out dressed for the evening and slipped on a pair of sandals, she noticed Lindy was absorbed in whatever she'd found on the web.

"Bathroom is yours. I'm leaving. Don't stay out too late, Auntie."

Lindy waved her out the door, and Michelle chuckled as she went down the hall.

Roberto seemed to know Seville almost as well as he knew Marbella, Michelle thought as he zipped down one of the side streets, leading them away from the central part of the city. In a few quick turns, he took them to another neighborhood that looked less like a tourist attraction and more like a place where the locals went to enjoy themselves.

Like most cities in Spain, Seville boasted a thriving nightlife. People still preferred their afternoon siesta breaks and late-night social life. She and Roberto arrived a little earlier for dinner than many of the rest of the people did, so they were seated quickly and had a table on the patio where they could have a private conversation and watch the sunset. Around them, the flowering bougainvilleas crawled across the stone walls surrounding the garden-like setting. A fountain at the far end gurgled and splashed, adding a touch of soothing sound to accompany a pair of crickets who were carrying on more of a conversation than she and her friend were.

"It's nice here, yes?" he asked as he gazed around the area. Another four tables were set up on the tiled patio, but they were the only ones seated there at the moment.

"Yes. Have you been here before?"

"I have friends and a cousin who live here, and they've brought me to this place a few times. The food is excellent, and a little later, there will be musicians, but by then, we'll probably move on to the Flamenco club." He opened the menu and translated a few of the less common dishes for her.

One of the choices was stuffed octopus, and she frowned as he said it. "No, it is good. You need to be adventurous when you travel. Try something new."

"Maybe if you order it, I'll try some of yours," she replied, her nose wrinkling. "But for me, I think I would prefer something not so unique."

He pressed his lips together as if to keep from saying something he might regret, then asked, "How about goat? The spiced goat stew is very good. Once you get the meat tender, it is quite tasty."

"Next, please."

"I see… Nothing too out of the ordinary for the señorita. There is a great chicken dish with saffron and chili served over rice. It isn't too spicy."

"Maybe," she conceded. It sounded like a possibility, or maybe just a steak would be nice.

After a bit more kidding around about the menu, she settled on the chicken dish. Roberto ordered sangria for them and a tapas plate to munch on while they waited for the main course. She loved being in Spain and being with her travel boyfriend.

She wondered if her aunt was correct and the romance tasted sweeter when you're abroad, but was not sustainable when you're away from the magic of it all. Once you got to know each other and everything became ordinary, perhaps the relationship lost its luster, as Lindy suggested.

Possibly, her aunt simply didn't find the right person. Maybe Lindy's travel romances were simply flings, and she never intended for them to go any further. Would that apply to Colin also? Her aunt seemed to like the Englishman quite a lot, and she could tell he was fond of her. No, she thought, maybe her aunt was afraid to let her emotions go that far.

As much as she liked Roberto and enjoyed being with him, she didn't expect this to be more than a friendship. It might, she hoped, survive the separation once she went back home. She had plans, and they didn't include settling down in a tourist town on the coast of Spain. Time, however, could lead her a different direction, and they might one day connect again. So, she would just enjoy the moment and savor being in a romantic country with the handsome young artist.

After a delightful dinner, Michelle sipped a coffee and asked, "What do you think is going on with your painting here?"

He shrugged. "I don't know what to make of it. I would like to actually look at the canvas to see if the strokes are like mine, or if it was copied. I don't suppose it would be possible to get in the man's house without breaking in."

She shook her head. "I thought the same thing, but he has a housekeeper and a steward who probably live there. So even if he's out with my aunt this evening, the house would be watched."

A devious thought slipped into her mind. "Wait. What if I went back to the house while Marchant was out and told the housekeeper I lost my bracelet last night, and perhaps it slipped behind the cushions in the living room? I could slip it off, then pretend to find it after a search. You could come in as my friend, make an excuse to go to the bathroom, then pop into the gallery and take a quick look, so even if the housekeeper stays with me, you would be in the clear."

"It's risky, Michelle. What would happen if we were caught?"

"I don't know, but isn't it worth it?"

"Do you know the street address?" he asked as he considered it.

She nodded. "I wrote it down to give to the cab driver last night." She pulled a piece of paper out of her small purse. Thank goodness she'd used the same one tonight.

He looked at it, then pulled out his phone to key in the address and studied the GPS map. "Nice area of the city. Okay, let's see if your plan will work."

Forty minutes later, they pulled up at the curb of Marchant's villa, and Michelle slipped her bracelet off and into the front pocket of her slacks.

"The gallery is the second door off the lobby entry. The painting is in the back of the room on the left side, just before the corner. Do you have a flashlight, so you don't turn on the lights in the room?"

He held up a small laser light on his key ring.

She raised an eyebrow. "That's not much."

He flashed it once toward the wall, and it illuminated about three feet of it.

"Okay. More powerful than it looks."

He followed her up to the door, and she rang the doorbell,

then waited nervously for an answer. When the housekeeper opened the inner door, she smiled at her. "Hello, I was here last night with my aunt."

The woman gave Michelle an uncertain nod as she looked her over like she was trying to place who she was.

"I lost my bracelet last night, and I didn't notice it until I got back to my hotel. Then I didn't have time to come by earlier, so I'm hoping I might be able to check in the living room for it?"

From the confused look on the woman's face, Michelle thought she might have exceeded the woman's English vocabulary. The housekeeper peered at Roberto, who stood slightly behind her.

Jumping in, Roberto related the whole thing in Spanish and explained he was a friend. She asked a question or two, and he pointed to Michelle's left wrist and repeated her story.

Although she looked nervous about allowing them into the house, she stepped back to let them pass into the hallway. Escorting them to the main hall on the right, she turned on the lights and stood back as Michelle went to the chair where she'd sat at first on the previous night. While she ran her hand down around the cushions and pretended to search, Roberto spoke to the housekeeper and asked to go to the bathroom. She took him to the hallway and pointed to a room at the end of the hall, flush against the back staircase.

While she was out of the room, Michelle used the opportunity to shove her bracelet down between the cushions on the sofa where she and her aunt had sat when they returned from the gallery. When the housekeeper came back in, she was hunting on the floor under the chair.

The señora objected, gesturing to indicate the floor had been vacuumed and nothing was on it. Michelle cast a forlorn look at her and proceeded to pull at the cushions on the sofa. As she was trying to buy more time for Roberto, he surprised her by appearing in the doorway. Was he done already?

"Anything yet?" he asked as he came over.

"No. I have that sofa to check yet." She pointed to the one where she'd planted the bracelet.

The housekeeper began to look a little nervous about them, and Michelle imagined she envisioned them knocking her out and stealing from the house. She quickly shifted to the first cushion on the couch and began running her hand along the side of it.

Roberto took the next cushion, reaching into it to help her out. He looked surprised, then grinned as he pulled the bracelet from the crevice. "Is this it, Michelle?"

She faked a look of joy and exclaimed, "Yes, it is. You found it!"

He turned to the housekeeper to show her and explained it was the missing bracelet. They thanked her profusely, and Michelle slipped her a little money for her assistance.

"It was a gift from my father," she gushed as she tucked it into her little purse. "I would have been devastated to lose it."

Roberto translated, and the housekeeper smiled at them, then shut the door, happy to have them out of the house.

"What happened? Is it your painting?" Michelle asked when they got back to the curb. Roberto gave her a hug, pulling her close, then whispered, "It wasn't there."

"What? It had to be." She couldn't believe it.

"I found an empty space where you said it would be, so I checked the entire room. It was gone." He released her and climbed onto the motorcycle. "So, Flamenco club?"

She nodded and climbed on behind him. *So, all this had been for nothing? Why had Marchant moved it? He'd said it was part of his private collection. God, I hope my aunt never finds out I came here tonight.*

Chapter 16
❦ Lindy ❧

While Michelle had gotten ready for her evening with Roberto, Lindy did some research on both Marchant's gallery in Paris and on Pablo de Sintra. Of the first, she found quite a bit of information and good comments as well as reviews from people who had purchased paintings from the gallery. A quick financial look indicated the gallery appeared to be reputable and solvent. The catalog of paintings it handled also indicated it might prove a good match for her work, but still, an undetectable thing niggled at her.

As for de Sintra, not much information was readily available. A few images of some of his paintings reinforced her belief; his painting style duplicated Roberto's too much to be a coincidence, yet she couldn't see the connection. One of them had to be copying the other. According to the information, de Sintra was an old man, in his seventies, and his paintings only began showing up in the past five years. His biography said he began painting late in his life and developed his talent quickly. Although from the Basque region of Portugal, he now lived and worked in Lisbon.

After Michelle left, Lindy sent a text message to Colin to contact her, then took a quick shower, dried off, and went to the wardrobe to select her dress for the evening, a light blue, silk sheath dress with cap sleeves, and laid it on the bed. She pulled on her underwear, just fastening her bra as her phone rang. She glanced at the caller id and thumbed the answer key. "Hello, Colin. How is Italy?"

"Beautiful, but missing something without you. What's up?"

His voice was flirty and upbeat, and his words made her heart beat a little faster as her blood warmed. He missed her.

"Sorry to bother you when I know you have a lot on your plate, but I need a favor if you can help me out. I think you have better contacts than I do and can help me with something." She paused, took a deep breath, and then explained the situation with the paintings and what she'd seen. "Too many things look identical, and even if de Sintra copied Roberto's work or vice versa — although Roberto swears he did not copy anyone — even the brush strokes look the same. I would like an expert's opinion, and I figure you might know someone in Europe."

As Colin remained quiet a moment, she tensed, thinking he might say he didn't have time or the contacts, but then he said, "I think I know just the person. A mate of mine, one I've worked with a few times, is an art expert in Paris for a gallery there. I will be heading that way in a couple of days, and I'll have him take a look. I have Roberto's canvas you loaned me, and I'm certain there must be one of de Sintra's in the city we can view and photograph for comparison. If there's something dishonest going on, I'm certain we can get to the bottom of it. Just leave it to me, and I'll let you know what we learn."

"I knew you were the man for the job," she purred into the phone. "A regular secret agent. How's the scouting going?"

"Very well. I think I have three possible locations that should make the producers happy and two more to look at tomorrow. Then it's back to Paris to check out a studio there. And finally, I'll head back to Spain. Are you enjoying Seville?"

"Absolutely, but it would have been so much better if you'd been here."

"What about Marchant? You wouldn't have had dinner with the gallery owner if I'd been along. This could be an opportunity for your work, and it would have been a shame to have missed it. So long as it's only business."

"Do I detect concern or a touch of jealousy?" Lindy teased.

"Maybe a little. I miss talking to you… and other things."

Her breath caught, and a cascade of thoughts flowed through her as her heart swelled. Good lord, was she falling for this man? Was she doing exactly what she told Michelle not to do? This was a travel fling, not something she could expect to last. But he plucked her heartstrings like a guitarist with a skillful touch drawing out every desire.

"Me, too." Her voice carried a catch in it and pitched a little lower than normal

"How long are you in Seville?"

"Another day, then we're moving on to Portugal."

"Lisbon? Hmm, maybe I can look at a couple of locations in the area. Look, just be careful, and don't worry about the painting thing. I'll be in touch, and we'll figure it out, okay?"

"You got it. Until I see you again…" Her voice trailed off, and she made a kissing smack sound into the phone.

"Mmm-wah back," he said, mimicking it.

A wistful sigh escaped her lips as she hung up. She did miss Colin, not necessarily a good thing. She would be foolish to allow herself to fall for anyone who was likely a fling and not looking at a lasting relationship, but Colin kept surprising her and giving her hope.

She shook off the feeling and grabbed her dress, then slipped into it, adjusting the fit a little as it slid on her curvy body. She added a matching pair of low heels, then studied her reflected image in the mirror on the wardrobe door. The aqua color resembled the Mediterranean sea on a summer day and set off the creamy tones of her skin. She added a touch of lavender shadow to highlight her eyes and topped it off with a light Kashmir-rose-colored lip gloss. She'd pulled her hair up into an elegant French twist and teased the front bangs forward to give her a sophisticated, yet youthful look.

Marchant's appreciative looks at Michelle the night before hadn't gone unnoticed, and she was determined to divert his attention away from her young niece. With a satisfied expression, she grabbed her floral-print black shawl, picked up her matching clutch handbag, and went down to the lobby to meet her date.

Alain waited for her at the bar, a mojito in his hands as he chatted with the bartender. Again, he wore a casual beige suit with an open-collared pale yellow shirt setting off his tanned skin. He spotted her and flashed a big smile as he stood and held out a hand in greeting.

"Melinda, you look beautiful. Would you like a drink before we leave?"

Lips curving in pleasure, she took his offered hand and sat on the cushioned barstool next to him. "I'll have a small sangria, please." She crossed her legs at the ankles and placed her bag and shawl in her lap, creating a demure image.

"How was Italica today? Was it crowded?"

"No, it was not busy at all, and we had a wonderful visit. I was there a couple of decades ago before it had been excavated, so it was a totally new experience for me to see it now. I am very impressed."

"The setting is quite beautiful, don't you think? It would make a wonderful painting." He sipped his drink and watched her over the rim.

"Funny, you should say that," Lindy answered. "With those lovely tiles inspiring me, I took some photos with the idea of painting a scene from the Roman period in mind."

He raised an eyebrow and grinned. "I would like very much to see it. Shall we head for dinner? I have a taxi just arriving."

The restaurant wasn't far from the hotel, but Lindy was happy she didn't have to walk it after the day at Italica. Within ten minutes, the taxi pulled up to a striking three-story building showing yellow plaster wall panels set between long runners of red brick. Each level displayed windowed rooms with wrought-iron railing enclosing small balconies. At the ground level, the huge glass windows displayed the name Restaurante Oriza above an ornate design in the glass.

Inside, the place was warm and welcoming with more ironwork, while glass brick dividers and orange drapes accented the golden colors. The head waiter welcomed Alain as a friend and showed them to a table in a quiet corner where they could talk privately. Alain ordered a bottle of wine then suggested a tapas platter for a starter.

"Good plan," Lindy said. "I love experimenting with the different hor d'oeuvres. The chefs are so creative. What is good on the menu here?" She lowered her eyelids seductively and curved her lips into a coy smile as she spoke.

Alain ate it up, returning the smile and opening his menu to the entrees. He suggested a seafood dish with shrimp and grilled cod, proclaiming it to be excellent. She agreed that it sounded wonderful. Once the food was ordered, Alain got to the business of the evening.

"Have you given more thought to the idea of placing a few of your canvases with my gallery? I think it would be a very good match, and your work would be well received."

"I checked out your web site. You do carry an eclectic collection of artwork and artists, so it does look like a place where some of my work might fit in well. I would like to know a little more about the actual business deal. What percentage does the gallery take? Is there a time limit on the agreement? Tell me about the contract."

He barked out a brief laugh. "I like a woman who cuts to the chase. Here's the deal..." He refilled her wine glass, then proceeded to detail the financial part of the agreement, what he expected from her as the consignor, and what she could expect from the gallery. Lindy nodded as he talked, taking in the information and comparing it to other deals she'd taken. When he'd finished, she said, "Well, Alain, your proposal sounds very reasonable, and I am inclined to offer two pieces on consignment with the terms you outlined. If they do well, and we feel it is to both our advantage, then I might consider additional ones."

"Excellent. You select the art and send me a short description, the canvas size, and your asking price, and I'll take it from there. We'll send you a contract, and you send us the paintings. What could be simpler?"

"Nothing, I guess. I look forward to this partnership."

He raised a glass, and she tapped it as they drank to the deal. She'd barely taken a sip when the tapas arrived. They admired the delicious-looking creations before they began devouring them. Alain laughed a little over the awkward way to eat crab rolls as oozed butter down his chin. Lindy decided to be more clever and not pick one up with her fingers. Instead, she used the cocktail fork to stab one and nibble at it as she held it over a plate and leaned forward. The move, calculated or not, revealed more of her cleavage, and Alain noticed, his eyes sliding to the ravine between her breasts.

She raised her eyes to his, then said, "You know, I was thinking about the artist you mentioned last night, and I wondered about the painting you have at your home by him. Is it one of his early works?"

"Pablo de Sintra. Yes, it was one of the first pieces he did. I acquired it recently. It is quite lovely, isn't it?"

"I believe you mentioned you discovered him and brought him into the art world. How did it happen?"

His eyes narrowed a little, and he seemed to hesitate before answering. "Very simply. I saw this older man sitting in front of a shop on the Casa de Blanco in Perdido. He had three or four paintings displayed around him. They caught my eyes because of the composition and the vivid colors, so I took a closer look and began talking with him. Once I learned his history, I decided to buy one of the paintings to show some colleagues. They loved it, and it grew from there. You said you saw some of his paintings in New York, I believe."

"Yes, at a small gallery. If I recall right, there were six of them on display in one of the petite galleries. Like you, I was struck by the colors and the composition, but I didn't think more of it until later." She tried to keep it simple; a casual interest in the artist was all.

Being honest, she acknowledged she hadn't remembered anything about the artist until Alain had brought his name up the previous night. Although she did think Roberto's paintings had reminded her of something she'd seen before, she hadn't connected him with the paintings from New York.

"But you weren't impressed," Alain said as if he could read her thoughts. "You studied my painting closely last night, and I wondered what had attracted you."

She sipped her wine, thinking about how to phrase her answer. "The painting intrigued me. As I said, I liked the composition and the way the light is handled in it, along with the smooth direction of the brush strokes. You say he's an older man, but he has fine control of the brush, which is unusual for someone who has not done a great deal of art. So, I think he might have a storehouse of other paintings from a younger time in his life. Don't you wonder about it?"

Alain laughed briefly. "Yes, I do, and I did ask him about it. If he has any, he's locked them away and is not willing to show them to me or anyone else. Perhaps his practice pieces were not good enough. Or because he was a poor man, he simply used the same canvases over and over."

"I don't suppose you would be willing to sell me that painting? Wasn't it called *'La Señora de Laundressa'*?" Lindy asked.

His mouth turned down as his eyes met hers. "No, I am sorry. I ended up selling it to Jose this afternoon as the painting I was expecting for him did not come in today, and he was quite taken mine. Maybe I will keep the new one instead, or it may be available in a few days." He smiled charmingly and leaned back. "Would you like to go to a Flamenco show? There is a dance-theater close to here, and a show will start around eleven."

"It sounds lovely, but I don't want to get back to my hotel too late." She glanced at her watch to see it was ten-fifteen already.

"The show is only one hour," Alain replied. "And it is one of the best in the city. Surely it is not too late for you."

"Well, when you praise it so much, how can I not go?"

The theater was a few blocks down from the restaurant, which was below the Alcazar, which loomed over this section of the city. On their side of the street, the grounds and hills of the royal palace sprawled toward the structure at the top. They were closer to the central district than she'd thought.

Alain took her arm and led her across the street to a small courtyard where an outdoor cafe served coffees and sweets, and just beyond it was the door to the club. A brightly painted sign proclaimed Flamenco in bold lettering. Just within the door, they found the theater box office.

As he paid for the tickets, Lindy looked at the photos on the walls of the dancers in performance. They included handsome men, some in their mid years, dressed in the snug pants and short jackets so typical of the Spanish male dancer while the women wore the extravagant dresses with long trains and shorter front hems to show their feet as they dance.

Their seats were to the back at a small coffee table with a deep red velvet cushioned love seat for them to share. A cocktail waitress brought them each a glass of sangria to enjoy then moved on to the other patrons, some of whom were already seated while others were just arriving.

This is cozy, Lindy thought, noting no one was behind them, but the place was so small they still had an excellent view of the stage.

As the lights dimmed, Alain slipped his left arm around her shoulder, pulling her a little closer to him. She tensed a bit and resisted moving over. He tugged a little harder.

"I thought this was business," she whispered.

"No harm in combining it with a little pleasure, is there? You are a beautiful woman, and it's a romantic setting, so what is the harm in a little affection?"

"A little? None, but don't expect more."

"No, of course not." But his fingers tightened more around her upper arm.

Lindy tried to relax as the show started with explosive guitar music and the tap of the steel-toed shoes on the wooden floor in sharp staccato. The lights flashed on the stage in yellow and red bursts as the dancers came out.

In form, the Flamenco, which is sometimes referred to as the Gypsy dance, is similar to tap dancing in about the same way Irish dancing is to it. They all use metal plates on the shoes, and they dance taps or stomps on the stage. With Flamenco, there is a lot of heel and toe work, so the rhythms are important, and the dancers use the taps to tell the story. Lindy was as fascinated watching it now as she had been when she'd first seen it.

By the time a slower-paced piece of music started, Alain had advanced even closer and now tried to pull Lindy into his lap. She pulled back, putting a few inches between them.

"I said no," she said in a loud whisper. While it bought her a few moments of respite, it was short-lived before Alain began advancing again. She felt his mouth nuzzle against the nape of her neck, and she twisted away again, trying to get some distance between them.

By the end of the second dance number, Lindy had enough. She pulled her shawl around her arms, picked up her handbag, and excused herself, saying simply, "I have to go."

She saw the confused look on Alain's face as she moved past him and made her way along the wall to the exit. He didn't come after her, perhaps he misread her intention. She didn't care. She hurried to the exit and out in front of the open-air cafe where she saw a taxi sign and stood next to it, looking for an open cab. In a few minutes, one pulled in, and she gave him her hotel address.

She arrived within a few minutes and heard the muted sound of her phone ringing and felt it shake in her handbag as she paid the driver. Going inside, she pulled it out and saw the caller number, then switched it off. Alain. She didn't want to talk to him right now. He'd not taken no for an answer, and while she might not have minded the advances under other circumstances, right now, her mind was on Colin, not the gallery owner with whom she might one day do business.

Stepping off the elevator, she felt her purse jiggle as the muted phone vibrated. Probably Alain again, she thought and ignored it. She stepped into her room, flipped on the light, and looked around. No sign to indicate Michelle had returned yet, but she still had a few minutes before her curfew.

She ignored two more calls on her phone and changed into her nightgown. When Michelle wasn't in by the time she came out of the bathroom, she checked her phone and saw one of the calls was from her niece. All of them had left messages.

She hit the play button and listened as the first came up.

"Melinda, what happened? Are you all right? I thought you'd gone to the ladies' room and had one of the girls check for you, but you were not to be found. Please call me back." Alain's voice sounded mildly concerned.

The next call was his also, his voice a little more angry as he said, "I assume you have left me here without a word. Call me when you get this message."

The third, which must have come in while she was in the bathroom, was Michelle. "Sorry, Aunt. We're running just a little late. I'll be there before one. Roberto is refilling his gas tank right now."

At least one worry was answered, and the girl had been thoughtful enough to call.

The last call was Alain, and it was brief. "Call me. I am concerned."

She climbed into bed and closed her eyes as her head hit the pillow. She didn't even hear Michelle come into the room.

Chapter 17
cs Michelle so

They had breakfast at the hotel rooftop restaurant at mid-morning. Roberto joined them before they'd even made it through their first cups of coffee. He looked chipper and refreshed, Michelle thought, although she felt a little tired still. She'd been surprised her aunt was already asleep when she'd arrive the previous night, but glad for it anyway.

The show at the Flamenco club they'd gone to see had run longer with the enthusiastic crowd urging the dancers on. She hadn't even glanced at the time until it was well past eleven, then she'd had to pry Roberto away from the place. Next, he said they had to stop for fuel or his bike wouldn't make it back to the hotel.

"What could I say then?" she asked her aunt when she told her about the delay as they munched on breakfast rolls.

"Not much," Lindy agreed. She cast a stern glance at Roberto. "You, on the other hand, should have filled your fuel tank before you went out."

"You are right," he replied. "I have no excuse. But I apologize for getting her back late."

"So long as nothing bad happened, it's forgivable. Just don't do it again. But you had a good time, Michelle. What did you do?"

"Dinner and a Flamenco show," she answered. The rest of the evening's activities were not to be reported. "What about you?"

"Same thing, only I started later, discussed business, and returned here earlier than you did."

"It was a long dance show," Roberto said in explanation.

"And in a different area of Seville," Michelle added. "We went to a more local area than where tourists go. The restaurant was wonderful, and we ate outdoors. Then the dancers were just amazing. They're so powerful and energetic. I even tried dancing with them, but I couldn't keep up on the simplest steps."

Lindy's eyebrow shot up as she shot a glance at Roberto. "Please tell me you took video."

His head drooped a little. "Sorry, no, I didn't think to do it."

"I am so disappointed in you." Lindy's mouth turned down.

Michelle giggled. "I wouldn't have let him keep it anyway, Auntie. I was that bad."

"Well, how am I supposed to get some embarrassing material on you for blackmail purposes, young lady?"

"So, are you doing the gallery deal with Marchant?" she asked, deflecting the conversation back to her aunt.

"I'm still thinking about it. It sounds fair, and I think my paintings would do well in his gallery, but I need to give it more thought and run it past my lawyer."

"Maybe I could get a few of my paintings in with him one day if I ever get some national recognition," Roberto commented. "I should have Arturo talk to him."

"Arturo?" Michelle gawked at him. "Arturo barely gets you any commissions except for those that fall in his lap. I think you need to get a better agent. Don't you think so, Aunt Lindy?"

"What she said," Lindy replied.

"But he is my friend, and he does a lot of the legwork for me."

"It isn't about that," Lindy said. "You need someone with contacts, and that is where an agent is valuable. They know who and where to show your work and can help you to get the best price for it."

"Do you use an agent?"

"I have three agents. One for my book covers, one for gallery paintings, and one to book conventions and art shows for me. They all specialize."

For a moment, Roberto gazed at Lindy as if she were a goddess. "Can you help me find a good agent?"

Michelle studied her aunt's face as she thought about her answer. His question put her on the spot.

Finally, she replied, "I might be able to. After this trip is over, I can talk to a couple of people. You need to be able to show some of your work in a gallery. Do you have photos of all your commissioned paintings as well as the more unique ones?"

"I do," he said.

"Send them to me. I'll see what I can do."

After breakfast, Roberto slid his chair back and stood. "Thank you. I will send them when I get home. I need to get back to the coast, so I'll leave now. Are you around here longer?"

"The rest of the day," Lindy answered. "Then, we're heading for Portugal."

Michelle's head whipped around as she gaped at her aunt. Portugal? Where did *that* suddenly come from? She thought they were going to go shopping then on to another town a little further northwest.

But she stood when Roberto did and walked with him to

the elevator to go to the ground floor. He took her hand, rubbing the back of it with his thumb, sending little tingles up her arm. She got into the lift with him. As the door closed, he punched the button for the lobby, then he pulled her toward him and wrapped her in an embrace before he leaned in and pressed his lips to hers.

When the elevator opened on the ground floor, they still held each other and exchanged one last kiss. At last, Roberto let go, and said, "I will contact you soon, *mi carita*."

Then he stepped away, striding across the suddenly too small lobby. Michelle lingered, watching his receding back before she pressed the button for the top floor again.

"Portugal? Today?" Michelle sputtered as soon as she returned to their breakfast table. "I thought we were staying here another day or two."

"To do what?" her aunt asked and refilled her coffee cup from the pot on the table.

"There are a couple of museums you mentioned. Wasn't there a park near the plaza you said we could explore before we left?" She flopped down in the chair across from her aunt and picked up a piece of melon from the platter on the table. "Has something happened that you want to leave so soon?"

Lindy's face got her contemplative look. "Well, I think Alain is trying to get a little too close for comfort, and I'd just like to avoid him."

"What do you mean too close?"

Her aunt's lips shifted to a scowl. "He tried to seduce me during the Flamenco show we went to last night. At the back of the theater, no less, and he wouldn't take no for an answer."

"So, you'll just run away? Like a shy teenager?" Michelle

teased.

Lindy stuck her tongue out at her. "You're right. I did just want to get out of town rather than talk to him again. But we can stay one more day. The Museum of Arts and Traditions is quite interesting. We can see it this morning, as well as the park near the *Plaza de España* this afternoon. And there is the Museum of Fine Arts if you really want to see it."

"Yeah, I think I would. I'm beginning to appreciate the finer aspects of the classical paintings more and more. Maybe they have something more by that Pablo guy."

Lindy's eyes widened as her brows lifted. "De Sintra? That Pablo guy?"

"Yeah. I mean, if one painting is similar to Roberto's style, might there be more?" Michelle wished she could tell her about her excursion with Roberto to look at the painting at Alain's, but she couldn't admit to her aunt they had pulled that kind of deception and had nothing to show for it.

A slow smile grew on Lindy's face. "I like the way you think, Niece. There might be something, but I think he may be too contemporary for the museum here."

She finished her coffee and led the way to the elevator. "I need to change shoes into something more suitable for walking."

An hour later, they stood outside the Museum of Fine Arts, and Michelle gaped at the entryway with awe. The magnificent, two-story-high entry boasted four decorated half-pillars against the marbled walls, and the arch over the entry was capped with two cherubs, one on each side. Above was an alcove with the Virgin Mary and two disciples kneeling in prayer, so she assumed. A wrought iron entry filled the top of the arch with a solid bar bottom reading *Museo de Bellas Artes*.

"It looks like a church entry," she said as Lindy stepped beside her.

"Funny you should say that, but it *was* originally a convent. The building goes back to the sixteenth century when it was used by the Order of the *Merced Calzada de la Asunción*. Now, it houses the artworks of some of the finest Spanish artists from the Middle Ages to the last century. I don't think they've expanded to include any of the more recent ones, but we can check the list of artists displayed when we go in."

As it turned out, her aunt was correct; no artists past the mid-twentieth century were displayed inside. But the paintings were magnificent, and Lindy explained a lot about paints, and the lighting in them gave her a whole new appreciation for them. When she wasn't enchanted by the paintings, she was mesmerized by the ornate and elegant gallery ceilings.

At one point, her aunt's phone made a subdued buzzing sound, and Lindy excused herself, leaving Michelle alone to gaze in awe at a fifteen-foot-high, or so it seemed, painting depicting a medieval-looking scene. Such amazing treasures to have lasted so many years after they'd been painted; the artists now long dead, and yet, their work still so alive hundreds of years later.

For several minutes, it altered her perspective on life, and what was achieved in the short time a person might have. She wanted to be an actress, and if she made it to film, then her work might survive a century or two, but would it last as long as these paintings? Would Roberto's work achieve this kind of recognition? Or even her aunt's? Lindy's work covered books and was in many libraries, while her original paintings were in less limited distribution. But if Marchant wanted to display and sell them, would it elevate their value?

At that moment, she felt insignificant in the grand scheme of things. To be remembered, she needed to achieve something memorable.

When Lindy returned, they continued to go through two more galleries before they decided to take a lunch break. Lindy said a tapas bar near the main entrance had many recommendations when she'd checked on her phone, so they headed that direction. They crossed the plaza to *Calle Monsalvo* and went up a block or two to the small, but clean and welcoming bar.

They ordered a tapas sampler and sangria light, which only had a little alcohol in it rather than the stronger version. As they waited for their lunch, Michelle asked about the phone call.

"It was Alain. I thought I would ignore it. But I've ignored his last six calls, and I figured he would just keep calling. I told him I was not pleased with what happened last night. He apologized and said he had drunk too much, but isn't that the usual excuse when a man oversteps his boundaries?"

Michelle shrugged. Maybe.

"Anyway, I told him I was seeing someone and did not appreciate his advances. Then he asked about the gallery deal, and I told him I would be in touch, which I will when I decide." She took a big swallow of the drink as if to wash away a bad taste in her mouth.

The waiter, a young man about Roberto's age with a cheerful smile and striking good looks, brought the tapas platter filled with an assortment of meats, fried pies, shrimp, and slices of spicy tortilla, plus marinated olives and cheesy artichoke hearts, all of which looked and smelled delightful. They gorged on the food, eating more than was wise when they had a busy afternoon planned. As Michelle finished off the last meatball,

Lindy leaned back in her chair and sipped her sangria. If her aunt were a cat, Michelle thought she would be purring at this moment.

"A siesta would be good about now," Lindy said, closing her eyes and tipping her head farther back.

"It does sound good, but the garden waits for us, and the sun does not. We have lots to see yet."

Reluctantly, her aunt opened her eyes and sat forward. The waiter brought the bill, and Lindy tipped him well. Then they went to the larger street to hail a taxi.

Almost a continuation of the Plaza, the gardens were a sprawling creation on the former palace grounds of San Telmo, an area donated to the city by the Duchess of Montpensier, and featured exotic-looking flowering bushes, ponds, fountains, and statues. Michelle took photo after photo as they walked along the pathways. She posed a few times for Lindy to use her better camera for the shots.

At the Lion Fountain, Michelle sat next to one of the lion statues so she could get close and lay her head against it for a photo. The detailing on it was exquisite. When she stood next to it, the statue wasn't quite as tall as she was, but close.

"I think these are life-sized statues," she told her aunt. "They look as if the artist had magically encased the lions in stone."

Lindy nodded. "I agree. They are quite lovely, aren't they?" She snapped a close up photo.

"Why did they choose lions?"

"Well, I imagine it's because the lion symbolizes power and authority. That's why it's a royal beast and on many banners and flags." Lindy paused to think about it a little more.

"Do you ever think about your legacy?" Michelle asked.

"What?" Her aunt looked puzzled by the question.

"What you'll leave behind when you die. What will people remember about you? Will your art be around for centuries? Those kinds of things." She still thought about the old paintings and the existential thoughts that had filled her there.

Lindy's pensive face showed she had caught the gist of Michelle's question. "Now and then, I do. I probably was about your age when I first addressed the same questions. What will I leave behind to tell anyone I ever existed? I have been an artist ever since I can remember, Michelle. I started drawing when I was five or so. I mean really drawing, not just scribbling with crayons and a pencil, but creating art at that age. There was never a question in my mind that I would do it for a living. By the time I was a teenager, the assumption was a reality. I'd already started selling my artwork and got my first few book cover commissions by the time I was fifteen."

Michelle's eyes grew wider as Lindy talked, and she realized how long her aunt had worked at her craft. How long she had known what she would do.

"One day, when I was about twenty and going to school in Paris, I stood in the Louvre and marveled at all the great art of various kinds around me. Art from the masters, some of whom were acknowledged as greats in their lifetimes, and others who lived in poverty, fighting for the money for their materials to produce what their souls drove them to do and didn't gain the recognition until after their death. And yet, centuries later, they were revered as some of the greats to have lived and created.

"It was humbling, and I almost cried as I thought, what do I have to offer that can possibly be worthy of this? And my answer was nothing. I had nothing that could even compare. But then I looked at the works of Andy Worhol and thought, I don't need to compete with them. I am who I am, and if I am talented and produce something that touches someone's heart, then I am successful in this life. And maybe some of those works will be passed on to others, and time will not forget me."

"I know it won't, Aunt Lindy. I think art is enduring, don't you?" Michelle said, tearing up as she spoke. Her aunt had shared her same fears and found solace in what she did. Michelle realized she must forge her legacy also.

With a gentle smile, Lindy took her hands and squeezed them in reassurance. "Michelle, we don't build our lives with the concern of what will remain after we're gone. We do what we love as much as we can, and we find peace and fulfillment in the goal. If we are good enough or make the right human connections, then we are remembered."

"Thank you, Aunt Lindy." Michelle hugged her, her emotions riding at the top of her heart, and so grateful for the understanding of her ambitions and her passion.

Her aunt hugged her back and pressed a kiss against her forehead. "You may not be from my body, but you are my child. You have the soul of an artist and the compassion of a saint. You will do well in your choices, my dear girl."

Michelle felt the tears spill from her eyes then, running down her cheeks and dampening her aunt's blouse. She loved her so much and had needed this understanding so desperately. Her parents were so practical and didn't understand the passion driving her. They tolerated her desire to be an actress, a stage performer, but they didn't really understand it.

When she tilted her head up to meet her aunt's eyes, she saw the tears glistening in them also, and they smiled at each other. Lindy squeezed her a little closer, then they turned and walked, hugging each other at the waist, toward the next section of the park where the statue of the park's benefactor sat in a floral setting.

Michelle's heart overflowed with love for her aunt, and for this wonderful summer trip, which she now felt was a key point in her life. While she has resented not being able to go with her friends at first, she now felt grateful for all the magic, love, and compassion of this time with her aunt. And for meeting Roberto. Somehow she knew he would be her lifelong friend.

They ate their evening dinner in a garden restaurant near the Alcazar, sitting at an outside table and looking up at the lights from the building, it suggested another time in this magical place.

"It's all so beautiful," Michelle said. "The buildings, the art, the whole city is magnificent. Castles in Spain... It's like a fairy tale."

Lindy's eyes twinkled as she spoke. "We will have to see Avila and Segovia before we leave Spain. So far, my dear niece, you have only seen southern Spain, the Moorish-influenced cities. Towards the north, you will see the European ones, and one of the most romantic-looking castles in the country. But Avila is a fully-walled city, so medieval it remains a perfect example of the era."

Michelle sipped her drink and asked, "Why is Spain so different from other countries? What makes it seem so magical?"

"Part of it is because the country retains a lot of its past. Where other countries in Europe were bombed and partially destroyed during World War II, Spain was untouched. It was a neutral country, so none of the battles happened here, leaving the castles and towns safe. The other part is the people. They are happy, party people who enjoy life. Not that the people of other countries don't, but the Spanish, they believe in it wholeheartedly. Listen around you."

She paused, and they listened as the lively Spanish music from a strolling band drifted to their ears. The music had a beautiful tempo and called to them to come dance and come party.

"It's a *ronda*," Lindy said. "An inviting tempo calling to you to come out and be part of the world around you. This is what makes Spain special."

Impulsively, Michelle raised her glass to a salute and said, "Viva, Spain. May I visit her often and always remember these wonderful days and nights. Thank you, Aunt Lindy, for opening my eyes."

Lindy clicked the glass as tears glistened on her cheeks.

What adventure awaited them next in Portugal? Why had her aunt decided to divert their trip there? She had her suspicions, but so far, Lindy hadn't given her an explanation.

Chapter 18
∞ Lindy ∞

While the weather had been stunningly beautiful in Spain, the opposite greeted them as they neared Lisbon and the Portuguese coast. The windshield wiper clicked at a foxtrot tempo as it worked to keep the rain from becoming a solid river on the glass. Lindy slowed down even more as they began to encounter more traffic, and the reasonably short drive to the city grew into more of an ordeal.

They approached from the south, coming in on the IP5, and ahead, barely visible through the rainy haze, rose the tall towers of the *Ponte 25 de Abril* or the Bridge of April the 25th. As Michelle squinted at the twin, tall towers, she commented, "Those look awfully familiar, kind of like ..."

As her voice trailed off, Lindy finished it. "The Golden Gate Bridge. It does resemble it very closely since it is also a suspension bridge, built in the same way, and is painted in the same golden-red paint as its counterpart in San Francisco. In fact, some people refer to it as the Golden Gate of Portugal."

While the bridge seemed close, it still took them another thirty minutes to get onto it. In reality, it looked even bigger with six traffic lanes layered and two train levels. Below them, glimpsed now and then through the weather and the bars of the golden cage, they could glimpse the Tagus River flowing out to the Atlantic Ocean. Lindy tensed a little with the strain of getting into the city, and she wasn't particularly fond of crossing large bridges like this, but she took deep breaths and concentrated on watching out for the traffic.

Once they were across, she relied on the GPS navigator to guide them to their hotel, the Metropole near the city center. When Michelle had sent a text to Roberto telling him they'd delayed leaving for Lisbon, he'd gone to work and located a hotel for them in the city. He had a friend who knew someone, and all those contacts paid off in a hotel reservation they might have gotten without help.

She pulled the car into the nearest parking spot to the hotel, labeled check-in parking only. A bellman with an umbrella came up to greet them and escorted the ladies into the lobby, holding the curved dome over the heads the entire way. Once inside, Lindy breathed a sigh of relief to see it was a high-quality hotel with elegant, old-world furnishings. Deep cushioned chairs and love seats formed a conversation square in the lobby, and a bar sat off to the left. All the comforts, she conceded. The kid did okay.

As she checked in, Michelle went with the bellman to get their luggage from the car. In a short time, check-in was completed, and they were back with a luggage cart hauling their three suitcases and a backpack.

"What about the car?" Lindy asked. "Where do I park it?"

"It's being taken care of," Michelle answered. "They have a valet park it in a nearby lot, and they will have the keys for us at the valet desk any time we need it. I think this may be like Sevilla, though, just leave the car parked and take a cab around town."

"You're probably right," Lindy replied as she'd been

thinking the same thing and was relieved she didn't have to find a parking garage in the downpour.

Their room was spacious and looked very comfortable with a pair of oversized twin beds with elegant golden spreads, and a stack of pump-looking pillows piled on top. Michelle didn't hesitate, throwing her body into the center of the nearest bed.

"I guess I get the window one, then," Lindy said with a laugh. She strolled over, pushed the sheer under-curtain to one side to look out, and peered out at the gray fog of the storm with hints of the coast peeping through. When the rain cleared, it would be spectacular. Sitting on the bed, she felt the mattress yield to her weight, and her mouth curved into a pleasing arc. They had memory foam beds. Perfect. She should have Roberto arrange all of their hotels.

They had gone without lunch, relying on their large breakfast in Seville to carry them through to Lisbon, but now, at nearly three-thirty in the afternoon, Lindy's stomach rumbled, demanding attention. She checked to see if the hotel had a restaurant and perked up when the desk told her the bar served tapas all afternoon.

In far less time than it took to cross the bridge, they were seated in a booth in the bar with a cocktail table holding soft drinks and a plate of freshly grilled shrimp with garlic and lemon. The waiter set down a dish of grilled zucchini, mushrooms, and artichoke hearts along with tiny little cocktail forks to spear them. On the side were rounds of yeast bread to soak up the oil and garlic sauce.

"Heaven," Lindy breathed as she bit into a shrimp. "This is heaven. The first time I traveled to Portugal, they brought the whole shrimp—shells, head, and all—and you had to break them apart before you could eat them. It wasn't for the squeamish, and up until then, I had generally gotten my shellfish cleaned, so it was a challenge to get my dinner."

"Oh, no," Michelle grimaced. "I don't know if I would like that. A girl could starve."

"I learned quickly. It's not too bad to take them apart, but you have to keep ignoring the eyes."

"Please, Auntie. I'm trying to eat here." She stuffed another shrimp tail into her mouth and followed it up with a mushroom.

"So, what would you like to do in this historic city?" Lindy pointed at the tourist booklet they'd gotten when they checked in that listed most, if not all, of the tourist attractions in the city.

"Well, the Belem Tower, for one, since it is so close, but not if it's raining. And there's the Commercial Center, Geronimos Monastery, the Bernardo Collection Museum, and lots of other places. What do you think is best?"

"Definitely Geronimos and the museum. The Commercial Center is not a shopping mall, but it is an interesting place as I recall. There is also an art market street where you will find artists and galleries. It's not too far from here. If the weather clears tomorrow, much of this is within walking distance. In some ways, being in Lisbon is like being in San Francisco. The city is hilly, it's by the ocean, and it is filled with many interesting places in a small area."

"It sounds like fun and also calls for my most comfy shoes, I think."

After they finished eating, they went back to their room where Lindy read through some material on the artists' quarter and looked up one address in particular. She didn't want to do anything to alert her niece to a problem, but she definitely wanted to visit Pablo de Sintra's studio. Located on a side street of one of the main thoroughfares of the art district, it would be easy to find. Public transportation could get them within a few blocks of it.

Michelle took her phone and slipped off into the bathroom. It didn't take a genius to know she was calling Roberto.

"Tell him, hello, and I like the hotel," Lindy called after her.

Michelle waved her left hand at her in a silencing motion as she shut the door.

While Lindy was amused by her antics, she thought fondly on her own days as an impulsive teenager with romantic notions. But had she changed, really? She picked up her phone and displayed her messages to see a text in from Colin. She'd missed the notification buzz downstairs. It was a brief note – *in Paris, saw my friend, will have report tmrow. Talk soon.*

She felt ridiculously happy to hear from him. He seemed such a solid, reliable man – something she'd seen little of in her relationships. Maybe *that* was part of the attraction. She sent a short text back. *Safely in Lisbon. Heavy rain. Tourist thing tomorrow. Miss you.*

Just around sunset, the rain started to let up, and Lindy checked the area around them for any nightlife. A *fado* club was just a block away, so they decided to go there.

"What is *fado*?" Michelle asked as they huddled together under a borrowed umbrella from the hotel.

"It's a form of music popular in Portugal. I suppose you might call it a melancholy type of singing, usually with guitar accompaniment. In Ireland, they would probably call it a dirge. The songs are usually about the sea or lost love or being horribly poor, basically, all the things that make people unhappy."

"Sounds delightful," Michelle said drily.

"We don't have to stay long, but you should at least hear a

few songs to see what it's like. The singers are often very good, and it is compelling in a strange way. We'll have dinner at the club, then we can see if there is anything else we'd like to do."

The place was tucked into a corner building and up a level to the second floor. Like the Spanish Flamenco clubs, it was set up with tables facing a small stage and was dark, being illuminated primarily by the candles on the tables. Once they were seated at a table close to the front, the waiter brought a short menu and recommended the house specialty, which was pork done in *Alentejo* style with potatoes and asparagus. While Michelle went for a house salad, Lindy ordered the octopus salad, which garnered a disgusted look from her niece.

"It's all right. I'll let you have a bite."

"Don't do me any favors, Auntie." Michelle requested a soda instead of trying the local punch, which was a lot like sangria.

As the salads arrived quickly, they began to eat. Lindy noticed Michelle glancing at her salad as if she expected a tentacle to crawl across the table and onto her plate. She stabbed a little round piece of octopus with her fork and offered it to her niece. "Try a piece. It's not rubbery, and it tastes quite good."

Michelle frowned at the offering. "That doesn't look like octopus. It's white meat."

"It's been cubed, and most of the suckers removed so it doesn't look like anything more than cut up fish. The flavor is very mild and mostly picks up the dressing and spices in the salad."

With obvious reluctance, Michelle took the fork and bit a tiny piece off the offered meat. She looked like she expected it to gag her, but her expression changed to something more neutral when she realized it wasn't awful.

"Didn't I tell you?" Lindy said as Michelle ate the rest of the piece.

"It's okay," she admitted. "But not anything I'd get excited about."

They had just finished up dinner when the *fado* singer came onto the stage. A guitarist followed her out, taking a seat on a chair behind her. He hit one string to give her a starting note, and then she began singing with a powerful and emotionally charged voice. The words, of course, were in Portuguese, but she managed to convey the worry and grief in it as she sang. The guitar joined in after the first two lines and added a soulful sound to the music.

"The power of the music is to be able to touch the part of your soul that responds to the sorrow in the song and to identify with it even if you don't understand the lyrics," Lindy whispered to Michelle. Just the melody and the voice pulled tears to Lindy's eyes, and she could feel the longing and sorrow in it. Michelle sat with her eyes down, looking at her hands beneath the table rather than at the singer, and Lindy wondered if she was texting with one of her friends. Whatever. She couldn't blame her for not being enthused with this part of the adventure, but at least she'd been exposed to it.

As promised, after three songs, all of them sounding pretty much the same, they left the club and headed back to the hotel.

"Shall I look for a dance club or something else for the evening?" Lindy asked.

Michelle shook her head. "No, I'm kind of tired tonight, so an evening in would be good. It looks like the rain is stopping, so if tomorrow is clear, we can get an early start."

Lindy agreed. She felt just about worn out after the drive today and those draining songs. She'd forgotten just how depressing a *fado* could be.

Lindy awoke to sunshine coming in the window and a clock reading six. Early to bed meant waking up early, although it appeared Michelle still slept. She took advantage to get showered before her niece got up. Then she checked her phone's GPS to make sure it showed Lisbon. By then, Michelle was up and heading to shower.

She decided their first stop should be the Belem Tower since it strictly meant a photo stop and look around the monument. Situated nearby, but on the shore, they would need to take a bus to it. That would be easy to do in the earlier hours of the morning since the other places they might go wouldn't be open for at least three hours.

After eating from a selection of pastries and fruit with the strongest coffee in the world in the hotel breakfast room, they went to the bus stop and boarded within a few minutes. The ride went fairly quick even though many of the customers were heading to work, so it made frequent stops, but then, they weren't in a hurry, so that didn't matter.

The Belem Tower itself perched at the edge of the water on the far side of a semi-circular tiled plaza. It looked like a gray stone medieval tower fortress, which was what it had been. The tower was surrounded on three sides by a curtain wall with round towers in them. In all, it resembled a small castle.

"Once it guarded the mouth of the Tagus River," Lindy said, reading the information from her phone. "It was actually built on an island near the shore, but the river shifted."

"It's really a work of art," Michelle said as she took several photos and marveled at the detail work that went into the fortress. "The builders really liked to decorate everything, didn't they?"

"Yes, I guess they did. They liked to have beauty and form in their work, even castles and fortresses. They were functional, though, and the features that look like embellishments often served a purpose, such as those cross-looking window openings that allowed archers to shoot arrows at the enemy without exposing themselves much." Not that Belem seemed to have any examples of that particular building feature, but it did have triangular notches that might have served a similar purpose. Still, given where they were positioned, they were more likely to be venting or drain holes for the privies.

"Can we go in?" Michelle asked as she pointed to an entrance that appeared to be open to the public.

"I guess we can."

As it turned out, they were a little early, but they used the time to stroll along the waterfront, take photos, and enjoy a hot cup of coffee from a street vendor. By the time they returned, the entrance was open, and they began exploring the area. On the bottom floor, they found round openings for cannons to fire on any ships entering the harbor, although none of the cannons remained now.

Lindy read that it had been used for an art exhibit after the renovation in the 1990s and eyed the space with new appreciation. Upstairs were chambers that had been used by the governor, or so the pamphlet she'd picked up read. In the center was a water well to provide for their needs. Several round holes in the floor could be used to drop oil or other objects on an enemy below.

"I wonder if they ever had to use them," she commented to Michelle before they headed up to the King's Chamber and found more of the holes in the floor.

"It looks like they planned for this type of defense on each level," Michelle answered.

But the chamber was lovely and had a balcony that let them look out toward the shoreline.

"I wonder what it felt like to live in a place like this. It seems cold and barren, although the fireplace is gorgeous." Michelle wandered over to have a closer look.

"When someone lived here, the walls would have been hung with tapestries that would give them warmth as well as beauty, and the floor would probably have been covered in rugs. But it would definitely be lacking in amenities by our modern standards. Also, it had a military purpose, so it was well-defended, and probably the guards' quarters were not as nice."

On the top floor, they could look out across the Tagus River to where the ruins of a companion tower sat on the far shore. That one didn't fare as well over time. A light breeze caught Michelle's long hair and brushed it across her face just as Lindy snapped a photo. She glanced at the displayed image on her camera.

Beautiful. So photogenic...the girl could be model. She could see why Roberto had photographed her for his paintings, even without using her face specifically, she was a well-formed young woman, proportionately speaking, and had an uncommon grace.

"Time to move on," she told her. "The Commerce Center is open, and we have lots to see."

She started down the stairs with Michelle following. They hurried to catch a tram that stopped near the Tower before it pulled away, and Lindy dropped into the nearest open seat to catch her breath. It had been a long time since she'd had to dash for a tram. But it took them to the west side of their destination, depositing them just steps away from the plaza. The Commerce Center was now a transportation hub for the city.

As Lindy warned, the *Praça do Comércio* was not a shopping zone but housed many offices that were related to the commerce of the city. Lindy explained that at one time, Lisbon was an important trade and shipping city and still did a lot of import and export. Once this plaza might have been filled with traders selling their products from other lands and financiers would be arranging for expeditions.

As the largest shipping plaza in the city, it had great importance, and the detail of it was breathtaking. An arched gallery ran all along the U-shaped building that faced the estuary. Bright golden yellow paint covered the upper level of the building, suggesting the wealth that the trade center represented. In the center was a statue of King Jose I seated on his horse, stomping the symbolic snakes.

"That's a ginormous statue," Michelle said, gawking at it. "It's at least as tall as the Belem Tower and probably as wide."

"Go up the stairs and stand by it for perspective, and I'll take a photo," Lindy suggested.

Michelle shrugged and did as she asked, skipping up the steps, then turning and still not even coming to the base of the actual figures below the king and his horse.

Behind the statue was the *Arco da Rue Augusta*, the arch leading to the Augusta Road, which was even taller than the king's statue. It looked to be easily four stories tall before you got to the trio of figures on the top. By the time they'd walked around the entire plaza and gone down to the marble stairs, called the *Cais das Colunas*, which lead to the water, they'd pretty much looked at and photographed everything to be seen at this location.

They sat on a bench and rested their tired tootsies as they contemplated their next move. Lindy took off a shoe and rubbed at her ankle feeling the stain that all the walking put on it. The sprain wasn't totally healed.

"Why doesn't the language sound like Spanish?" Michelle asked as she listened to a couple of Portuguese men discussing something nearby. "It has a hint of it, but also a hint of French, doesn't it?"

"While it's a romance language, and it has the same root as Spanish, it developed separately with words and pronunciations varying. I speak a little Spanish, but while I can read and understand some of the Portuguese, most of it is very difficult for me." Lindy paused to put her shoe back on and tie the laces. "And you're right; a little French probably came in from the Basque regions. Certainly, *rue* is French for road while *calle* is Spanish. Now, if I lived in Spain and I visited Portugal often, in a short time, I might pick up the differences, and it would become easier. Or so I've been told. So, are you ready for some lunch?"

They found a little café a short distance from the plaza that sold sandwiches along with a little fruit cup, so they sat at an outdoor table and ate. Lindy checked her GPS to locate the art district, which she was anxious to visit. However, right next to the plaza was the Lisbon Art Museum, and they couldn't pass that up, could they?

A little over two hours later, they left the museum and headed several blocks over to the main street of artists. Not quite like the sales street in Spain where you could find many little street shops, this one had a few galleries and some individual artists living in the area. The buildings were like many old city ones with three or four stories of apartments above the shops that rose over the narrow streets. It seemed very dark in the afternoon, even though several hours of light remained in the summer day.

Lindy gazed at the graffiti on many of the storefronts, some of it artistic and some not. Some looked like protests or political statements, and some were just nasty. She watched Michelle's eyes grow wider as they picked up their pace to a gallery just ahead. Michelle stayed close to her, and she felt that at any moment, her niece might actually reach for her hand like a little girl.

She opened the gallery door, ushering Michelle in and pulling it closed behind her, then a sense of relief filled her. The scent of oil paints and a sweet wine reminded her of art studios in Paris. Inside, the store was small and somewhat cramped with three rows of three tables set up in the middle to make aisles. Canvases tilted back against easels along each row, and the walls around the room featured two rows of large paintings. A friendly-looking woman greeted them and invited them to look around with a wave of her hand.

Giving her an acknowledging nod, Lindy went to the left side and began walking down the path between the end row of tables and the wall, taking time to look at each painting and assess the talent of the artist. She automatically glanced at the signature in the corner, looking for any that she might recognize, but all on that row were unknown to her. A large number of them were street scenes and tourist spots around Lisbon that were aimed at tourists. She doubted they sold many to foreigners in this area of town. Michelle tagged along behind her, reluctant to get separated in any way.

She turned and ambled up the next row, eyes roaming from one row of easels to the other. She spotted one painting that was signed by a name that was clearly neither Spanish nor Portuguese, but other than that, the artists all seemed to come from this area. The last row yielded more of the same, and she didn't see the signature she was looking to find. She thanked the woman in her not-so-good Portuguese, and they left the shop, continuing on down the road.

Another shop came up on the right, and she looked in, then decided that the dark, Satanic-looking images were not what she had in mind and backed out of the entry, nearly bumping into Michelle. A little farther down, she spotted the street sign she was looking for then turned onto an even narrower street. Ahead of them, one of the buildings connected to another on the other side with an arch over the road that provided more living space to one or both of the residents. Just in front of that building, Lindy saw a hand-lettered sign that read *De Sintra*. She took a deep breath. Maybe they were about to get some answers.

She turned to Michelle and said, "This is the studio of Pablo de Sintra. He should have a few paintings on display, but we need to be casual about this. Don't ask any questions or make any comments while we're in there. If a painting looks similar to Roberto's, note it, but keep it to yourself until we leave."

"Do you think he's copying Roberto's work then?" Michelle asked in a low voice.

"I think it's one possibility. Just don't give any indication that something isn't right. If something is going on, something illegal, we don't want anyone in this shop to know. Can you do that?"

"Of course," Michelle replied. "I'm an actress."

"Right," Lindy drawled out and opened the door to the

studio.

Darker inside than she had expected, the walls bore a few paintings, and an easel with a partially completed work sat at the back of the room. A door at the back led to private quarters and the facilities. A middle-aged woman, sitting at a table to the right side, worked on embroidery and barely glanced up at them when they walked in. Three other floor easels sat along the left side of the room; each displayed a painting.

Lindy gravitated that way and paused before the first painting. The style differed from Roberto's and didn't seem like de Sintra's either. The overall images were not proportioned well, the colors a little muddy, and the strokes entirely wrong. It was not signed, but it didn't strike her as a professional painting. Perhaps de Sintra held workshops.

She moved to the next painting and examined it. Clearly a work in progress, the basic image was partially painted. It resembled one of those popular wine and painting parties where an instructor guided people through a simple design. Also not signed, she noted. As she moved to the next easel, Michelle touched her arm and pointed to a painting on the back wall.

Lindy nodded, cast a cursory glance over the third amateur canvas, and moved toward the one Michelle had spotted. Her niece followed behind her as she came close to it. Yes, this one looked like Roberto's work – and de Sintra's. She lowered her eyes to the signature at the bottom and recognized it as the same as the one at Marchant's house. She studied it, noticing a bit of a moist glisten in the paint. Painted recently, while the rest of the canvas was dry. So, presumably, de Sintra had signed it after the paint dried. Unusual. She studied the signature for a minute or so.

She also noticed Michelle staring intently at the painting,

studying every detail. She stepped away and addressed the woman at the table, asking in Spanish, *"¿Es esta pintura de Señor de Sintra?"*

The woman raised her tired-looking brown eyes up long enough to glance at the canvas Lindy pointed to and said, *"Sí."*

"Es muy bonito. ¿Cuánto cuesta?" she asked. *It's beautiful. How much is it?* She figured she might buy it for evidence if her hunch was right.

"Desculpa. Já está vendido." The woman shook her head. *Already sold,* Lindy interpreted the Portuguese.

"That's too bad. I really like it." She smiled and turned her attention back to the paintings on the wall while the woman went back to her embroidery.

Lindy stepped in front of Michelle, blocking the woman's view of the painting and whispered to her niece to take a photo with her camera phone, no flash. Done, she moved to another canvas on the wall and checked the signature. Also by de Sintra and another with the same warm style, detailing, and colors so common in Roberto's paintings. She looked at the signature area and thought she detected something unusual. The next painting was also one of de Sintra's and followed along the same lines.

She turned back again to the woman at the table. *"¿Se venden estas dos imágenes también?"* *Are these sold also?*

Again, she raised her head and nodded.

"¿Está el pintor en este estudio?" Lindy asked if the painter was in the shop.

"Não. Ele estará amanhã. Volte."

Lindy puzzled over her reply for a moment before realizing what she'd said. *Volte* ... was that like *vuelve*? Return? "Oh, he'll be in tomorrow," she said as she connected. *"Obrigado."* Thanks had been one of the first words she had learned in Portuguese.

"Come on, Michelle. We'll need to come back tomorrow to see the artist."

Glancing again at the painting on the back wall, Michelle paused a half minute more, then followed Lindy outside.

As soon as they were away from the shop, Michelle grabbed her left arm and pulled her closer, then whispered, "That was Roberto's painting!"

"You're sure?"

"Yes, I'm positive. It's the one stolen the other night. I watched him finish it."

"Don't say anything else until we're well away from here. You never know when the walls have ears in these narrow places." Lindy kept her voice low and guided them back to the cross street leading to a tram stop.

She had been certain something shady was going on, but given this evidence, it seemed it was more than she had expected. De Sintra wasn't copying paintings; he was buying them, changing the signatures, and selling them as his own. She wanted to check the dates on his first sales versus the dates Roberto started selling his private commission paintings, and she bet they would match up.

Chapter 19

༼ Michelle ༽

"So, what do we do next?" Michelle asked her aunt as soon as they were back in their hotel room where, presumably, it was safe to discuss the situation. "Is this guy copying Roberto's paintings or what?"

Lindy dropped into the chair by the window and slipped off her walking shoes. "No, my dear. I think he's stealing his paintings and putting his name on them. I can't be sure, but a couple of things indicate it's a possibility apart from the fact you recognized a painting he wouldn't have had time or access to copy."

"The most recent one. But the other two you looked at seemed to be from the same artist." Michelle stretched one leg out on the bed and leaned back into the pillows. "Would it be possible for him to duplicate his style? Why would he do it? What would be the value of copying an unknown street artist from Marbella?"

"I don't have all the answers, and Colin is checking out the hunch I have. He has a friend who is analyzing the actual strokes and paints on a canvas of Roberto's and one of de Sintra's. I think he will find they're the same. An artist has a unique style with a brush, not just with the colors, form, lighting, and blending of the paint on the canvas. This combination can be duplicated by another artist to some extent, but no one can be one hundred percent the same. Combined together, these elements are the signature of a soul. A talented art expert can look at a painting by a master and tell you who painted it without ever seeing the name scratched on it."

Lindy held out her hand. "Let me see the photo you took. It may not be light enough to see well, but if I can get it enhanced, it might show what I think I saw."

"Which is?" Michelle asked as she handed over her phone.

"Recent paint in the signature on the canvas. The rest of it was dry, but not that." Lindy called up the image, studied it a few moments, enlarging it a little with her finger. "It's pretty dark, but maybe..." She keyed in something, and Michelle heard the familiar beep as it connected to a line.

Satisfied, Lindy handed it back to her, then picked up her phone and opened an incoming message. "I'm going to send it on to Colin. Why don't you send it to Roberto and ask him if this is his missing canvas, just to verify it?"

While Lindy mailed it to Colin, Michelle sent a quick note to Roberto telling him they'd spotted it today in Lisbon, and was it the same painting? She was pretty sure she'd hear back from him soon, but she decided to scurry down the hall to get ice and a couple of sodas from the machine.

When she came back, she found Lindy had changed into a lounging dress and was rubbing cream on her aching feet. She glanced up and saw the drinks. "Thanks, sweetie. Although I might rather have had room service from the bar. I could use a good, stiff drink tonight."

"Want me to call for one?" Michelle set the ice bucket down and filled a glass, then poured soda into it for herself. She glanced at her phone and saw a text message had come in from Roberto. It was brief: *Yes. Where is it?*

"Roberto confirms it was his. He wants to know where we found it. Shall I tell him?"

"No, not yet. I don't want him to get too upset about this until we know more. Once I have the whole story and talk to Colin, then we can decide what to do about it. I can't go accusing a man of theft and illegally selling a painting as his own without more proof. I wonder if Marchant has any idea his painter from Sintra is a phony."

Michelle nodded, wondering the same thing herself. How could he just accept all those paintings were done by this artist who suddenly appeared on the scene? She needed to talk to Roberto without her aunt around. She took a sip of her drink, then dug into her purse as if she was looking for something.

"Oh darn it, I seem to have used the last of my lip balm. I'm going to go down to the gift shop before it closes to get another tube. Do you want anything, Aunt Lindy?" She hopped to her feet as she asked.

"No, I'm fine... On second thought. If they have one of those little bottles of wine, then pick up one of those. I think you're legal in Portugal. If not, then I'll call for room service."

"White?" Michelle asked, waited for the nod, then went out the door.

Once she was in the lobby, Michelle went to one of the nooks set up with matching loveseats facing each other, pulled out her phone, and called Roberto. She wanted to talk to him directly, not just texting. A smile touched her lips as he answered.

After a few moments of greetings and saying how much

they missed each other, she got down to business. "Listen, I think my aunt suspects something illegal with the paintings. I can't tell you everything. She doesn't want to go into detail until she knows more, but I wanted you to know something weird is definitely going on."

"It has to be my painting, Michelle. You saw it. You recognized it, yes?"

"Of course, I did. I watched you paint it. I have no doubt about it, and I told my aunt as much. She said Colin is doing some checking for her."

"I have to come there," he said, his voice dropping into something determined and serious.

"Wait a bit. When we know something, I'll call you, then you can come."

"All right... *Carita*, I miss seeing you. Today, I started a painting with you in the garden. It will be amazing." His voice softened as he said this, and her heart fluttered like a hummingbird's wings.

"I can't wait to see it." Even as she said it, she wondered if she'd get the opportunity. She sucked in a breath. "Talk to you as soon as I know more. Miss you too."

She ended the call and hurried to the shop to get the lip balm and wine. While she was at it, she grabbed a package of cookies and an English movie magazine with Kit Harrington on the cover.

Chapter 20
‹⁂ *Lindy* ⁂›

As soon as Michelle had left the room, Lindy pulled out her tablet and began making notes, looking up timelines, and piecing the puzzle together. She felt certain de Sintra bought Roberto's paintings either through a middleman or through Arturo. Since Arturo shipped the paintings rather than delivering them in person, she was pretty sure he'd never met either de Sintra or the middleman.

Once the painter had the canvas, he removed Roberto's signature, touched up the painting there, and signed his own name larger than Roberto's so any flaws from the process would be obscured by the new signature. She'd wondered why he signed with such a large flourish, and now she knew.

Figuring no one would ever connect his work with an obscure street artist in a tourist city, he could market the paintings as his own without anyone suspecting. Certainly not the likes of Marchant, who was a dealer, but no expert. With this much figured out, she placed a call to a friend in New York. She glanced at the time and felt certain she could catch Stephanie at work.

When she picked up, Lindy greeted her with the usual banter, gave her a quick rundown on where she was, and what she was doing, then got to the meat of the call, explaining the situation with Roberto. "Here's the deal, Stephie. I believe there's fraud being committed on the part of de Sintra. Can you find out everything you can about him? I can get basic information on the internet, but I know you have other sources. His work is being marketed through a gallery in Paris owned by Alain Marchant, who also wants to market some of my works."

"Of course, I can look into it. I'll get back to you when I have something, but it may not be until the morning. Is that okay?"

"Yes, fine. I don't know what I can do about this from here, but if I can prove anything, then I can take it to the police in Spain or maybe here in Portugal."

"This might even be an Interpol case," Stephanie said. "Is there a separate Euro police force these days?"

"I don't know. I hadn't given it any thought before now," Lindy laughed, then she heard Michelle at the door. "Thanks for doing this. I'll let you go now." She ended the call as soon as Michelle stepped through the door.

"Was that Colin?" her niece asked.

"What?" She glanced at the phone, still in her hand. "No, I was checking on something. I see you got the wine and some other things."

"Yes, they have English magazines, and I thought I'd see who and what was hot in film in the UK. Starts out with a pretty good cover." She flashed the front of the magazine toward Lindy, then let out an exasperated sigh when Lindy didn't recognize the actor. "I forgot. No *Game of Thrones* background, so you wouldn't know Jon Snow."

Lindy shrugged her shoulders. Was he an actor in the show? Maybe she should pay more attention to the television trends.

Michelle dropped her 'zine on the bed as she handed the wine to Lindy. She held up the rolled bag of Galletas Maria cookies. "I also bought cookies, crunchy ones. They look pretty good. I think they're like shortbread."

"They'd go better with cocoa than wine," Lindy said. "Why don't we go for dinner, and you can save those for dessert?"

"Sounds good."

"Did you talk to Roberto?" Lindy asked and watched as Michelle's hand hesitated a moment before she set the cookies down.

"Yes, just a couple of minutes. I thought it would be better than texting, and it was. He's positive the painting is his. He's hopping mad about it. He said he wanted to come here, but I told him to wait until we had more information."

"Good. We need to have proof or something more solid to go on, although I'm not sure what it might be. I'm really hoping Colin turns up something definite."

They went to a nearby restaurant and ordered the house specialty, which happened to be shrimp with garlic butter sauce. Like family dining for two, the waiter brought a platter of roasted vegetables, including zucchini, potatoes, artichokes, and bell peppers, along with the pot of shrimp and thick, crusty bread to soak up the sauce. Lindy hadn't realized how hungry she'd gotten until the food arrived, and they both dug in with hearty appetites.

"Omigod, this is so good," Michelle said between bites of shrimp and bread. "I absolutely love the food over here. The seafood is great. The flavors are pure magic."

"It's the seasoning," Lindy commented. "Some spices here are different from home, and it's influenced by Moroccan food as well. It's a big change from your daddy's beef and potatoes menu, isn't it?"

"You can say that again. You know how Dad is."

"Yeah, I do. I'm delighted I've been able to introduce you to the wonderful flavors of the world." She paused and gazed at her niece with misty eyes as her emotions surprised her. "I mean it, Michelle. I am so glad we had this trip together. It's been a joy to spend the time with you."

"Even though I worried and upset you?"

"Yes, even through that. I haven't been around most of the time you were growing up, and I think I should have gotten to know you better sooner. We are very similar, you know. Both creatives and looking for the elusive bubble to success."

"But you have it," Michelle objected. Her eyebrows lowered as she looked puzzled.

"I do, and I don't. I have success as a fantasy and romance artist who creates book covers. Some of them are seen by more people than those who will ever see a painting by Degas. But even though I have awards and have won accolades, I don't really have the recognition of the art community. I'm an outsider in their arena."

"Is that why you want to put your paintings in Marchant's gallery?"

"To some extent. If I display there with other well-known artists and my work sells, then it might attract more attention."

"What about your personal life, Auntie? Don't you long for a loving partner? Someone to share your success with?"

Lindy turned her eyes away as her smile faded to a more serious line. "I haven't had good luck there. I meet men, and I date a lot, but finding someone who is constant and is someone I wish to be with always hasn't happened. I've come close, but it's always ended badly. I don't think there is anyone for me."

"I don't believe that. There's someone for everyone. I know there is. You can't give up. Colin might be the one, you know, if you give him the chance. But you have to let him in …" Her voice faded as her phone chimed at her, and she glanced at it to see the caller, then back at Lindy.

"Go ahead and take it. I need to go to the loo anyway." She slipped out of her chair and started across to the marked facilities as Michelle answered the phone in a low voice. Lindy guessed it was Roberto. Who else would call her at this time?

When she returned, Michelle said nothing about the phone call, and Lindy figured it wasn't any of her business to ask. If Roberto had any new information, then her niece would have told her. They finished dinner off with a delicious orange almond cake, a wonderful match with their spiced cocoa.

Lindy woke before Michelle the next morning and quietly slipped into the bathroom to get through her routines before the girl woke. In fact, she hoped she could get dressed and slip out without her this morning. She had things to do which she preferred Michelle not be involved in.

As she came back out, dressed for the day in a pair of trim dark gray slacks and a cream-colored blouse, she saw Michelle had rolled the other direction, away from the window and still seemed to sleep soundly. She scribbled a note telling her she had errands to run and would be back around one. Putting the note on the breakfast table where her niece was sure to see it, Lindy slipped out of the room, stopped for a sweet roll and a morning coffee, then took a taxi back to the art district and the studio on the *Rua da Tristeza*.

The place had just opened when she walked in. The same

woman sat behind the same table and held her embroidery ready to begin working on it. Lindy smiled at her and asked if Pablo de Sintra was in yet. The woman stared at her a moment as if she didn't recall her from the previous day, then she told her to wait. Or at least, Lindy thought she'd said it.

She disappeared through the door at the back of the studio where it seemed to lead to steps upstairs if the short glimpse Lindy got meant anything. As she waited, she went over to look at the painting at the end of the row again and studied the signature a little more closely. Yes, she was certain the paint below had been touched up a little, perhaps giving the impression the artist had made an error and had to redo the signature on the painting although her gut was telling her Roberto's was obscured under the new signature on it.

She heard footsteps behind the door and moved to the middle aisle of paintings and wandered down them, giving the impression she was looking at them again. The woman came through the door alone, walked back to her table, then said, "*Una houra.*"

One hour. Presumably, she meant de Sintra would be there then. She told the manager or clerk or whatever she was that she would return to see him.

Leaving the shop, she went back to the crossroad and found a cafe where she could get a cup of tea. She checked her email, hoping to see something from Stephanie, but nothing had come in yet. There was a short text message from Colin: *Have news. Will talk to you soon.*

She texted back, saying she was eager to hear it and to call if he got the message in the next half an hour. Michelle hadn't called or sent her a text, so she trusted everything was okay there. After she finished her drink, she started back toward de

Sintra's studio, taking her time and checking out the shop fronts as she went.

When she got back, she found the artist in the shop. At least, she presumed the portly, elderly man sitting by an easel at the back of the shop was de Sintra. The woman was not in the shop, so Lindy made her way to the fellow and asked if he was Pablo de Sintra. He nodded in the affirmative, and she offered her hand.

"Do you speak Spanish?" she asked in the language.

"*Si*," he answered and added, "Also, Basque, French, and Portuguese. We learn many languages in this area."

"I am Melinda Morton, an American artist. Mainly, I do book cover paintings, but I studied in Paris many years ago." Why did she feel she had to justify her status to this man?

He smiled at her, his eyes crinkling at the corners, and motioned to a stool to sit. "Good, good. For us to make a living doing something we enjoy is very good, yes?"

"Yes. But if I read your biography correctly, you didn't actually start painting until about ten years ago? Is that true?"

"It is. I work as the brickmaker for most my life. Then the shop close down, and I have time for something else. I dabble with paints many years but not done pictures with them. So, I decide to paint scenes such as this one." He motioned to the painting she'd looked at the previous day.

"It's a wonderful painting. What was your inspiration for it?"

His eyes grew wistful-looking as if they were about to water. Come to think of it, they looked like he didn't focus very well. Lindy notched up things about him as things hinted he didn't paint anything at Roberto's level. Judging from the way he rubbed at his fingers and the stiffness of them, she believed he had arthritis in them. His hands had shaken a little when he had taken her hand.

He went on to tell her how he'd witnessed a young woman with her children in a Spanish village, and she'd inspired the painting. He'd returned to the studio and drawn her from memory.

"How fascinating," she said and wanted to ask him what village it was – like maybe Mijas? But she already knew he was lying. "I love your technique, Señor. Are you working on a painting now?"

"Not now. I wait for inspiration. Perhaps a beautiful woman, like you, might spark the idea."

"You flatter me. I hoped I might buy one of your paintings, like this one here." She motioned to the canvas.

"It would honor me to sell, but, sadly, this one is already sold. All my others also. I am fortunate they sell almost as they are done."

"Truly fortunate," Lindy agreed. "Perhaps I might get on a waiting list to buy ..."

Just then, the embroidery woman burst through the back door with a man who looked like a dock worker with big muscles and a frown on his face. She pointed at Lindy and said something in Portuguese. Lindy interpreted it as, "That woman has been snooping around here. Claims to be an artist and insisting on seeing de Sintra."

Lindy got to her feet and backed toward the front entrance as she spoke. "What? What is going on? I only wanted to meet the artist. Is that a problem?"

"Maybe you be too nosey," the man said in broken English and stepped forward. "What business do you do here?"

"I'd hoped to buy a painting." What was this? Did de Sintra

not sell from his studio?

The artist looked puzzled by this as the woman encouraged him to go to the apartment upstairs.

"Who send you?" the man demanded.

"No one. I simply admired his work and thought I could buy a canvas. Don't people come here to purchase?" She was almost to the door, but the man was only a few feet away.

The door opened behind her, and Lindy whirled around, fearing another attacker at her back and turned into Colin's arms.

"There you are, darling," he said, smiling at her. "I misread the address you gave me." He pulled her around to the door, giving a little wave to the man who had stopped when he'd come in. "We've got to run now. An appointment with Lady Michelle, you know."

He guided her out the door and down the street. Behind them, the man stepped out and watched them go.

'What are you doing here?" Lindy asked as he hustled her along.

"Rescuing you. What were you doing in there?"

"Trying to figure it out," she replied. "I know de Sintra didn't paint any of the paintings I've seen, and I don't know if he ever did. His hands aren't steady enough for the quality."

They rounded a corner, and Colin glanced behind them, then pointed to a car and opened the door for her. Once he was in the driver's seat and maneuvered the car into traffic, he said, "You're right. Roberto painted those, all of them. Every painting my friend in Paris looked at showed the same hand had created them, and that hand was the kid from Marbella and Mijas. De Sintra is making a fortune buying the paintings from Roberto and passing them off as his own."

"I knew it! But why was the big guy coming after me? I only wanted to talk to de Sintra, maybe buy a painting."

"I think they must consider you a threat. The old fellow the woman hustled out of there... Was he de Sintra?"

"Yes. He was very pleasant, and I thought we had a nice chat going, but it was clear his hands are arthritic, and they shook too much for him to paint a steady brushstroke. But I didn't threaten him or anything," Lindy protested. "It doesn't make sense."

"Unless someone else knows who you are and thinks you might present a problem to the arrangement," Colin said, then turned the car toward her hotel.

"Who? And what are you doing here? I mean, I'm glad you came when you did, but why are you in Lisbon?" She just realized he should be on his way to Mijas if he was just in Paris.

"I left Paris early yesterday, got to Mijas, and talked to Roberto. We drove in last night. Michelle said you had probably gone to the studio again, so I came over here."

She gaped at him. "Wait a minute! Roberto is here also? I thought Michelle told him not to come until we had more information."

Colin shrugged and pulled the car into the hotel entry. "After I told him what I'd found out, he couldn't be stopped. Those are his paintings, after all."

The hotel doorman opened the door for her, and Lindy climbed out, waiting with a tapping toe as Colin spoke to the man, tipped him, and came around to join her.

"So, am I the only one who doesn't know what you've learned?" she complained in a low voice.

"Let's go up to my room to discuss this, dear. You weren't here when we got up this morning. See what happens when you sneak off."

"I didn't sneak off," she muttered, but she didn't resist as he took her arm to lead her to the elevators.

Another couple joined them in the elevator, so they said nothing more until they were off the elevator and entering the room. "Tell me what you know," Lindy demanded, anxious to find out what he'd turned up.

Colin's room was the mirror image of hers, except it had a loveseat in it next to a computer table. He told her to sit, opened a bottle of orange water, and poured a glass for each of them, then sat at the table.

"Here's what I found out. As I said, the paintings my friend examined — and he looked very closely at several from the past four years – were all painted by the same artist. The style, color, detailing, and any other measure you can look at, all looked exactly the same as Roberto's paintings. Even Roberto's cheap for-tourists paintings show the same detailing and style. We have no doubt he is the artist."

"I still don't understand why the woman accused me of causing trouble," Lindy said as she thought about this. She has suspected this. Likely a middleman handled the transactions unless Arturo betrayed Roberto and was helping to swindle him. "Did you check out Arturo?"

"When I told Roberto, we went to talk to Arturo. He confirmed everything he'd told us before. He never met the person who ordered the commission paintings, and he'd had repeat orders from three different people and addresses. One was in Madrid, one in Seville, and one in Lisbon."

"Was the one in Lisbon to Rue da Tristeza?" If it was, then we have him, she concluded.

"No, it was a different address here. But it doesn't mean

they weren't being cautious."

"They?"

"We believe all three addresses are drop points for the canvases, and several people are involved in this."

"Incredible. I wonder if Alain is aware of this."

"Alain?" Colin asked.

"The Paris gallery owner, Alain Marchant. He was the first to push de Sintra's work through shows and his gallery... Oh, dear." Her face paled as she realized the implication.

"We may have found a link," Colin said and turning to his laptop, quickly called up the web page for Marchant's gallery. "Let's take a look, shall we?"

They went through every information page on the site, looked at every art expert who advised the gallery, every listed employee, and of course, Marchant and his company officials. Once again, Lindy noted the man she thought she recognized and mentioned it to Colin, who made a note of the name. The dates Marchant started handling de Sintra's work lined up with the time the art world first noticed him, but then she heard Alain say he had discovered his work by accident and began promoting him.

Colin frowned. "What if the artist he discovered was actually a young man from Spain, but the story of an elderly man, who was a male Grandma Moses, made for a more promotable option? What if he came up with the plan to pass Roberto's work off as this old fellow from the Basque country?"

"You can't be serious, Colin. Why would he even think of such a crazy scheme?"

"Consider it a moment, Lindy. Just the back story would arouse interest in the press and around the world. Allowing he could get his hands on custom paintings from a very good artist, then he could present them and make them into a collectible piece of art from an artist who may not live many more years. It boosts the value with the possibility of the number of paintings being limited and the uniqueness of the man's history. What did de Sintra tell you he did for a living before he started painting?"

She sighed, not liking where this was going. "He made bricks in a factory."

"A brick maker. I think the concern with you being at the studio is they knew you were an artist, and it wouldn't take long talking to de Sintra to know he wouldn't be able to create those canvases. I'd bet the signature on the paintings isn't even his. It's theft. Pure and simple theft."

"I can't believe it." Lindy stared at the page of photos where Marchant was arriving at his gallery opening. In one, she spotted a familiar face right behind him as he stepped away from his car. She pointed, "That's the man from the shop who was coming after me. He's Marchant's bodyguard!"

Colin nodded, his expression dark with a grim, tight-lipped mouth as he said, "You're sure?"

She nodded.

"Then, we have proof enough to go to the authorities on this. And this man, who works for Marchant, threatened you."

"Which authorities do we take this to – the Spanish or the Portuguese?" She glanced at the web site again. "Or the French?"

"I would say this might extend to Interpol," he replied. "But we can start with the Portuguese since we're here. Let's have some lunch sent up while we build a timeline and statement to take to them, then we can get Roberto and go down to the local office."

Chapter 21
Michelle

Aware her aunt was up early and getting ready to go out, Michelle feigned her sleepiness as Lindy went about her preparations. Roberto had texted her during dinner to let her know he was coming to Lisbon and would be there in the morning. Even though she'd told him to wait, he said he was already on the way, so she wanted to be at the hotel when he arrived. Her aunt's plan to go to the studio on her own worked out well for her. She smiled a little smugly into her pillow as she heard the room's door shut.

She gave it a few more minutes, then tossed the covers back and headed for the bathroom to get ready. After a lukewarm shower to wake her, she wrapped a towel around her body and grabbed the blow dryer to get her long hair at least partially dried. By the time she dressed, she had a text on her phone with a short message: *In town. c u in 15*

The timestamp was less than ten minutes earlier, so he would be arriving any time now. She straightened the covers on the bed and tidied up a little, wishing she had time to get coffee and a pastry before he arrived. As she picked up her aunt's robe, she heard the knock on the door.

"One moment," she called out and hurried to hang the garment in the closet. Then she peeked out to see it was Roberto, and she was surprised to see Colin standing behind him. She released the deadbolt, letting them in. Roberto gave her a brief hug and a peck on the cheek as he came in, which she returned, then looked at the other man. "Colin, I wasn't expecting you so soon. I thought you were in Paris."

"I was, but I got back to Mijas last night and found Roberto to get a few questions answered, so here we are."

He smiled at her and pointed to the bathroom. "May I?"

She nodded, then turned to Roberto as Colin went to the little room. "What's up? Why the sudden rush to get here?"

"Colin and I talked last night, and I had to come." He placed his left hand over his chest and spoke forcefully. "Someone has stolen my work and erased my name. I have to fight this."

Her heart melted in sympathy, and she threw her arms around him, pulling him close. "I'm so sorry. But Aunt Lindy and Colin are both working to find out the whole story. We shouldn't do anything until they can obtain proof."

"What more proof?" His eyebrows drew together in his anger. "The man has my painting, right here. The one stolen from my studio! Bad enough, he bought the others and took my name off, but he didn't even pay for this one!"

"I know, but you can't just go in there and accuse him."

"She's right," Colin said as he came out of the bathroom with the toilet flush still sounding behind him. "Let's get all the details worked out, then we can get the authorities. Is Lindy down getting coffee?"

Michelle glanced at him and thought he wouldn't be happy with the answer. "She left earlier this morning and left me a note. I think she's going to de Sintra's studio to talk to him."

"What? No, no ... This isn't good. Do you have the

address?"

Michelle nodded and called it up on her phone.

"I'm going after her. She might not be safe." He grabbed the notepad by the desk, ready to write down the address. As soon as he'd scribbled it down, he hurried to the door then paused to say, "You two stay here until you hear from me. Don't do anything. You understand me, Roberto?"

He nodded, then Colin left.

"Probably good advice," Michelle said. "Let's go get coffee and rolls and wait for him to get back to us."

Roberto sulked, his body still tense and anxious to take action. He looked tired, dark circles below his eyes, and he probably hadn't slept much on the trip to Lisbon. "Did you drive?"

"Colin did."

She nodded, caught his arm, and pulled him along with her to the hallway and the elevator downstairs.

They drank two cups of coffee, and she had the desired sweet roll while they waited for Colin to call or text them. Picking at a napkin with his fingers, Roberto told her what had happened when he and Colin had confronted Arturo about the commissioned paintings.

"The only thing Arturo is guilty of is not asking enough questions of these patrons who wanted to purchase my art. I can't really fault him for that. Fortunately, he did keep a record of all the requests and copies of the emails and letters. Over a dozen people contacted him for commissioned pieces, and you don't grill a paying customer about why they want the painting. We found three repeat customers, though, and combined, they ordered seventeen paintings."

"But why steal the last one?" Michelle asked as she tried to piece together the whole operation. Her aunt was right; middlemen were involved in the scheme, but stealing from Roberto was a dumb thing to do.

He shook his head. "I don't know. Maybe one of the people involved took it because it was commissioned, and they needed it right away. So they stole it before I was ready to hand it over."

"Still doesn't make sense. If they were in a hurry, why is it still in the studio here?"

Roberto shrugged. They both checked their phones again to see if they'd missed a message. Michelle sent a text to Lindy's phone, asking if she was okay. Now she was getting worried. Colin had been gone for about an hour, and neither he nor her aunt responded to their phones.

Abruptly, Roberto sprang to his feet. "I'm going down there. You wait here for your aunt. I can't sit here and do nothing any longer." He began walking toward the hotel lobby.

"No! Wait a moment." Michelle picked up her phone and ran to catch up with him.

"If you're going, I'm going with you."

He hesitated, then reached back to catch her hand as she drew almost even with him.

Roberto flagged a cab in front of the hotel, and Michelle rattled off the studio's address again. In less than thirty minutes, she stood just outside the studio as Roberto paid the driver, then led the way into the small, dark space.

As soon as they were in, Michelle cast her eyes toward the back of the studio where Roberto's painting still sat on the easel. The back door was open, and a light shone through from the alley. The odor of stale garbage wafted in with a draft. She saw no sign of her aunt or Colin. Her nerves spiked, and tension crept up her neck.

Roberto spoke to the same lady who'd been there the previous day. Her embroidery work spread across the table in disarray as if it had been thrown down instead of neatly placed, and the woman herself looked disconcerted to see Michelle and another visitor to the shop.

Even though she didn't understand much Spanish and even less Portuguese, she did hear Roberto say something about de Sintra. Asking to see him, maybe? The woman responded with something equally as unclear, and he shouted something back at her.

"Roberto, it's here!" she said, grabbing his nearest arm and pulling him toward the painting.

He said something sounding more like an order to the woman, then he followed her toward the painting. Before they got there, he saw another one on the wall and went over to peer at it. His face darkened as he grumbled, "I just finished this one recently. Another one Arturo sold. Look, he barely covered my name and hasn't signed it yet!"

Michelle paused to look where he pointed and saw the paint appeared smeared and retouched. Even she could see it.

She touched his arm and pointed to the one at the end, the stolen painting. He took one look at it then grabbed it off the easel. "This is mine. I painted this. Where is the bastard who stole my work?" He whirled and glared at the lady who was on her phone, calling someone.

"We need to go," Michelle said, her stomach growing nervous. She was pretty sure the clerk wasn't calling de Sintra to come chat. Where the heck were her aunt and Colin? She'd thought, for certain, they would be here at the shop.

Unexpectedly, two men ran into the room from the back hall. One made a quick grab for Michelle, and she shrieked out a cry. He wrapped his muscular arms around her chest, pinning her to make it hard for her to fight him. A goon of a man, at least in Michelle's mind, he was easily six inches taller than she was and had a good fifty pounds on her. As he yanked her backward off her feet and dragged her, she glimpsed a bigger thug struggling with Roberto and saw the painting fly out of his hands and to the floor.

Michelle dug her heels in and took a deep breath to let loose a howling scream when the clerk slapped her face, then pressed a strip of duct tape over her mouth. The goon forced her into a chair, and the embroidery lady ran the tape around her mid-section and arms to hold her in the seat. Legs still free for the moment, she tried to kick the goon, landing at least one successful hit before he grabbed her ankles. He and the woman secured her ankles to the front legs of the chair. Then the brute pulled her hands together, and the woman wrapped them firmly in tape.

All the while, Roberto fought against the thug, trying to land a punch or at least kick him someplace where it would count. As his eyes turned toward Michelle, his rage returned, and he screamed something in Spanish and attacked the man anew. The clerk stood nearby as the goon went over to help subdue Roberto. Another man stepped into the room from the back.

She recognized the build as soon as she saw his shadowed form. Alain Marchant. She wanted to scream, but couldn't make more than a muffled sound. Roberto turned toward the newcomer and also recognized him from the photos on the web site. Furious, he made a lunge toward Marchant only to be grabbed by the goon before he could get his hands on the art dealer.

She watched in dismay as Roberto fought like a trapped wild cat, his arms flailing with his hands reaching to claw at Marchant while the goon held him and tried to haul him back. Roberto brought his right hand back over his head and scratched at the goon, scraping a fingernail down one side of his face and drawing blood. Then the thug hit him over the head with a wooden mallet. Roberto reeled and tried to retaliate until the hammer struck again. He went out like a light, dropping motionless to the floor.

Michelle gasped and sucked in the sticky tape, nearly choking on it. Through tears in her eyes and a muffled cough, she stared at Roberto's inert form on the floor, trying to see if he was breathing.

"Bind him up and let's get them out of here, Sasha," Marchant said in French if Michelle interpreted it correctly.

He strolled over to Michelle and bent down to right in front of her face. "I should have known you and your aunt would be trouble, especially after you showed so much interest in de Sintra's painting. Now I need to figure out what to do with you two as well as this painter. You've made quite a mess of my operation."

Goon and the other thug picked up Roberto, who was now bound with tape at his arms and ankles with a piece over his mouth and carried him out the back door. In a few minutes, they returned, picking Michelle up in the chair and carried her along the same route which ended at the opened rear door of a parked van.

They lifted her into the van and secured the chair to the side with ropes. From this position, she could see Roberto but could do nothing to help him. Several canvases wrapped in bubble wrap were at the front of the van, and soon they brought another two out to join them. Were they all Roberto's? she wondered. At least two, and probably three, in the shop were his, but were they running this same scam on other unsuspecting artists?

Although she didn't see her aunt in the van with them, she couldn't assume Lindy hadn't been captured earlier. Maybe Colin had gotten her out before it happened. Now, what was Marchant going to do with them? Oh, crap! Why hadn't she talked Roberto out of coming down to the shop?

So many questions went through her mind, like where are they taking us? What happened to my aunt? Did Marchant grab her and take her somewhere else? What had he said – "I knew you and your aunt would be trouble..."? Did he already have her? What about Colin? Then, what the hell do I do now?

As she watched, the thug added another painting to the load in the van, then Marchant came out to inspect the cargo, and he glared at her. He turned to the goon, who was just behind him and said, in English, so she could hear, "We will need to take care of the aunt and her friend who were here earlier today. I'll leave it to you to handle while Sasha takes them away. I'll decide what we'll do with them once we have them all."

She could only shoot glares at him as he turned and walked away while Goon closed the doors of the van.

Her heart dropped to her stomach as the van began moving. She felt the turns and bumps in the road and figured the driver was taking them out of the central Lisbon district. The windows in the back had been blocked with dark curtains, and a wall separated the cargo area from the front seat, so she couldn't see anything except the shape of Roberto lying on the floor where they'd dumped him. As the vehicle moved onto a highway and began to pick up speed, Michelle felt like crying and screaming, but she couldn't do either.

She stared down at Roberto's unmoving body and felt the despair of being unable to do anything and not even knowing if he was alive or dying. And dammit, she was so uncomfortable her body was beginning to hurt.

After what felt like several hours, Michelle's body felt numb even though she wiggled her toes, flexed her ankles, and moved anything she could from her neck to her knees to try to keep her circulation flowing. During this time, she'd heard a muffled moan from Roberto and saw his body trying to move, but not being able to move to even a sitting position since they had trussed him up so much.

At least he was alive, she thought and made an answering muffled noise to let him know she was with him. Judging from his increased attempts to move, she concluded it might not have been a good thing to do as it seemed to aggravate him.

She'd had plenty of time to mull over their predicament during the drive. Once the initial fear had subsided, she could think more positively. They were still alive, which mean Marchant might not be intending to kill them. Or at least, not right away, or he would have had Sasha Thug take them out of town and do it, then dump them in the ocean or some other place where they wouldn't be found easily. So much for her positive-thinking. Maybe he figured to bargain with them, like promising Roberto he would keep her alive if he continued painting. But it would mean imprisoning them somewhere. Was he was taking them to their prison or to kill them?

Eventually, the van slowed and turned off the main highway and made another turn. To the right, she thought, probably going inland, assuming they'd been traveling up the coast from Lisbon. As they went, she detected the smell of rain and wet soil and heard drops hitting against the van. After about another thirty minutes or so, it turned again, then went for another long spell before slowing and turning once more onto an uneven road.

It bounced along, every bump jarring her body painfully until it came to a halt, then the sound of the door opening. A few tense minutes passed as Michelle expected the back to be opened at any second, but the van bounced again, and the door shut. The van moved forward for several feet, and the process was repeated. *Opening a gate,* she thought. The driver had to get out to open and close the gate after they went through. She was pretty sure they were almost at their destination.

When the van stopped again, the engine died, and she heard the cab door open. She braced herself and waited until the back doors opened, and the low light of near dusk and a dark cloud-covered sky backlit their captor. As her eyes adjusted, she could make out trees and some mountains in the background. She didn't see any buildings or houses, so they were in the countryside.

Ohmigod, is he going to kill us here? Her heart jerked, feeling like it had slammed into her ribs. She couldn't breathe as she tried to gasp for air.

Sasha climbed into the van, cut the ropes tying her to the side of the van, picked her up, chair and all, and set it at the edge of the opening. He jumped down, then lifted her again and carried her around the side of the van where an old-looking farmhouse stood alone except for a barn about fifty feet farther on.

Grabbing a dolly from the van, he set her on it and began wheeling her toward the barn. A light rain came down, soaking them both as they covered the ground, then he set the dolly upright, opened the barn door, and turned on a light. He brought her in then took her to the back corner of the barn where a small shed-sized building with a standard door sat. He opened this, and she panicked. He couldn't be putting them in the elevator-sized space. Then he wheeled her in, and she realized it actually was an elevator.

At the press of a button, they went down at least twenty feet before the door opened onto an underground concrete bunker. One side held food storage and other supplies, like a larder, and another section held a vault, which was closed at the moment. The back section was a solid wall with only a heavy metal door across it.

Thug opened this and took her inside, then left her there, turning back to get Roberto, she presumed. So confident of her inability to escape, he didn't even bother to close the door as he left. He was right, of course. If she hadn't been able to break even a hand loose in the past few hours, she wouldn't manage an escape in the short time it would take him to bring Roberto. Then what?

She gazed around the room to see what it actually looked like. A small room in the right back corner looked like it could be a bathroom, and it might even be big enough for a shower. Next to it, a wooden wardrobe with a 1940s look leaned against the wall. Farther up on the right side, a small propane stove and an electric heater crouched up against the wall. A wooden dining set, also looking like it came from another era, provided a flat surface to eat. Four uncomfortable-looking beds with only thin mattresses over wooden frames lined the left wall.

Perhaps it had been built during World War II and had been a bomb shelter. Although she guessed it might have originally started as underground storage for canned goods, produce, and other farm items, it had been converted. It might have been expanded from its original size, but she was certain, this section was added later and intended for someone to be able to live down here if necessary. Now, she feared it would be their prison.

A thump along the stairs caught her attention, and she looked to see Sasha Thug dragging his helpless victim into the room. Her eyes met Roberto's and the downturn of his eyes told her how sorry he was to have dragged her into this. She shook her head a little to say no. It wasn't completely his fault. She could have stayed behind, but she and her aunt had a part in it also.

Sasha whipped out a knife and cut her arms free from the chair, allowing her to move them a little. Then he cut the duct tape securing her ankles to the chair legs. He stood back quickly, then turned to Roberto, cutting the tape holding his legs together, then cutting the ones at his wrists.

Michelle tried to gain her footing, but her legs were so numb she nearly fell over and barely managed to sit back in the chair without knocking it about. Shifting her legs to try to get her circulation moving again, she watched as Roberto struggled to get to his knees. Like her, he could scarcely move. Sasha pointed to a bookcase near the stove where several bottles of water and a loaf of bread filled the top shelf. Below, it held several books, and nothing else. Then he gestured to the old icebox, and she looked at it. Once he was sure she'd seen them, he left them, slamming the door and bolting it behind him.

They were prisoners now, and this was all they had. Bread and water, wrists bound together, and mouths taped. Clearly, he expected them to release themselves now. Standing with more caution than the first time, Michelle took a tentative step, then another toward Roberto. When she got close, she knelt and walked on her knees the rest of the way. He was upright but looked exhausted. She motioned to him by twisting her head and jerking it back, indicating she wanted him to yank the tape from her mouth.

He looked puzzled at first until she half turned and wiggled her fingers, trying to show pulling. At last, he got it and nodded. She worked her way behind him, then lowered herself onto an elbow to get her head even with his hands. Positioning herself, she leaned forward until his fingers touched her face, and he felt around for the edges of the tape. Once he caught the edge, he pulled at it with two fingers getting a grip underneath it. Then he began to slowly pull it.

Not one to want to prolong the pain of taking the tape off, Michelle jerked her head sharply, hoping his fingers gripped it well enough they wouldn't slip before it came off. It tore loose, and she gasped with the pain. It didn't quite pull loose as part of it hung across her other cheek.

"It's not quite off. I'm going to lower my face again. Yank it the rest of the way," she told Roberto.

In a couple of minutes more, the tape was gone, and she could get a look at the tape around his wrists. She needed something to work with.

"Do you have anything in your pockets I can use to cut?" she asked.

He shrugged, then nodded. Maybe.

She worked around to his right side and poked a couple of fingers into his pocket, feeling around. Her fingers touched a set of keys, then a piece of folded metal. She gripped the keys and pulled them out, dropping them to the floor where she could see them. Two of them – his house key and his motorcycle key. Maybe she could use one to break through the tape. Then she reached in again, almost giggling at the awkward situation.

"Don't get the wrong idea about this, mister," she said with a touch of humor in her voice. "I'm just getting whatever this metal is out of here. I hope it's a pocket knife."

She pulled it loose, dropped it next to the keys, and turned to look. A set of fingernail clippers.

"Oh, great. We're all set if we have a hangnail." Her voice lacked enthusiasm, then she perked up. "But it might be enough to start a tear in the tape. Duct tape tears easily once you get it started."

Determined, she shifted around again and picked the clippers up, struggling to hold and open it at the same time. At least it was the type with a little pointed blade and a bottle opener. It might be enough.

Roberto shifted his position toward her so his wrists were almost within reach of hers, and they started inching their way toward each other. Michelle sat on her butt now and slid back as close as she could to Roberto. It wasn't quite enough with his feet still in the way.

"You need to spread your legs apart more," she said.

A foot bumped against her as he complied, then she slid in closer until she felt his body against hers. She reached with her fingers touching his hip.

"Which way do I move?" she asked.

He answered her by shifting his body down a little and to the left, then she felt his fingers brush against her hand. "Okay, that's it. Hold right there."

Working blindly, she held onto the clippers and felt with her left fingertips for the gap between his wrists where she could make a cut into the tape.

"Damn! Almost dropped them," she muttered as the clippers slipped, and she barely gripped them again. "One more time." She tried again, sliding the bottle opener blade between them and feeling Roberto tense as a little liquid flow told her had she nicked his hand.

"Sorry," she mumbled and concentrated on cutting the tape. With a poke at it, the pointed tip cut into the material, and it began to give. "I think I've got it."

She began working the blade back and forth, tearing the tape until she could grip it and begin pulling. It came off in strips and took a few more minutes before she'd pulled enough so the rest came off with only a little more effort.

Once his hands were free, Roberto tore the tape off his face, then turned to free Michelle's hands. "I'm so sorry, Mica. This is my fault."

"No, it's not. We're all in it together. And they're going to try to capture my aunt and Colin as well. We have to figure something out." Now she'd voiced it, she felt tears welling in her eyes.

Roberto pulled her into his arms and kissed her eyelids as he whispered, "There has to be a way. He won't kill us. I'm sure he wants something."

She nodded. "Your talent. You're Marchant's success story even though it's under another name." She laid her head against his chest as he rocked her in his arms.

Chapter 22
⍨ *Lindy* ⍨

After lunch, Lindy went up to check on Michelle and Roberto, assuming they would be there or at least have left a message. At the same time, Colin returned to his room to call someone he knew who had contacts at Interpol. She looked for Michelle as she entered but quickly realized no one was in. She looked around for a note or something to tell her where they'd gone.

Nothing.

She dialed Michelle's cell phone, but it went to her voice mail. "Michelle, it's your aunt. Call me when you get this. Colin and I want to talk to you and Roberto."

She picked up her purse and went downstairs to the little coffee and pastry shop in the lobby to see if they were there. She paused at the entrance for a quick look around to see only a few people in the shop. She hesitated, then stopped the waitress and asked in Spanish. "Excuse me. I'm looking for my niece. I wondered if you had seen her in here." She pulled out her phone and showed her a photo of Michelle.

The waitress, a girl about her niece's age, looked at it closely, then nodded her head. "About two hours ago, just before noon. She was here with a young man having coffee. They seemed to be arguing about something. Then they both left. He went out first, and she ran to catch up with him. I think they went toward the front door."

Lindy thanked her then went outside to the hotel entrance and found the bellman there, the same man who'd been on duty this morning when she had required a cab. She repeated the question to him and showed him her picture.

He nodded, "She and the boy took a cab from here. I haven't seen them come back yet."

Thanking him, she went back inside and called Colin's number, which was busy. She grabbed the next elevator to his floor and knocked on the door to his room. She was beginning to get anxious. If she put herself in Michelle's place and Roberto showed up, what would they have done? Obviously, coffee first and a discussion. They argued. About what?

Colin opened the door, a look of surprise on his face. He hadn't expected her back this soon, and he was still on the phone. He stepped aside for her to come in, then spoke to someone in French for a few more moments before ending the call. He turned to her, the question on his face.

"The kids are missing," she said in a rush. "They went down to the coffee shop about two hours ago, when I was at the studio, and you were on your way. They had coffee, argued, then Roberto left in a hurry, and Michelle ran after him. They caught a cab, and I can't get hold of her. Her phone is going to voice mail."

"Where did they go?" he asked. "Did anyone know?"

"No. But where do you *think* they would go? If you were Roberto, where would you go?"

He connected the dots quickly. "The studio."

She swallowed hard as he confirmed her thoughts. "What do we do, Colin? If they just went to check on the painting, they would be back by now. If Roberto made a scene ..."

"We're going to the police." He caught her hand, and they hurried out to get a cab.

A little less than two hours later, Lindy stood outside the studio, took a deep breath, and opened the door, stepping into the place with confidence. The clerk looked up from her embroidery and raised an eyebrow at her, no outward sign of alarm.

"Excuse me," Lindy said in Spanish. "I'm looking for my niece, the young lady who came with me yesterday. Have you seen her today?"

The woman stared at her with an unreadable expression then said, "I did not expect you to come back here after causing the master such upset this morning."

"I know. It was unfortunate, and I meant no harm. I thought we were getting along well. But my niece is missing, and I thought she might have come here. I would not bother you otherwise. Please, did she come here?"

The woman's eyes narrowed. "Wait. I was not here all the time. Let me check with the master."

As she hurried through the back door, Lindy looked around the room, seeing the empty easels and open spaces where the paintings had hung on the walls. They had moved all the canvases. Walking toward the easel where the stolen painting had been, she noticed a few red spots on the floor. Not paint, she thought, as she knelt to touch it, feeling a bit of moisture in it still although it looked mostly dried out. Blood, maybe. They showed the dark, maroon-looking shade blood took on when it dried. She sniffed at it and noticed a faint odor to it.

"I think this is blood," she said in a low voice, then straightened as she heard footsteps from the other side of the door. She braced herself.

The clerk flung the door open, and a strong-looking man a little taller than she, not big like the one from the morning, stepped through it.

"Anna says you are looking for your niece. There was a young woman here today with a disruptive young man. It could have been her, yes?" He spoke very good English, and Lindy thought he looked familiar. His expression was serious and concerned, but he didn't seem dangerous. Dressed in a neatly pressed gray shirt and black slacks, he looked more like a businessman than the bouncer from the morning, but she was cautious.

"It sounds right, yes. Her friend had arrived in Lisbon this morning. Do you know where they went from here?"

"The man was upset, and they were arguing when they left here. I am sorry, I have no idea."

She might have been inclined to believe him, but something shiny under the table caught her eye as she turned away from him. She had bought Michelle a Damascene gold bird pendant in Toledo at the start of their trip, and if she was not mistaken, it sat in the shadow of the easel, barely visible.

She wished she could pick it up, but she couldn't accomplish it without being too conspicuous. She lowered her eyes in disappointment and said, "Thank you for your help. Please tell Señor de Sintra I apologize for the incident this morning. I meant no disrespect."

She started to turn toward the door and ran into the arms of a bean pole of a man who grabbed her, pinning her arms to her side as the woman dashed to her table.

"Let go of me," Lindy cried out. Jerking hard, she struggled to break free of the man's grip. She yanked her arms to get in a position to kick his ankles or bring a knee up into his groin. From behind her, she heard a ripping sound, then the first man brought his hands over her twisting head and wrapped a long piece of duct tape over her mouth and half-way around her head. Then he tore another piece and secured it.

"If you quit struggling, this will go much easier, Miss Morton. I don't want to have Javier knock you out."

Not risking the threat, Lindy dropped her fighting posture and slumped her head. She didn't like it, but she couldn't do any more at the moment. If she were unconscious, she wouldn't learn any more about what had happened to Michelle and Roberto.

The man holding her, whom she presumed to be Javier, eased his hold on her. The two men pulled her hands to her back and taped them together. She stood rigid as they patted her down, checking her pockets for a cell phone. Her handbag had gone flying off her shoulder when Javier had grabbed her.

"Better," the dapper man said. "Now, we will go for a drive in the country. You wanted to see your niece. I will take you to her."

Lindy's heart jumped to her throat. They had Michelle! How they would get out of this mess, she didn't know, but at least she would find her.

They led her to a car behind the shop, opened the back door, and told her to get in. Javier got behind the steering wheel, and the other man slipped into the front seat, half-turning to keep an eye on her. Like she could do anything with her hands tied behind her. The only saving grace for her now was the tracking device planted in her shoulder. She hoped Colin and the detectives could follow it.

As they drove north from Lisbon, Lindy shifted her body a

little more onto the seat, which drew the dapper man's attention for a moment until he saw she was no threat. When he turned away, the angle on his face triggered an image in her mind. She'd seen a photo of him on the associates' web page at Alain Marchant's gallery. Dammit, he worked for Alain! Was the gallery owner part of this scheme?

She leaned her head back against the window edge and gazed out at the sea until the car exited the highway and turned inland. In spite of her situation, she drank in the beauty of the Portuguese countryside with its outcroppings of oak trees, open fields, and small towns where even little houses seemed to have colorful tiled entryways. Like the Spanish, the Portuguese were experts at making ceramic tiles, called *azulejos*, which were tin-glazed and painted. They displayed them with great pride, but long ago, she'd learned, they also helped with temperature control as well as decoration. On her first trip to Portugal many years earlier, she'd had several cases shipped to her home in New York and applied to the walls of her apartment.

Then, she realized her captors had not blindfolded her, which worried her. If they allowed her to see where they were going, then did they plan to never release her or the two kids, if they had them both? Were they planning to kill them?

The road now led toward Coimbra, then they shifted to a smaller road headed into a more rural area, and the progress slowed a little. After about twenty or so kilometers, Javier turned the car again onto a country lane, which took them to an isolated farmhouse with a barn almost the same size as the house. Dapper-man got out and opened the gate onto the property, then closed it after the car had passed. They drove around to the back of the house, where Javier parked the vehicle.

They had reached their destination, more remote than Lindy had hoped, and she worried if the tracking device would be able to send a signal from the location. Dapper-man opened the back door and waved her out. "We go to the barn," he said and gave her a little shove toward it.

With the sun descending rapidly into the west and the shadows growing long, dusk would soon plunge this remote corner into darkness. Not a pleasant prospect.

Lindy stumbled a bit as they walked across the uneven ground to the barn, and Dapper growled with impatience. With her arms tied behind her back, Lindy found her balance slightly off and tried to keep from tripping while keeping up with the man's pace. Once they reached the barn, he opened the door, flipped on lights, caught her left arm at the elbow, and pulled her straight toward the right back. He opened a smaller door to a cubicle structure, which turned out to be an elevator. They entered and it dropped them to a lower level.

Lindy recognized the bomb shelter ahead of her as soon as she stepped out. Dread settled in her stomach, and her knees turned to jelly as Dapper shoved her in the small of her back. He opened the door and pushed her into the room, then slammed it behind her.

She stumbled in, almost losing her balance, and pulled up short as she saw Michelle and Roberto at the end of the big, low-ceiled room. From their half-out-of-the-chairs positions, it seemed they had started rising from the table as soon as the door clicked open, but they hadn't made it further than to their feet before the door had been shut again.

Now, Michelle ran to Lindy, crying out, "Aunt Lindy, are you all right?"

Lindy straightened and met her niece's eyes straight on

with an annoyed look. *Tape over my mouth, wrists bound, and she asks if I'm all right?!*

"Sorry," the girl said as she understood, then hurried to get the tape off her mouth. "I didn't think."

As she pulled it loose, Lindy sucked in a breath as the tape pulled her skin and yanked out pieces of her hair even though Michelle tried to remove it off gently. Confining her anger and pain with thoughts of wrapping the woman at the shop in a cocoon of duct tape, Lindy tried not to jerk or yell about the loss of some of her hair.

Roberto had followed behind Michelle and pulled his nail clippers out his pocket to begin removing the tape from Lindy's wrists.

"What happened?" Michelle wadded up the tape and tossed it toward a trash can in the kitchen area.

"What do you think? I went back to the damn studio looking for you two. It was a trap."

As Roberto pulled the tape off, Lindy flexed her wrists and arms, getting movement back to them. "You shouldn't have gone there. I wanted you to stay at the hotel where you were safe."

"It's my fault," Roberto said. He put the clippers back in his pocket and put an arm around Michelle's shoulder. "I wanted to go, but she didn't want me to go alone. I didn't listen to her arguments. He had my paintings, and all I could see was the theft. I was angry." His eyes dropped to the floor as his face reflected the regret he felt.

Following Michelle and Roberto, Lindy walked over to the table and sat as she gazed around the space. "A bomb shelter and four cots. Looks like they were prepared for us. I assume they will try to get Colin next."

"Will he come looking for you?" Michelle asked.

"Tea?" Roberto offered at the same time.

Lindy turned her glance to the table where a teapot, two cups, and a plate of cookies sat. Her lips tugged to a bitter upturn. They had been having tea when she had been thrown into the shelter.

"Yes, to both of your questions. Tea would be welcome, and Colin will be looking for me." She leaned in close to Michelle so she could whisper, "Is this room bugged? Do you know?"

Michelle's eyes grow wider, and she shook her head as she answered under her breath, "Don't know."

Lindy sat back and cast her eyes around the space, looking for any possible cameras. She didn't see anything obvious, but with the little spy devices these days, one or two could be hidden. Best not to chance it.

Instead, she asked, "How long have you been here?"

"Maybe four or five hours," Roberto answered, setting a cup in front of her. "It's hard to tell. No clocks, no watch, nothing to give us a clue."

"Right," Lindy agreed. "It would have been about the time I realized you weren't at the hotel. We must have just missed you."

"You and Colin? He found you?" Roberto asked.

She nodded. "So what about food here? Do you have some?"

"We have bread and water," Michelle said and pointed to the shelves. "And cookies. The 'fridge is pretty empty, but we have a toaster oven. I don't know if they're going to bring us anything else. Or what they plan to do with us."

"I guess it depends on if they want Roberto to continue painting or if we're all liabilities. Since they brought us here, I am guessing whoever is in charge isn't sure of the plan yet."

"It was Marchant," Michelle said with a hiss in her voice. Her eyes blazed as she leaned closer. "He was at the studio when his two heavies grabbed us, and he directed Sasha to bring us to this place."

Lindy's blood raced as her niece confirmed Alain Merchant's direct involvement in their abduction. Not just involved, she amended, but probably in charge. "Damn. We pretty much played right into his hands, didn't we? I'll bet he knew we had a connection with Roberto, and his meeting up with us at the plaza was no coincidence."

"I gather the door is the only way out of this room," she whispered.

"As near as we can tell," Michelle replied, her voice as low as Lindy's. "We haven't checked behind everything, though, but..."

Lindy nodded. "It's possible there might be a way out." She would check out the whole area, including the ridiculously small bathroom, and any vents coming into the room. They had to have vents, didn't they? She couldn't just sit here and hope Colin and the police came to her rescue, especially when she was pretty sure the transmission from the tracker wasn't getting out of this bunker's walls.

She began with the bathroom, noted the tiny sink and old toilet. And the obvious fact it allowed very little room to even turn around. She saw a narrow vent above the toilet, almost to the ceiling. At barely the size of a legal mailing envelope, it wasn't big enough for any of them to get through it. She climbed up on the edges of the toilet to see if she could determine if the tube behind it was any bigger, but it was too dark to see more than a couple of feet. She did spot a glimmer of light coming from the side toward the kitchen area. Maybe it was another vent.

Jumping down, she washed her hands, then exited and went to the kitchen. The only thing in the area which might need venting was the small refrigerator. She looked around it and didn't see anything right off, but then something caught her eye. A section of the wall behind the appliance looked like it had been plastered over more recently than the rest of the room. She could just make out the uneven edges of an area about three feet square. Maybe it was an emergency tunnel from the bunker to the surface and the owner had sealed off. If it remained clear, they could use it to get out.

Straightening up, Lindy called Roberto over and opened the 'fridge to pretend to look in it. As the kids had said, there wasn't much in it. A little butter, a jar of already-opened jam, and a small container of cream. Well, at least they wanted them to have cream for their tea and instant coffee. As Roberto leaned in to look, she said, "Look behind this near the baseboard. Do you think it looks like a sealed opening?"

Then she took out the cream and went to the hot plate to heat the tea water again. As she went about the business of making another cup of tea, Roberto checked out the space and went back to the table to sit.

"It looks like it could be," he replied as she returned to the table.

"Can we get it open?"

"Maybe. There isn't a decent knife in the drawer here, just smooth-sided ones and they can't cut anything. I have the tiny knife blade in my clippers, but nothing else." He didn't sound too enthusiastic.

Lindy nodded. "We need to move the refrigerator out from

the wall a little to get behind it. If our watchers have any cameras within the room, I haven't spotted them. Do either of you see any possible places they might have placed one?"

"I've been through everything on the bookcase, and it's clean. Also, the food shelf. Nothing there either," Michelle said.

"I will check the beds now," Roberto volunteered. "I do not think anything is on them, but I will look carefully."

Lindy stood, then leaned forward with her hands on the table. "I'm going to just walk around the edge of the room looking for anything in the ceiling or corners suggesting it could be a camera. Michelle, check the counters and the refrigerator along the top and at the bottom in the vent. They may just be cocky enough to figure this bunker is so secure they don't have to worry about it, but I want to be sure."

As Lindy turned and began a slow circle of the room, looking at the ceiling and letting her eyes travel over every blank surface in the room, Michelle checked out the counters, opening drawers and cabinets, and running her fingers over the surfaces. Meanwhile, Roberto checked out the bed frames, even the mattresses and edges of the pillows.

Nothing adorned the walls in here, no clock or paintings or anything else giving the impression of anyone living in it. Nothing to actually hide a camera in. Perhaps they hadn't planned to take them, and they weren't set up for surveillance. And maybe they thought they didn't need it with the room seeming so secure.

Lindy motioned the others to the small refrigerator, where they worked together to slide it away from the wall. She squatted down and ran her fingers along the slight ridge she could barely detect.

"Try to cut through the wall here," she told Roberto,

showing him the very thin line. "I think if you can get it started, then it will be easier to follow the rest of it."

He nodded, pulled out the blade on his nail clippers, and started to try to dig the not-too-sharp point into it. He switched to the sharper point on the can opener blade to get the initial cut into it and rocked it back and forth several times to get a good gash into the wall.

"It looks like it is just a thin layer of plaster over a wooden panel," he said.

"Let's hope it's big enough to get through, and it leads to an emergency exit or venting tunnel," Lindy replied.

As Roberto worked at cutting around the panel, Lindy sat with Michelle at the dining table. She brought her niece up to date on what she and Colin had learned about Marchant's business and stealing Roberto's work. She didn't tell her they suspected other artists might be victims of the scam, and at this point, they didn't have proof.

Roberto slid out from behind the refrigerator, his right arm covered with tan plaster dust. Brushing it off, he grabbed a bottle of water from the shelf and came over to the table.

"Need a break," he said in a low voice and sipped at the water. "I have the first side and partway across the bottom of the panel cleared off. It looks like it will be about as big as you thought. We should be able to get through it if there is a passage behind it."

"I'll take over for a while," Lindy said, holding her hand out for the blade.

Roberto reached into his pocket, pulled it out, and pulled the dull, short blade out. "Good luck with it. It is only a little sharper than those knives they gave us. But it still managed to rip the plaster off the wall."

She grinned as her hand closed on it, then she sauntered to the opening behind the refrigerator, sat down on the floor, stuck the blade in the long slot of the opening Roberto had already done, and started sawing against it. She felt the plaster tearing – sawing wasn't the word. It took more muscle power than the actual blade to force it through the tiny crack between the wood and the concrete wall. After just a short time, she began to appreciate how much energy Roberto had expended in doing this.

She worked at it for about an hour to cover the way across the bottom, and her shoulders already ached with the effort. She turned the blade to go up the other side, poking and digging to try to get it started. Going up would definitely be harder than coming down or going across, she concluded. She pulled the bottle opener blade to get the pointed tip, ran her fingers up the slight bump to where she thought the top was, and began poking and digging with it to make a hole in the plaster.

She felt certain the very old plaster afforded the only reason they made any progress. She suspected it might be close to fifty or sixty years since the tunnel was closed off, and whoever owned the place just sealed it themselves. Once it was painted, no one would really notice the flaw in the wall.

Once she had the opening started, she went back to the larger, but duller blade to begin pushing it in and down the crevice. Like Roberto, her arms were covered with fine dust, and she could feel it on her face as she leaned close to see her work as she cut.

Muscles trembling with all the exertion, she paused, leaned her head against the wall, and closed her eyes. What seemed like only a few moments later, she felt someone touch her shoulder, and she turned to see Michelle's face right next to hers. Had she dozed off?

"Take a break, Aunt. Let Roberto work on it some more."

Lindy straightened and dragged to her feet, handed Roberto the clippers, and switched places with him. She pulled herself toward the table, stiffness and aches in all her joints accompanying her. Michelle brought her a bottle of water and a slice of toast with butter and jam.

"Any idea how long it's been?" she asked.

Michelle shook her head. "No. It feels like much longer than it probably is. It could be the middle of the night, or it could be morning. No way to tell. They'll kill us, won't they?"

"We can't be sure, but it certainly looks like it's their only option. They might try to persuade Roberto to continue painting for them by using us as leverage. Or they might just cut their losses. They have several paintings for Pablo de Sintra stored up. After all, he is an old man. He could stop at any time or even die."

"What about Colin?" Michelle asked. "He's looking for us, right?"

She nodded. "And it seems they haven't nabbed him yet. But we're a long way from Lisbon. I don't know if he was able to follow me."

"You knew we'd been taken when you went to the studio again, didn't you?" Michelle's eyes grew wider as she began to piece it together.

"It was the only thing that made sense," Lindy answered. "We figured they had to have something to do with the two of you vanishing. So I went into the studio with hopes to get some clues. I saw your bird pendant on the floor there, and I knew. I had to let them grab me to find you. Colin was watching me from a distance. But he might have lost the car before we got this far."

"He'll still be looking," Michelle said. Her eyes held hope.

A sharp curse in Spanish and a scuffle of noise came from the 'fridge area, and Roberto sprang to his feet, his hand bleeding.

"What happened?" Michelle asked as he went to the counter to grab a paper towel to wipe it, then wrapped more sheets around it.

"I caught it on a sharp edge," he muttered. He sat down and put pressure on the wound. "It may be a lock or clasp of some sort."

"Let me see," Michelle demanded and reached for Roberto's hand.

He pulled it back. "It's nothing, *carita*. Just a little cut, but it bleeds quite a bit."

"We don't have anything to wrap it with unless I can salvage some of the duct tape to hold more of the paper towels on," Lindy said as she went to the trash can and began digging through the pieces they had pulled off. She found a large enough piece to make a couple of strips of one-inch-wide tape.

Meanwhile, Michelle got another paper towel and folded it into a bandage. In a short time, they crafted a make-shift bandage for Roberto's hand, cleaned up the cut, which was not serious, and wrapped it.

Then, they turned their attention to the door behind the refrigerator.

Chapter 23

☙ Michelle ❧

Michelle watched her aunt go back to working at the opening as she looked for the latch where Roberto cut his hand. She marveled at the older woman's resilience and calm in this situation. Her stomach churned, and she couldn't help thinking about the likelihood of a bad outcome if they couldn't escape. While she hoped Colin had managed to follow her aunt, she also worried he might be coming alone, and he, too, would be captured. Then who would look for them?

If she or Lindy didn't call her father in a couple of days, he would be alarmed and begin searching for them, but would there be any way to trace them? She feared not. And if Marchant had them killed, it would be unlikely their bodies would be found any time soon. Their only real hope meant getting out of this room and finding help nearby. She didn't want to consider how unlikely the scenario looked.

She heard Lindy grunt, then a thunk-like sound, and a scrape of metal. She took a few steps closer to the 'fridge in the hope of seeing something other than her aunt's back. The scent of moist dirt filtered into the room, along with a slight stir of air.

Lindy sat back and cast a crooked smile at her. "We have a passage of some sort behind this door. From what I can tell so far, the area just beyond it is like a culvert, although there is concrete right next to the basement."

Roberto came up behind Michelle and peered over her shoulder. "Can you see a light at the end?"

"No, it may be dark outside or even a cover at the other end," Lindy answered, sliding back and getting to her feet. "Do we have any kind of a flashlight?"

"I always used my phone," Michelle said. "But they took it."

"Same here," Roberto replied. "But I saw some candles in a drawer under the counter. They're not big, just little church ones you put out for prayers."

"Get them," Lindy ordered as she pulled out the matchbook she'd spotted in the drawer. "At least, they left us matches to light them."

Roberto handed her four of the votive-sized candles, which she stuck in her front pants pockets. She took off her neck scarf and tied it around her hair. Then she grabbed a butter knife and added it to her pocket. "Okay, I'm going to crawl through the tunnel to the end to see if I can get out. You two stay here and keep watch. If anyone starts to come into the room, shove the refrigerator back against the wall and tell them I am in the bathroom. Stall as long as you can."

"Be careful, Aunt Lindy," Michelle said and hugged her briefly before Lindy got to her knees and crawled back into the darkness.

Lingering by the refrigerator, she watched as a candle burst to light, then the flickering began moving down the tunnel and out of sight. Michelle turned and slid an arm around Roberto's waist. Automatically, he laid a protective arm over her shoulders and hugged her to him.

"I hope my aunt finds a way out," Michelle mumbled. She didn't want to admit she was frightened, but the fear sat in the middle of her belly, reminding her she and Roberto had gotten themselves and her aunt into a serious situation. Still, she tried to remain hopeful. If Lindy didn't come back, then they would both try to get out the same way.

"So far, our captors have left us alone," Roberto remarked.

"Yeah, not even bothering to talk to us or to bring any food," Michelle agreed. "We have enough bread to last a couple of days, I guess. That probably means they will be back within twenty-four hours, don't you think?"

"It's probably night," Roberto said. "They won't come tonight. The best thing to do now is to try to get some sleep. Your aunt will either make it out or come back. There's nothing more we can do to help her."

"One of us should stay awake," Michelle said. "If someone comes, we need to hide the opening behind the refrigerator."

He glanced back at the clearly out of place object, then said, "You sleep first. I'll keep watch."

She gave his waist a squeeze. "Wake me if anything happens."

With the worries and fears, she didn't think she would fall asleep easily, but she stretched out on one of the beds and pulled the light blanket over her. Roberto turned off half the lights in the room, so only the kitchen area was lit. She turned her back toward it. As she ran the problems though her mind like a litany, she dropped off the sleep.

The sound of a chair moving woke her a little while later. She sat up, her head groggy as she focused in on the room. She'd hoped the whole kidnapping had been a nightmare. Roberto sat backward in the chair, arms resting across the top as he watched the door. He must have slid it causing the noise.

"Is anything happening?" she asked in a low voice.

"No. I don't think so. I thought I heard someone outside the door, a man's voice talking loudly. But I couldn't hear what he said."

She slipped out of bed and crossed to join him, squatting down by the chair. "Do you think he's coming in here?"

He shrugged. "I don't know. I have not heard anything else. He may be talking to someone, but he's not near the door."

For the next few minutes, they remained as they were and listened for any noises coming from outside. It seemed as quiet as it had been since their abductors had brought her aunt into the room.

Suddenly, scuffling noises and shouts rose up outside.

Michelle sprang to her feet and dashed to the refrigerator to follow her aunt's orders. Roberto came right behind her, and together, they shoved the appliance back up against the wall.

More shouting and sounds of activity continued as they fled to the sofa in the room and sat facing the wall as if they had been there all night as they waited for the door to open.

A burst of something sounding like automatic gunfire came from outside the door. Roberto yanked Michelle to him. Her heart pounded as she pressed against his chest, she could feel Roberto's racing as well.

What was happening out there? Were they coming for them now?

Then the sound of clanks as the locks on the door slid back. With a creaking sound, the door started to open. Michelle caught her breath.

Chapter 24

∝ Lindy ∞

As Lindy crawled into the narrow tunnel, she paused to pull out one of the candles and struck a match, lighting the wick. A dim light illuminated the area just in front of her so she could see about three feet ahead.

Bugs scrambled from the light, heading to hiding places. She gave them a few moments before she began advancing down the space. As near as she could tell, the tunnel had been shoveled out, long uneven streaks in the clay-like dirt suggesting it had been a painstaking process for whoever had done it. But the bottom was reasonably flat and not too difficult to crawl across.

As an escape tunnel from the barn, it hadn't been wide or tall, but a pure emergency exit. She had no idea how far it extended or which way it went, but Lindy shoved ahead and hoped the air was not limited, and the end wasn't sealed.

After what seemed like hours of crawling, but was only about fifteen minutes, she paused to catch her breath and get off her knees for a few minutes by sitting and stretching her legs out. She shifted her shoulders and stretched her arms as much as she could. Lighting the second candle, she snuffed out the little bit left of the first one and set it in the ground. If one candle lasted only a little over fifteen minutes, then she only had enough light for an hour. Would it be enough?

She could crawl in the dark, but she was reluctant to do it. Any small creatures in the tunnel scuttled away from the light, and she didn't want to meet them by crunching them with her knees. She pressed on, now and then pushing a cobweb aside with the butter knife she'd brought with her. Not much of a weapon, but still useful.

As the second candle began to sputter out at fifteen or so minutes farther on, she paused for another rest and leaned against the wall, rubbing her thighs and calves against the strain of the long crawl. She worried about what might be happening back in the secure room. Were the kids safe? She gazed back the direction she'd come, seeing just a glimmer of the light from the room beyond, so she knew they had not closed off the entrance.

Lighting the third candle, she resumed crawling, her body moving slower now. She grew tired and thirsty, sweating from the effort. How far had she come? Five hundred yards? Six hundred? Where did the tunnel lead?

She shuffled her knees along another ten or so minutes when she glimpsed a wooden barrier at what looked like the end of the tunnel. Encouraged, she picked up her pace, ignoring the aches and pains in her knees and a cramp in her right calf. She would welcome a long soak in a hot tub after this. With the candle almost to its end, she came to the structure she'd seen. A square door about the same size as the tunnel blocked the end of it.

As the candle flickered out, Lindy leaned against the wood and listened for any sounds coming from the other side. Nothing. No voices, no noises of any sort. What was on the other side? She ran her fingers over the wood, catching a splinter and jerked her hand back. Bending her head down, she attempted to pull it out with her teeth.

She managed to grip it, but it broke before she could remove it, so she had to suck it up and leave it in for now. She found a loose piece of the wood and pulled at it until she managed to get a lengthy section off. It felt dry to her touch. She pulled out her last candle, lit it, and examined the piece of wood. About eight inches long and an inch wide by a half-inch thick, it looked like it might burn. She used the candle to get the end flaming, then extinguished the candle to save it for later.

Holding her makeshift torch up, she examined the door looking for a way to open it. Hinges held it to a wooden frame on one side, and they looked old and rusty. She tried the butter knife to pry them loose. While she felt some give, they wouldn't yield enough. She shoved against the boards, using her shoulders, but not getting adequate leverage to apply enough strength to it.

She set her torch into the dirt and worked her body around so she could kick the door, then levered herself up on her elbows, lifting her hips, and kicked as hard as she could. The first blow cracked one of the boards, so she targeted it with the second and third kicks. The wood broke, but she couldn't see anything through the gap in the wood. She leaned close, hoping her eyes might adjust to whatever light might be there. She felt air moving on the other side and breathed it in. Whatever waited ahead, at least, it had an open space with air.

After a few moments, she resumed kicking, tackling the next slat, and kicking until she broke it. By the time she broke the third slat out, the others had begun to tilt and shift in the frame allowing her to remove them with little effort.

Lifting the wooden torch, which had now burned half-way

down, she held it out in the space beyond the door and tried to see what might be in it. She saw the outline of a machine, maybe a tractor. She could smell manure and hay.

Shoving her head through the opening, she saw the sky overhead and could feel the dampness of moisture in the air. She hauled herself the rest of the way through and looked around as her eyes adjusted to the available light. The tractor sat in a row of a plowed field about five feet from her. She glanced behind her to see the raised bubble of ground, which hid the tunnel's entrance. Beyond it, the barn and the farmhouse sat in a straight line from it. She had traveled about a thousand yards from the bomb shelter under the barn.

Now, she had to stay out of sight and make it to the long line of bushes flanked the house on the right. From there, she could use them for cover while she worked her way to the road.

She bent low, and ran across the field, hoping no one was looking this direction. She made it to the edge of the bushes and started to work her way into them when one of the men burst out of the back door, slamming it behind him. Peeking through a break in the bushes, she saw him coming her way in a run, and she crouched lower, working her way into the bushes as much as possible.

Lindy considered stopping and holding as still as possible, but the thrashing of the bushes at the other end persuaded her the man wouldn't hesitate to tear the entire row of bushes out to find her.

She moved on, picking her way through as quickly as possible. Branches slapped her in the face, thorns pricked at her arms, and she kept going. She could hear him moving closer, as oblivious to the resistant bushes as she was.

As she came near the end of the driveway, she burst out of

the bushes and ran for the dirt road, her feet flying as fast as they could down it. She didn't have to look back to know he was right behind her. She heard his shoes hitting the dirt and could tell he was gaining on her.

Abruptly, something hit her, and she stumbled, falling to the ground as his arms locked around her thighs. As she face-planted in the dirt, she realized he'd tackled her. She tried to flip over to face him, her hands fisted and pounding at him, barely making any contact.

It was Javier, a man much heavier than she was. In fury and desperation, she struggled to hold up against him. He grabbed for her hands, catching both at the wrists with one hand, leaving the other free to slap her hard.

"Stop fighting," he growled, "or I will punch you senseless."

In response, she tried to head butt him but came up short. He flipped her over in the dirt, pulling her hands behind her and snapped a plastic band around them, tightening it to lock her down. Then he yanked her up and hit her in the jaw, sending her head in a jerk to the left.

As he pulled back his hand to deliver another hard punch, a man's voice said, "Hit her again, and I'll kill you."

A British voice. Colin. Lindy couldn't believe it. Down the road, four more men clambered out of darkened cars and came running toward them.

"Stand down," one of them yelled in Portuguese. Lindy couldn't make out the rest of what he said, but Javier released her and rose to his feet, raising his hands over his head. As the officer cuffed Javier, Lindy rolled out of the way and sat up just as Colin stepped around them and rushed to her side.

"Are you all right?" he asked, slipping his arm around her

waist to help her to her feet.

"I think so," she managed to say though the pain in her jaw. "Bruised. Am I bleeding?"

Colin carefully took her face in his hands to examine her face and nodded. "Just a little. You have a split lip. You're probably tasting the blood. That jerk really clipped you in the jaw."

She started to react, then remembered and grasped the front of Colin's shirt as she said, "Michelle and Roberto are in the basement, a bomb shelter below the barn. They're locked in. We need to get them out. Hurry."

"It's okay. Calm down. We'll get them." He motioned to the other men, who now pulled in around them. One of them asked her about the basement. Another handed her a bottle of water and a cloth to wipe her face. Taking a sip, she told them everything about the shelter and the guards around it.

"Keep her here," one man told Colin, then the four of them headed toward the farmhouse first.

"No, they need to get the kids," Lindy objected, trying to pull Colin toward the barn.

"Hold on a minute, Lindy." He resisted her pull. "Let the officers handle this. They'll get them out as soon as they clear the house. The best thing we can do now is to wait."

"I can't just stand here and watch," she objected.

Colin wrapped his arms around her, holding her back as she tried to move forward. "They're safe in the shelter for now. They'll get them out in a few minutes."

"What happened to you? I was afraid you wouldn't come."

He squeezed her. "I lost your signal once you got here, so I pulled the car up and waited for the police to arrive. Then we weren't sure where you were until I saw you running toward the bushes. I was above the house on the road."

She fought her tears. "I thought you'd lost my signal and had no idea where I was."

His voice broke a little as he admitted, "I was worried, too. There's another house farther up the road and one across the street. I didn't know which one you'd been taken to, and I couldn't go barging in alone. Waiting for the police to get here was hell."

As he finished saying this, one of the officers came out with a man between them, guiding him toward the road as the other three officers headed for the barn.

Lindy recognized the man as he passed her; the suave guy who'd brought her out, the one she'd called Dapper-man.

He leered at her as he passed, but the officer herding him shoved him onward.

Colin pulled out a tissue from a pocket pack and began wiping Lindy's cut lip to get the fresh blood off. She watched his eyes as they darted across her face accessing her for any other damage.

"How bad is it?"

His lips curved up in a hint of a smile. "Not too bad, gorgeous. You're already getting some swelling and the start of a nasty bruise on your jaw. We'll need to get you checked out after this is over."

"Great. Now, can we get closer to the barn and the action? I want to be there when Michelle comes out." She tugged at his arm, ready to break away from him if he held her back again.

But he yielded this time, and they set a brisk pace back up the dirt lane. As she strode with Colin, his right arm around her shoulder, Lindy thought her brother would be very cross with her for this fiasco. But how could she know a young street artist in Spain would lead them into such a twisted adventure? Once more, she was grateful for having met Colin. If he hadn't come to her aid, who knows what kind of bad ending this might have had?

They stopped right outside the barn door, uncertain what the status was inside. The officers had gone in. Behind them, another vehicle, a police one, pulled onto the dirt road, sped up it, and halted just a few feet from the barn. Two more officers jumped out of it and ran into the barn. One paused long enough to tell them to stay back.

Itching to get inside and see what was happening, Lindy still feared the men guarding the shelter might try to take Michelle and Roberto hostage. This whole thing could still go sideways. She fidgeted, paced, then just couldn't stand back any longer.

She ran into the barn, heading back to the elevator at the back. Behind her, she heard Colin break into a run to come after her.

"Lindy. Wait! What are you doing? There's still danger."

She dashed into the elevator and hit the down button, the doors closing just before Colin reached it. "Sorry. I have to do this," she called out as they shut.

As the door opened, Lindy peered out before jumping out into the hall leading to the underground shelter. It looked clear, although she spotted the back of one of the officers at the corner. From his stance, she guessed he had his weapon out, ready to fire if needed. She dashed across to the wall and began working her way to the corner as quietly as possible. Before she even reached it, a pair of popping sounds erupted, echoing from the hall. Gunshots followed the noise, and she feared someone was blowing the place up.

Logic would have told her to run back the way she'd come, but she wasn't listening to her inner voice as she ran to the corner. The officer she'd seen had already dashed into the hallway in front of the shelter. As she came around the corner, she ran into a hall filled with smoke.

Coughing and eyes burning, she backtracked to the corner and almost ran into Colin as he hauled her into his arms. She pointed back to the corridor behind her and choked out, "Smoke. Lots of it."

He pulled her close to him as the shouts, more gunfire, and scuffling noises boomed from the hallway. She pointed to the opposite side of the wall facing the corridor. "Let's go over there, just to the edge, where we can see."

She yanked him toward it, his steps still reluctant to get close to the action, but moving anyway. From the edge, they could get a view of what was going on. For the most part, she saw smoke and the police wearing gas masks as they seemed to be throwing someone on the concrete floor while another man was shoved up against the wall. In a few minutes, the smoke began dissipating, and Lindy could see more clearly.

The officers had subdued and cuffed the men, pulling them to their feet. To her eyes, it appeared the door to the shelter was still closed as one of the officers scouted around the area, maybe looking for the key. Lindy started walking forward, aware she was going into an area she probably shouldn't, but she wanted to be there when they opened the door. One of the police told her not to enter the area, but she continued forward. Colin stayed a step or two behind her.

The officer in charge came over, planting himself in front of her. "Please go back, ma'am. This is still an active police zone, and I asked you to wait."

Tilting her head up to meet his steely stare with one of her own. "My niece in that room, frightened, and probably even more so after all this noise out here. I want my face to be the one she sees when the door opens. I won't interfere with your arrests, but I need to be there."

The officer glanced over her head to Colin behind her, then looked at her, his expression stern.

"You wait here. Do not go any farther until we get these men out of here and secure the area. Then I will call you forward before we open the door. This is the best I can do." His voice was firm, his mouth set in a stubborn line, but Lindy saw a hint of compassion in his eyes. She nodded her agreement and stepped back to stand with Colin.

While it seemed like a long time for them to get the two men out of the corridor and to make sure everything in the area was secure, only ten minutes elapsed before the captain motioned for her to come to the door.

A specialist checked the lock to make sure no explosives were hidden in it, then he opened the door. Taking a deep breath and putting a big smile on her face, she stepped into the room to greet her niece.

Michelle and Roberto stood in the kitchen area, and Lindy saw the refrigerator had been shoved back to the wall. As soon as they saw her, relief washed across their faces, and Michelle broke into a grin as she ran into her arms for a deep, grateful hug. Both of them dissolved into tears of relief as Roberto followed Michelle at a more restrained pace.

Out of the corner of her eye, Lindy saw Colin step into the room, moving a few feet around her. He held out a hand to the young artist and pulled him into an affectionate embrace. The nightmare had ended, but where was Marchant?

Chapter 25
ଓ Michelle ଓ

Sitting in an outdoor café in Marbella, Michelle sipped her sangria as she and Roberto shared a last "date" before she would be returning to South Carolina. She flipped a strand of hair from her face as she smiled at her friend.

He leaned back in his chair, watching her as if he was memorizing every detail of her face. His eyes showed amusement, but his mouth suggested something much more, a provocative smirk on his lips.

"You have plenty of photos and paintings to remember me by," she complained. "I need a few of you. So, I think we should do a photoshoot this afternoon with you as the subject."

"And some together as well. Selfies, yes?"

"Absolutely, yes."

His eyes twinkled at the prospect. For today, he'd not set up his street shop to sell paintings but had decided to spend the whole day with her. They'd walked the marketplace earlier with Michelle doing some last-minute gift hunting for friends and family back home.

The past two weeks had been hectic at times, with the police investigation in Portugal holding them there for another few days after their harrowing kidnapping. Her father had come unglued and threatened to fly over and bring her home immediately, but Aunt Lindy had finally calmed him down.

She and Roberto had given their statements, and he'd made his claim for the stolen paintings. While it had gone well enough. It had all taken time. On the plus side, Roberto found his paintings were worth a lot more than he'd been selling them for, although they were now known as the Pablo di Sintra Alias paintings. The story of the theft and illegal marketing of his paintings had made quite a splash in the art world.

He'd found himself the subject of a small amount of fame with interviews, television news, and a few galleries courting his work. In the meantime, he still sold some of his work from his street stall until the madness settled down when he could make some informed decisions about his future.

As for Michelle, she would be heading back home and on to college. She had a beautiful portfolio of photos taken by Roberto plus two paintings to take home. But she dreaded leaving him. So, this day together had a bittersweet feel to it.

After they finished their drinks, they walked down to the beach. Every time the scenery changed a little, whether it was the ocean or the charming café backdrops along the way, Michelle took a photo of Roberto... sometimes several when he was acting silly and making faces at her while she took them. She'd pulled out her small digital camera rather than loading up her phone with images. She didn't have much memory in it, and she wanted tons of photos.

"Now what?" she asked Roberto as he put an arm around her shoulders while hers wrapped around his middle. "What will you do?"

"I am not sure. I have many offers to display my work in galleries, and I am already getting bids for a few of the paintings. The police say they will track down the ones sold falsely." His eyes drifted to the Mediterranean, looking out into the distance where a cruise ship headed north toward Barcelona. "But those people were duped by Merchant, and I do not feel it is fair to take the paintings from them."

"I agree with your point. Only it's not fair to you that they bear another person's signature."

He shrugged. "Perhaps I will ask to have them returned so I can change the signature then return them." An amused smile bloomed on his lips. "It would be good, yes?"

They turned back toward the town after about a half-mile of beach strolling and worked their way back up the hillside to a garden set on a cliff looking down on the white-washed buildings. With the deep variegated colors of the sea beyond, it was a picture-perfect spot. Here, they drew close together, arms encircling each other, and Roberto took the camera to use his longer reach to get a selfie… and another… and another, until they had one they both thought looked good.

The café served tapas, so they ordered an assortment and enjoyed sampling the various flavors of the Spanish dishes. Roberto critiqued them more than Michelle, but in the end, they decided they were quite good.

"We should come back," Roberto pronounced then realized what he'd said. *She* couldn't come back with him. "Ay. I am sorry. It has been easy to forget you are leaving tomorrow."

Her heart had dipped when he said it, all the joy she'd felt at the moment dimming. Her lips shifted into a sad line. "It's all right. I had almost forgotten, too. I wish we could just make this day go on and on."

Her aunt had warned her about summer romances on foreign shores. She'd thought she had the right mindset but look at her now. A gorgeous, talented guy who cares about her, and she has to say goodbye. With over three thousand miles separating them, living on separate continents, how would she douse the fire of her feelings for him?

"I do, also. But we will remain friends, Michelle. This is not forever. We can talk on the computer, and if things work out with my art, I might one day come to America. You might come back here. We do not have to say farewell forever." He leaned across to press a hand to the side of her face, caressing it with tenderness. "I will never forget you, *carita*. I do not see a future without you in it in some way."

Tears gathered at the corners of her eyes. She wanted to stay so badly, to be with him for many more days. Maybe she could change her college and go to school in Madrid. At least, it would be closer.

His mouth moved towards hers, coming in for a kiss. Michelle lifted her head, ready to meet his lips, sighing as they touched. She wound her arms around his neck, diving into the depths of the kiss. Warmth spread through her, dipping toward her core, signaling her desire for so much more.

As he pulled his mouth away, he whispered, "You are so beautiful, *carita*. I want you so much, but I will wait for you."

In a way, she was relieved but also disappointed. She didn't know if she could have resisted him if he'd pressed for more, but he'd taken the decision away from her.

They left the restaurant and made their way to the garden area where they sat and gazed out toward the sea as the sun dipped behind the mountains to the southwest and cast an array of golden red shades across the sky, and they reflected in the waters. Even this far into summer, the lights lingered a long time as the young lovers sat with their knees pulled up and arms wrapped around each other to enjoy one last idyllic evening.

Michelle's head rested on Roberto's shoulder as his left hand rubbed at her knees in a soothing circle. This was perfection in her mind. She lifted her camera and took a selfie as he laid his head against her for the shot.

"I'll remember this moment forever," she whispered.

Content to just be, they didn't move again until after the last wisps of color left the sky, and the first stars began to appear in the night sky.

☙ *Lindy* ❧

As she lounged by the hotel pool, Lindy stretched her long legs out and let the sun's rays warm her body. The pool had been a little chillier than she liked, but refreshing nonetheless. On the lounger next to her, Colin stretched out as well, a light shirt barely wrapped around his torso to help prevent sunburn. The afternoon swim had been inspired, leaving them both relaxed and a bit drowsy after the excitement of the Portuguese excursion.

Marchant had been apprehended trying to flee Spain with a half-dozen faked paintings. Roberto hadn't been the only artist he'd bought work from then peddled under a different name. Some were worth even more than their budding young Picasso's, but with Colin's help, the real paintings were now in the capable hands of an agent who specialized in placing artworks in quality galleries for sale and display.

Lindy's jaw still had a slight tinge of greenish color from the bruise had mostly faded. Her muscles and bones ached a little from the fight, but it was minor. Every day, she thanked her lucky stars she had met Colin on this trip. And he'd come through when she needed him. They had another couple of days together here in Marbella before he needed to get back on the job, back to scouting locations and making deals with local agencies for their use.

"Sure you don't want to come scouting with me?" he asked for the third time as he rolled onto his stomach to let the sun dry his back. The shirt he'd put on looked soaked. "It would be fun. No kidnapping. I promise."

She chuckled a low sultry sound. "I don't know. One attempt in Morocco, a near success in Lisbon. I don't think I want to tempt fate a third time."

"You're not saying those are my fault, are you?" He sounded indignant.

"No, of course not. But I did happen to be with you each time."

He turned his head to her. "May I remind you, my dear, I was not the catalyst for those events. They all seemed to have stemmed from young Roberto of the golden brush."

A laugh escaped her lips before she could stifle it. "True. From the least likely person to be caught up in one of the strangest art appropriation schemes I've ever seen."

She closed her eyes. One thing still niggled at her mind- the man who'd attempted to grab her in the Kasbah. Did he fit into this plot as well? She tried to picture him, but she hadn't seen his face with enough definition. But his height and build... "Colin, I think the man in Morocco could have been the same as the man who grabbed me in Lisbon."

"What?" He hadn't followed her thoughts.

"The guy I called Dapper-man. He worked for Marchant's gallery. Could they have been on to me even then?"

He lifted his head to gaze at her. "It's possible, I guess. But he's been arrested with the others. Either way, you're safe."

"I am, but I would like to have my necklace back." She frowned and wondered if she could have the police in Lisbon check on it. She leaned back again, musing on the thought for a while.

"Well, if you aren't coming with me, where are you heading next?" Colin asked after a minute or so of silence.

She closed her eyes and thought about it. "Mmm, Paris, I think. Then probably back to my place in Chelsea."

Colin let out a low whistle. "You have a flat in Chelsea?"

"No. I own a home there."

He sat up and gawked at her. "Apparently, you're not a starving artist."

"I never said I was," she answered. "You just assumed it. And before you ask, I inherited the house from my great-grandmother twenty-five years ago."

"Well, la-ti-da. Tell you what, you can buy my dinner for a change."

Taken a little aback, Lindy grinned nonetheless. "Glad to treat a poor man to a meal."

"Poor may be right," he replied. "I appear to have misplaced my wallet."

Laughing, she reached into her pool bag and pulled out the missing item. "You left it lying on the bar when you bought the drinks, love."

He breathed a sigh of relief and took the wallet. "Well, now it appears I can buy you dinner after all."

She shook her head. "No, let me get it tonight. I know a place."

Three hours later, they sat down at an indoor table at an upscale restaurant on the *Plaza de los Naranjos* to enjoy an exquisite meal with one of the finest chefs in Spain.

"How did you swing this?" Colin asked in a loud whisper.

"I have contacts," she answered smugly. "I keep saying you underestimate me."

After they ordered an appetizer and drinks, they took a few moments to truly enjoy the beauty within the tastefully decorated building. High arches broke the room into separate dining areas, and colorful paintings of the city hung sparsely on the walls, so they didn't overwhelm the room.

Colin reached across the table to catch Lindy's left hand in his. "I really wish you'd change your mind about coming with me."

"Colin, I appreciate the offer. Believe it or not, I have my own work to do and fabulous art studios in both Paris and London. I can't do it out of hotel rooms while you're working."

With a touch of sadness in his smile, he squeezed her hand. "I guess we're both heading in different directions, aren't we? But we can keep in touch for now. This job I'm working will end in a month or so, and I'll be back in London. We can get together then if you like."

Lindy's eyes sparked at the suggestion. "I would love it, Colin." She'd been worried that she might not see him again. Not since a wild fling with a musician, almost ten years earlier had she found a man she wanted to be with more. She could almost imagine a future with Colin, but she wasn't there yet.

Tomorrow, Lindy would drive her niece back to Madrid for their last night together in Spain. The next day, Michelle would board her flight home while Lindy would take the train to Paris. Both of them would be leaving behind the men who had captured their hearts for the few weeks they'd been here. Not just a summer fling with Colin, she'd found a man who would stand by her when the going got rough. He was someone worth hanging on to.

After an exceptional dinner, they strolled out onto the square, working their way through the shops and cafés, enjoying the enticing scent of the orange trees sweetening the evening air. Block by block, they worked their way to the beach. Colin wrapped an arm around her, hooking her to him as she leaned into his embrace and wrapped an arm around his waist. He took moments to drop little kisses on her forehead, her eyelids, her cheeks, in a drawn-out tease as they strolled.

Ahead the last vestiges of the golden sunset danced in the gentle waves rolling onto the beach. Pausing, they removed their shoes, and Colin rolled up his slacks, then they resumed their leisurely stroll, his head resting against hers, along the edge of the beach where the water could lick at their ankles.

As they strolled, Colin's kisses finally landed on her lips, and the teasing touches shifted to passionate kisses demanding more. An inferno fired up in her core as they turned toward her hotel. Desire danced between her legs while her breasts tightened in anticipation as the kisses, deep and demanding offset by gentle and enticing, accompanied them all the way back and up the stairs.

They burst into the living room area, barely getting through the door before she tore at the buttons on Colin's shirt while he slipped his hands under her blouse to push it up. Shoving his shirt back, she ran her hands over his toned muscular chest, admiring his fit torso and teasing at the dimples just where his waist met his hips. Maybe a touch of fat there, but also a bit ticklish as he sucked his stomach in and twitched back from her fingers.

But then what was he doing to her breasts? His fingers danced lightly around one as his tongue licked the other. Sucking in a breath, she moaned with the feeling she would burst at any moment. Colin lifted her into a bridal carry to take her into the bedroom. Dropping her on the bed, he fell across her, his right hand struggling to unzip her pants while he levered himself up.

In return, Lindy worked to remove his slacks, her nimbler fingers getting a grip on the zipper and yanking it down. She could feel his erection, hard and demanding, pushing against her hand as she shoved his pants, underwear and all, down his hips.

A moment later, Colin succeeded in getting her pants off also, leaving her with just her skimpy thong to guard against his assault. Now, he slowed down to a slower tease, making her squirm as he paid special attention to her breasts and allowed one finger to rub against her panties at just the right spot.

Out of habit, Lindy reached to the lamp and turned it off as she wriggled with her growing eagerness. Colin's fingers and mouth explored her whole body, working up one leg, rubbing her thighs, then his mouth planted kisses across her abdomen, just above the thong line. She sucked her breath in with a gasp, sliding under him more. Rising up on his left arm, he reached across to turn the light back on.

"What? Why?" she asked in confusion.

"Because I want to see every beautiful inch of you, love." His eyes gleamed as he settled back to his task. "I want to give you a night you'll long to repeat in London."

Slipping out of her bed the next morning, Lindy pulled on

her robe and padded to the living room. She noted Michelle's door was closed, suggesting her niece had returned at some point during the night. She stepped out onto the little balcony that faced the sea and leaned against the door frame to watch the swell of the waves caressing the shore as the first glimmer of dawn began to lighten the night sky.

Along with the exquisite thoughts of the wonderful affair she'd had with Colin, a bit of sadness touched her, making her smile seem more wistful than joyous. This holiday had been like none other she'd ever experienced.

Soft footsteps sounded behind her, and she turned to face Michelle, who'd come out barefoot and in her short pajamas. She stopped by Lindy, leaning her head against her shoulder as she gazed at the sea.

"I don't want to go."

"I understand." Lindy shared the melancholy Michelle felt at this moment. She slid an arm around her niece's shoulders and hugged her. "It's a hard parting. I assume you'll be keeping in touch."

"Uh-huh. Hoping our paths cross again in the future. What about Colin?"

"The same. If it's meant to be, it will happen, my sweet girl. No matter what, we've both met extraordinary men here, and we've had an amazing adventure linking us all together."

"Nearly got us killed, you mean," Michelle said with a small smile.

"There is that. But it will bond us in ways you can't even imagine. What a wonderful holiday we've had." Squeezing Michelle even closer, she planted a loving kiss on her niece's cheek.

As she turned back to the room to begin getting ready to

leave, Lindy considered this the best holiday she'd ever taken in spite of the danger and intrigue. They had found an idyllic interlude in their lives along with a promising-chance at a beautiful future.

The End

Thank you for reading *Signature of a Soul*.

I hope you enjoyed reading the novel as much as I loved writing it. If you liked the book, I hope you will consider leaving your honest review at Amazon.. Reviews are important to both the writer and other readers. Whether short or long, thumbs up or thumbs down, they are deeply appreciated.

About the Author

Riona Kelly...

...comes from the southwestern United States, where she was raised until 21, then she migrated to California. She lived there for several years before moving back east all the way to Las Vegas, Nevada, and eventually moved north to the foothills of the Sierra Nevada Mountains. She enjoys painting, drawing, music, and living an uncomplicated life while serving the needs of her feline companions. She's a fan of figure skating and switched from roller skating to ice skating for fun. Writing is a passion so like it or not, expect more books.

 For more about Riona Kelly's books, visit her web site and sign up for her mailing list if you want to keep informed of upcoming books. She loves to hear from her readers, so drop into the Facebook page if you have comments or email her at: RionaKelly.author@gmail.com

Website

Facebook Page

http://www.RionaKelly.online
https://www.facebook.com/rionakellywrites

Amazon Author Page: https://www.amazon.com/~/e/B08541V2JB

Other Books by Riona Kelly

Bitter Vintage

A sudden death and a daughter's return yield a bitter harvest.

When Philip Claremont, the heir to the family vineyards in Northern California, is killed in an accident, his sister, Martinique, returns home for the funeral. She finds her father reclusive, her estranged half-sister in residence, and a mysterious person skulking around the property.

At the funeral, she encounters her brother's best friend and is reminded of her own close friendship with him. Like her, he has questions about Philip's death. Determined to get to the truth, Marti decides to stay and investigate.

As Marti begins piecing the information together, a story she never expected unfolds, placing her in danger. Will she be the next to die?

"Bitter Vintage" brings the suspense of treachery, greed and ambition along with romance and betrayal as the story unfolds against the California vineyards of the Napa-Sonoma region and the migrant workers' struggle for fair wages in 1964.

Echoes of the Past

A picture-perfect morning. A dead woman washes onto the beach.

Kathleen's summer research trip to Wales turns upside down in that horrible moment when she finds the body. Without warning, the intrigue surrounding the victim sucks her into an eddy of unanswered questions. Who was she? How did she come to be washed ashore? Was it murder?

That night, an enigmatic stranger arrives at her hotel, and with a brief encounter, he sets her trouble radar on alert. A man to be avoided. Only he seems to go out of his way to find her as their paths continue to cross. The more Kathleen tries to pull away, the more fate shoves her closer.

Through her growing fears, Kathleen wonders if she is tangled in a mystery that might endanger her life, but she doesn't anticipate the possibility of death.

The first book in a series of international suspense romance novels, *Echoes of the Past* is set in present-day North Wales with *An American Rose Abroad*.

Enjoy these other novels ...

from Pynhavyn Press

Funeral Singer Series – Paranormal/ Urban Fantasy

By Lillian I Wolfe

Music is a passion for Gillian Foster, a struggling musician with dreams of success. When an accident bestows a paranormal talent, her whole life takes an unexpected turn. Getting gigs as a funeral singer, she finds her conscious-self transported to an interim cemetery where she can speak to the recently departed while she is singing. She feels compelled to help the spirit complete any unfinished business.

But more than departed spirits haunt the transitional plane and they pose a threat to not only the souls in transit, but those still living as well. And they've identified Gillian as a danger. She's one soul against hundreds and she needs help.

Can she find others like her and rally enough to stop the spread of evil that can take everyone she loves?

The *Funeral Singer* series explores the overall theme as each thriller takes Gillian deeper into danger as she tries to help the departed souls cross to safety on the next ethereal plane.

Available to read now in eBook or paperback:
> *A Song for Marielle*
> *A Song for Menafee*
> *A Song of Betrayal*
> *A Song of Forgiveness*
> *A Song of Redemption*

O'Ceagan's Legacy: Book 1 (O'Ceagan Saga)
by Lillian I Wolfe (Sci-Fi Fantasy Adventure)

Trained by her grandfather to command, Grania O'Ceagan expects to one day inherit the family's space freighter, but first, she must prove herself worthy of being captain. Her ambitious brother Liam is nipping at her heels and wants a ship as well.

On the return trip from Earth to their homeworld, they take on two unplanned passengers and find themselves facing a disaster that could destroy everything. Can Grania muster her crew and apply all she's learned to save her ship and crew from impending destruction?

In Strange Waters: Book 1.5 (O'Ceagan Saga)
by Lillian I Wolfe (Sci-Fi Fantasy Adventure)

For a shapeshifter stranded on a distant world, water is life itself, the main thing making his self-imposed exile tolerable.

But Dari soon learns the waters of Erinnua are not like the seas of Earth. The sea life appears twisted and distorted. Swimming in it feels unnatural to his water horse form as he finds it disturbing and dangerous. Even the dominant underwater species may be suffering from the effects of a terrible human-caused accident. In fact, all life on the planet may be at risk if what he fears is true.

Can Dari convince the human colonists of the danger and work with them to prevent the disaster from threatening their world?

Time Walker (Time Threads) Book 1
By Lillian I. Wolfe (Fantasy Time Travel)

When a time traveler changes the past, it sets off events altering the future.

Mali's quiet night tracking the timeline is disrupted when an anomaly suddenly appears Somewhere in the past, someone changed a significant event. Now, she finds herself on a travel team sent to the 18th century to fix the problem before it snowballs into the future.

But repairing time is not as simple as it seems as Mali becomes entangled with secret agendas and her own past. Will Mali's era knowledge be enough to give her team the edge they need? Or will her lack of field training and personal interests result in disaster?

Splintered Time (Time Threads) Book 2

By Lillian I. Wolfe (Fantasy Time Travel)

After Mali's unsuccessful attempt to return Doyle to his own time, the pair find themselves a little farther in the future than expected. Electric automobiles, street lights, and hydro power generators make London a better place than the one they left. Has Varsi, the time traveler who is determined to stop the environmental issues that contributed to Earth's unlivable state, accelerated technology that far?

Determined to derail his plans before he annihilates her future, Mali chooses to pursue Varsi... as soon as she can control her time walking.

Book two of the trilogy picks up where *Time Walker* left off. Releases August 31, 2021.

Beginning in July on Amazon Vella

Episodic stories for on-the-go readers. Stories are posted episode by episode under the new token pay system Amazon is introducing in July/August. Formatted for your phone or tablet reader for grabbing when you have a few minutes to read

.

Cynara's Destiny

The first three chapters are free to read. This book is not available for Kindle or in paperback. It is currently exclusive to Vella.

When an alien force threatens, a sixteen-year-old sorceress must learn to use her birthright gifts to save her solar system. Cynara faces opposition and doubt regarding her theories about possible other world invasion from the planet's governors and she doubts her own ability to protect the whole the system.

Telepathically connected to her companion, a frost leopard, the team set off to discover the truth when crops start dying in the west and the river waters are fouled.

Les Loups-Garous (YA/Urban Fantasy Series)
By Angelina Fasano

Alpha's Song

Pack is power; pack is family.

In quiet little Kennington, Massachusetts, dark secrets abound and some are buried deeper than others.

Following the devastating death of her mother, Christa Ellsworth never expected to return to the town where she grew up, but five years later, she finds herself dragged back to the scene of her family's tragedy. Christa's plan to finish high school unnoticed comes to a halt following a chance encounter with a devastatingly handsome club owner she can't get out of her head. She begins to uncover the extraordinary truth about the town an unusual birthright that is now hers.

Now she must figure out how to unite herself with the alpha she was meant to be, while coming to terms with a betrayal that directly affects her.

Beta Rising

The Kingdom Will Fall..

As Christa begins to settle into her new role as True Alpha, she is confronted by new challenges to her authority and her pack...

She thought that with the death of Brendan, the threat of a Rogue was behind her. She is quickly learning that Brendan was just a pawn and another, more powerful foe is hiding, waiting to take what belongs to her.

If another Rogue wasn't enough, a different kind of werewolf has come out of the shadows and seems intent on making her and her kind extinct.

Can Christa manage to confront the new threat and destroy the Rogue?

Will she be able to survive the ultimate betrayal?

For Eleven Million Reasons (The Franklin Logs)
by M.L. Weatherington - Police Mystery

If you think winning the lottery is a dream come true, you need to read the possible dark side of publicized sudden wealth. In *For Eleven Million Reasons,* mystery author M. L. Weatherington takes you on a suspenseful ride of murder and intrigue as Lt. Arthur Franklin pursues a killer. Don't miss this thrill ride of a first novel.

idewiped! (The Franklin Logs)
by M.L. Weatherington - Police Mystery

Picking up from the first book, Lt. Arthur Franklin of the Lodi Police Department finds himself suffering from doubt and uncertainty as he recuperates from the injury suffered in his last case–the one that nearly took his daughter's life. Melissa has retreated more than Art, who has been seeing a psychiatrist, Amanda Burton, a stunning woman, and Art is undeniably attracted.

Meanwhile, a new murder has hit the streets of Lodi. Even though Art is on leave, his partner, Walt, wants to get his input on the case. With few clues to help them, it's a real puzzler. As things begin to escalate, Art is pulled into more than one mystery. Can Art help Walt solve the murder, and how does it tie in with a mysterious stalker at his house?

The Gentle Giant Returns (The Franklin Logs)
by M.L. Weatherington - Police Mystery

Crime is news, and everyone's ears perk up when blood is spilt. Art prides himself on solving these few and far between homicides and noting the case resolved in his personal and private Franklin Logs. It is a red spiral-bound notebook he keeps in his home office drawer. There are few entries, but every crime that he solved was personal to him, like finding a long-lost friend and bringing them home.

This is one of those times where Melissa, Amanda, Doc Wexford, Murphy, and Walt are trying to unravel a puzzle. The mystery is the loquacious African Grey Parrot, the tape recording, and, well, you will see as you get into the story. You, like all of them, want answers from Art, but he is not talking.

Find out why in *THE GENTLE GIANT RETURNS*

Sometimes Love's Just Murder (The Franklin Logs)

by M.L. Weatherington - Police Mystery

A chill in the November air mirrored Arthur Franklin's place in his life. He's turned his back on the only livelihood he's known, lead homicide detective at the Lodi, California Police Department to become the newest P.I. of Tango Investigations. Coming out of a drug overdose, he sensed everyone hovering, concerned and ready to step in to help. Problems sprang up when the only thing that has kept him focused, his daughter Melissa turned sweet sixteen.

All of his friends have his best interest at heart. They just want him to be happy and to get-a-grip. Art understands, but he feels that he's the same capable man he's always been. And confident in his gut that he was right about one thing... Madam X! Follow Art Franklin as he works his way through emotional firestorm after firestorm in SOMETIMES LOVE'S JUST MURDER.

Dead End (Franklin Logs) (Coming in 2021)

by M.L. Weatherington - Police Mystery

Coming in 2022 from Pynhavyn Press

From Riona Kelly
The Cat Whisperer
Tainted Truffles (Isla Thorne Mystery #1)

From Lillian I. Wolfe
Outer Rim (O'Ceagan Saga #2)

Pynhavyn Press
www.pynhavynpress.com